THE
REBEL
BILLIONAIRE

The Winters Saga
Book Five

IVY LAYNE

GINGER QUILL PRESS, LLC

The Rebel Billionaire

Copyright © 2017 by Ivy Layne

Find out more about the author and upcoming books online at www.ivylayne.com

CONTENTS

Also by Ivy Layne

THE HEARTS OF SAWYERS BEND

Stolen Heart

Sweet Heart

Scheming Heart

Rebel Heart

Wicked Heart

THE UNTANGLED SERIES

Unraveled

Undone

Uncovered

THE WINTERS SAGA

The Billionaire's Secret Heart (Novella)

The Billionaire's Secret Love (Novella)

The Billionaire's Pet

The Billionaire's Promise

THE BILLIONAIRE CLUB

CHAPTER ONE
CHARLIE

"You're fired."

I laughed.

Why wouldn't I? Aiden was joking. He couldn't fire me. I was Charlotte Winters, and we were sitting in the executive offices of Winters Incorporated. I'd been working for the family company since I was eighteen. I belonged here. Sometimes, it felt like this was the only place I belonged.

Aiden couldn't fire me. I waited for him to laugh along with me.

The laugh never came. He sat behind his desk, his usually warm, brown eyes chilly and impenetrable. Aiden was the only man I knew who could loom while sitting down. I fought the urge to shrink into my chair.

I'd seen him aim that cold stare at plenty of people—employees, clients, his ex-wife. Never me.

"Aiden, you're not firing me," I said, trying to force amusement into my voice. This was all a joke, right? Aiden held my gaze, unflinching. I sat up straight, feeling my own eyes go cold. "Is this about Hayward?"

Aiden paused for a split second before shaking his head. "This has nothing to do with Hayward," he said, meeting my eyes. He was lying. He had to be.

"You agreed that we had to turn him in. You went with me to the FBI. How can you fire me over it?"

Aiden's jaw was set as he said, "Charlotte, this has nothing to do with Bruce Hayward. You handled that situation perfectly and I'm proud of your courage."

"I don't understand."

"I already told you. You're fired. Security has cleared out your desk. When we're done here, they'll escort you from the building."

His words were a punch to the gut. Tears threatened. I knew that prickle in the back of my eyes. I bit down on the inside of my lip, my teeth cutting into the tender flesh so hard I tasted the copper of blood.

I would not cry. I refused. Swallowing hard, I stood, planting my fisted hands on my hips. I knew I was in real trouble when Aiden stayed where he was.

If this was a power play, he would have come to his feet and reestablished his dominance. If he was letting me take physical control of the room, it was only because he knew he'd already won. Fear was an icy wave cresting behind me. When it broke, I'd be lost.

I *was* my job. If he kicked me out of Winters Inc., what would I do? I didn't know who I was without the company. Not anymore.

Steel bands wrapped my ribcage and I couldn't draw a breath. Turning my back on Aiden, I inhaled slowly, digging my nails into my palms and dragging my emotions under control.

I'd learned the hard way to keep my feelings to myself. Always. Even with my family. No one saw my pain, my fears. No one saw me cry. Ever. Not since I was ten.

Aiden knew me better than almost anyone alive, and he gave me time to pull myself together. Also not a good sign.

When I thought I could keep my voice level, I said, "I'd like you to explain this to me. After years of giving everything I have to this company, I'd like to know why you think you can shove me out the door."

There, I'd done it. I was calm. In control. I was not about to scream and burst into tears. I was not going to curl into a ball and sob. And I was not going to kill Aiden. Not yet.

In the same cool voice he used when he'd fired me, he said, "Charlotte, keeping you on isn't what's best for you."

My voice as icy as his, I asked, "What's best for the company, or what's best for me?"

"For you. It's not what's best for you," he said.

A volcano of rage burned away the ice. What the fuck? Keeping a lid on it, just barely, I managed to grind out one word from between my clenched teeth.

"Explain."

Aiden let out a sigh and leaned back in his chair, dropping the chilly CEO persona. His eyes on mine had all the warmth I was used to from my big brother. It only made me more furious.

"Charlie. You've been working here since you were eighteen. It was bad enough when you were in school. Now that you've graduated, you work all the time."

"So do you," I said in a short burst of sound. He did. He worked every day. He was here first and was the last to leave. Except when I was here late. Or early.

He might have a point about me working too much, but I was no worse than Aiden and he knew it.

"But I love my job," Aiden said, his tone so gentle I had to fight back tears. "I love this company. I always have. And you don't."

"You can't fire me for not liking my job!" I shouted. "No one likes their job. That's why it's a job and not a hobby. This is ridiculous!"

I felt myself losing control, my fury and terror spiraling up and spewing out of my mouth. "You can't fire me because I don't love my job. I'm an exemplary employee—"

"You are," Aiden interrupted. "You're an excellent Vice President. If you weren't my sister, I'd be giving you a raise."

That little bit of complete illogic pushed me over the edge. I kicked my chair, sending it rolling to crash into Aiden's huge walnut desk. He didn't flinch. I pointed at him, stabbing my finger into the air to punctuate my rage.

"This is completely sexist. You're doing this because you want me to get married and start having babies like Maggie."

"That's absurd," Aiden said with a wince. "I do NOT want you to get married. Jesus. Not until you get better taste in men. And I'd rather not think about my baby sister having babies of her own."

"You wouldn't be doing this if I were a man," I said, sullen, my arms crossed over my chest.

"Charlie, how many senior executives do we have who are female?"

"Seven," I said, knowing the point he was going to make.

"Exactly. Just under half. And how many of those have families?"

"Five. So why me? Why are you firing me?"

I bit my lip to shut down the plaintive whine in my voice. I knew Aiden wasn't sexist. I was grasping at straws. I knew it wasn't my performance. I was good at my job, even if I didn't like it. If it wasn't sexism, then what?

Why was he doing this to me? Didn't Aiden understand that my job was all I had?

"It isn't about your gender, Charlie," Aiden said in that same gentle tone. "I'd do the same if you were Holden or Tate. Even Jacob."

"But not Gage?" I asked, half sarcastic and half trying to figure out what the hell was going through Aiden's oversized brain.

"Not Gage. Gage loves the company," Aiden said, his tone almost wistful.

"Then why isn't he here?" I said in exasperation, feeling my temper slipping its leash again.

"I never should have let you come on board, sweetheart. But you were so determined and I was selfish."

I sat in my chair abruptly, my anger down to a simmer. "Aiden, you're never selfish." He wasn't. Aiden was about two things—his family and the company. He'd open a vein for any one of us in a second.

"I was," he insisted. "I never pressured any of the others to join the company. I knew Holden and Tate would find their futures elsewhere. And Jacob loves business, but he needed to run his own shop. With Vance and Annalise, it was clear they had no interest in a nine-to-five job. I was right with all of them. Except you."

"Aiden," I protested, "You've always supported me. That's why I don't get this. You don't have to fire me. We can work something out. I'll cut back."

"I supported you, but I didn't look out for you. I was selfish. I always thought Gage would come home and we'd do this together. But he's doing what he needs to. I understand that. When you wanted to come on board, I should have told you no."

"But why?" I begged. "Don't try to tell me I haven't done a good job."

"I can't. You're bright and you have a head for business. No one works harder. But your heart isn't in it."

I shoved to my feet. "I'm not the only one here who isn't in love with Winters Incorporated."

"No, Charlie. But you're the only one who's my sister. I love you. And you're not happy. I can't be a part of that anymore."

"You don't get to choose that for me."

"Maybe not. I can't tell you what to do now. You're going to have to figure that out on your own. But I can tell you what you aren't going to do. And that's come to work tomorrow."

"I'll go somewhere else. There are a hundred companies who would love to give me a job." I wasn't being cocky. It was true. I might not love my job, but I was good at it.

Aiden shook his head, looking almost sheepish before the expression dissolved into a grim look that made me nervous. "You won't find another job in Atlanta," he admitted. "You'll have to take some time off to think about what you want."

"What? You blackballed me? How could you do that?"

Everything I'd worked for since I was eighteen was slipping through my fingers and there was nothing I could do to stop it. Hot tears streamed down my cheeks. Horror congealed in my stomach. I never cried. Not in front of anyone.

I wiped my cheeks with my palms, hurt and anger a hot, poisonous ball in my chest. I would have expected betrayal from anyone else before I would have looked to Aiden. He was more than my older brother. He'd practically raised me after our parents had died.

Through the blur of tears, I saw him coming toward me. I put up a hand to stop him. If he tried to comfort me, I was going to bash him in the head with the heavy Baccarat pen holder on his desk. All our family needed was for me to end up in jail for killing Aiden. After two suspected murder/suicides, we'd had all the scandal we could take.

I backed up, putting my chair between us. Biting hard on the inside of my lip to stop my tears, I said, "Back off. I hate you right now."

"I know you do, Charlie. I can live with that. But I miss you. I miss the Charlie you used to be. And I know you miss her too."

I held my breath, strangling my shout of rage. I stormed out of Aiden's office. No one commented on my red eyes as I rushed through the halls. Aiden had been thoughtful enough to have my desk packed into a box while we were in his office, the bastard. Security didn't exactly escort me out, but they were there, lurking.

Fucking Aiden. How could he do this to me? What did he mean, he missed me? He saw me every day!

At the memory of his face when I left, somehow both contrite and resolved, my vision flared with white hot rage so fierce I was blinded by it. I was not going to think about Aiden. I was not going to think about the scope of his betrayal or wonder how my beloved brother could have done this to me. If I did, I might swing the car around and go back to the office. If I laid eyes on him again, I'd kill him.

I barely noticed my family home as I sped up the drive. Located on ten wooded acres in the heart of Buckhead, Atlanta's most elite neighborhood, Winters House was a seventeen thousand square foot Mediterranean-style mansion.

At that size, it could have been imposing, but the warm,

creamy walls and red tile roof gave it the look of a historic Italian villa, both welcoming and impressive.

Built in a square around a central courtyard, the design made the big building intimate, as well as more secure. When I was a child, the inner gate had never been closed.

After my parents died, we'd all been grateful our home could double as a fortress. With so much of our family gone, we'd wanted to protect what was left.

I came to a stop in front of the black iron gate that protected the courtyard. Stabbing my finger at the remote to open it, I waited for the heavy gate to swing open, vibrating with anger and impatience.

Pulling in front of the tall front doors, I parked, taking my keys with me. I didn't want the staff to move the car as they usually did. I wouldn't be here long enough.

For once, I didn't give a thought to how things looked. I just wanted to get my things and get out. The home I'd always loved looked like a prison, complete with my brother as warden.

I loved Winters House. We all did, but everyone else had eventually moved out. I'd stayed, not comfortable leaving Aiden to rattle around in the big house by himself with only staff for company.

I was over it now. If I had to look at him at the dinner table, I'd stab him with a fork.

Lucky for me, I had somewhere to go. Funny how things worked out. A month before, I'd bought a rundown Craftsman-style home in the Virginia Highlands neighborhood. I don't know why.

Buying that house was the first irrational thing I'd done since I was a teenager. I didn't need a house. And while real estate could be a good investment, that was more Jacob's thing than mine.

All I can say is that the first time I laid eyes on that house, I wanted it. Now it was mine, and it was a mess.

The plumbing was shot, the front porch was falling apart, and the electrical wasn't much better. At least I'd managed to get the single bathroom on the first floor working. I just needed a sleeping bag and a mini-fridge and I could move in.

No one was home at Winters House, another stroke of luck on this unbelievably shitty day. Mrs. Williamson, the family housekeeper, must have been out running errands. There was a gardener, some day maids, and a cook, but they were nowhere to be seen.

I raced to my suite and slammed the door behind me, catching a glimpse of my reflection in the full-length mirror in my dressing room.

It was like looking at a familiar stranger, even after all these years. I had my mother's shiny auburn hair, but I wore mine pulled back into a restrained, professional chignon. I was her height and had the same curvy build.

I could still remember the scent of her perfume and the warmth of her hugs. I'd never be my mom, but she hadn't wanted me to be her. She'd wanted me to be me.

I had no idea who that was anymore.

For a second, I had a flash of another me superimposed over the view of my charcoal suit and sensible heels. Me at fifteen, a little plump, wearing a Misfits t-shirt and a paint splattered pair of Converse, a blue streak in my long hair.

Before my life changed for the second time. Before Elizabeth moved in. It was the last time I remembered being me. Really, truly me. But I couldn't go back. No one could.

If I didn't have Winters Incorporated, I had no idea how to go forward.

I stripped off the suit and pulled on jeans and a short-sleeved cotton sweater. No reason to be dressed up if I was unemployed. Especially if I was going to my house. I loved every decrepit inch, but the place was a mess.

Stuffing clothes and toiletries in a bag, I called Maggie. Magnolia Henry was my cousin's fiancée and my best friend. No answer.

Just before I could leave a message, I remembered she and Vance were out of town with Rosie, Vance's infant daughter. They'd said it was a business trip, but they'd brought along their new nanny and I'd teased Maggie that it was more a pre-honeymoon than a business trip.

She'd blushed so pink I'd known I'd been right. If she had any idea what had happened, she'd rush home in a second. I wasn't going to ruin their mini-vacation. I'd just have to handle this on my own.

I slung the bag over my shoulder and stomped down the stairs, taking a perverse satisfaction in letting my temper out. No need to be professional now. What the hell did I care what anyone thought? It wasn't like I had a job. I didn't even have the prospect of one.

Aiden had blackballed me.

My knees wobbled at the wave of fury. I couldn't seem to get my head around how thoroughly he'd destroyed my career. He knew I wouldn't leave Atlanta.

I love my city. Gage and Annalise aside, my family was here. My friends were here. I could probably find something if I were willing to move, but I wasn't going to flee Atlanta because Aiden was a controlling asshole.

I ground to a halt at the door to his home office. I wasn't above a little petty revenge. Not in my current mood. But what I had in mind wasn't petty. On the shelf behind his desk sat a crystal decanter filled with brown liquid. Aiden's pride and joy. He wasn't much of a drinker, but he did like his whiskey.

I'd never seen him drunk, but I often joined him in his office for a glass after a long day. We drank whiskey together, but not what was in that decanter. I'd never seen him touch the contents aside from a single glass the day it had arrived.

Carefully, I picked up the decanter and one glass, taking them both with me. He'd be furious. Maybe as furious as I was at being fired. Served him right.

I didn't stop to think until I was pulling into the cracked and overgrown driveway at my house in the Highlands. I unloaded my bags, locked my car, and took the crystal decanter and glass to the back porch. The covered porch circled the house, and most of it was rotted and unstable. The section outside the back door was safe enough, I thought.

I liked to sit out there, admiring my tangle of a yard and imagining what the house would look like when I was finished with it. I'd barely gotten started. Too many hours working and not enough free time.

I didn't have that problem now.

My stomach did an uneasy flip at the reminder that I was unemployed. It wasn't the money. Even accounting for the cost of the house, I had money. I'd been working for Winters Incorporated since my freshman year in college and I'd kept expenses to a minimum.

Hard to spend money when all I did was work. I still drove Aiden's car, the one he'd given me when I turned sixteen. I'd lived at home, so no rent, mortgage, or utilities.

He didn't even let me pay for groceries. I never went on vacation and I rarely shopped except for work clothes. Since buying suits wasn't my idea of fun, I kept that to a minimum too.

I was twenty-four years old with a flush bank account, but no job and no life. A tiny voice whispered that maybe Aiden had a point.

Screw that.

It would be a long time before I'd be willing to talk to Aiden, much less admit he might have done the right thing.

This was *my* life. I knew he could be controlling, but firing me was beyond insane.

Gritting my teeth, I poured myself a generous portion of whiskey into the crystal glass I'd stolen. At the familiar burn of the liquor, I smiled for the first time since I'd walked into Aiden's office a few hours before.

The whiskey was the best I'd ever had. At fifteen thousand dollars a bottle, it should be. Aiden had bought the Macallan Select Reserve Single Malt at an auction a few years before. He wasn't generally extravagant, but he loved this whiskey.

I took another sip and grinned, remembering the first time I'd stolen Aiden's whiskey. I'd been thirteen and gotten my backside tanned. Back then, the punishment had been worth it, though I'd thought the whiskey was disgusting. How things had changed.

Now I welcomed the smooth burn of the Macallan. Aiden had already delivered his punishment, so why not?

If he could yank my entire life out from under me, I could drink his ridiculously expensive whiskey. Even the crystal decanter was valuable. A special anniversary edition, it was worth almost as much as the contents.

Now, all he had of the set was a single glass. I drained every drop of whiskey from the one I'd stolen and refilled it.

I was going to get drunk on obscenely expensive whiskey and figure out the rest of my life later.

"Isn't it a little early for whiskey?"

The voice was smooth, dark, and luscious with a husky bite. At first, I thought it was the whiskey talking. Then I looked up.

Shit. Standing on the other side of the fence was my neighbor, the one Maggie and I called *Lawnmower Hottie*. The name was silly, but apt.

At first, I'd only seen him mowing his yard, always shirt-less, his chiseled body on full display. He was tall, taller than my brothers and cousins. At least 6' 6" and solid, with broad shoulders, lean hips, and long legs. All of him was covered in muscle and what seemed like acres of tattoos.

He should have scared me. My cousin Vance was big and had muscles and a bunch of tattoos. But not like this guy. Lawnmower Hottie was dark, with olive skin, black shaggy hair, and apple green eyes. I'd never seen him smile.

And I'd looked. I'm not going to admit how often I'd spied on him. I was Pavlov's dog. I heard that lawnmower start up, and I went straight to the window.

"How much of that have you had to drink?" he asked, nodding at the decanter beside me.

I looked from him to my half-empty glass before I answered. We'd never spoken, never exchanged more than a vague half-wave, but now was as good a time as any to get to know my new neighbor.

For once, I was feeling reckless, my anger and the whiskey mixing in my blood, tugging at my memories of another time, when I'd been another girl.

"This is my second," I said, holding my glass up to the light. "Do you want some? I don't have another glass. You'll have to share with me."

Lawnmower Hottie was over the fence in one fluid leap, landing on the balls of his feet, moving far too quietly for his size. This man was a predator.

Dangerous.

Before I could regret my invitation, he was sitting beside me, his spicy male scent blending with the whiskey and going straight to my head.

Had I said I was feeling reckless? The heat of his body warming my side, he took the glass from my fingers, his skin brushing mine, sending electric sparks shooting down my nerve endings at the brief contact.

My breath caught in my throat. His green eyes were as clear as glass as they studied the whiskey before he raised the tumbler and took a sip.

Up close, he was a study in contradictions—the clarity of his green eyes gemlike, the line of his jaw aggressive, a perfect match for those bladed cheekbones. And his mouth. Lush and full, it was the mouth of a lover, a mouth made for kissing.

I found myself leaning into him, his lips a magnet. I started to pull back, to get myself under control. I was Charlotte Winters. Perfect Charlotte Winters. Perfect grades, perfect clothes, perfect job. Always perfect.

Not anymore. That Charlotte was gone. I was left with Charlie, and Charlie was unemployed, sitting on her back porch in the middle of the day drinking whiskey and thinking bad thoughts about kissing her neighbor.

Charlotte would get up, politely excuse herself, wash out the glass, and set it to dry beside the sink before she went off and did something sensible. But Charlotte wasn't here. And Charlie knew exactly what she wanted.

I didn't care if it was the whiskey, the crappy day, or just good old-fashioned lust. I knew what I wanted. Maybe not in the big picture. My life was in a shambles and I had no clue what to do about that.

But right there, with whiskey and desire fizzing in my veins and Lawnmower Hottie close enough to touch, I knew exactly what I was going to do.

Before I could think twice, I closed the distance between us and pressed my lips to his. Fireworks exploded behind my eyelids. He let out a grunt of surprise and his hands closed over my shoulders. He was going to push me away. Disappointment stabbed through me.

Then I opened my mouth to his, my tongue stroking across his lower lip, and he pulled me closer, my breasts pressing to his broad chest, his mouth slanting over mine, taking control of the kiss.

My blood sang and my body was molten. He tasted of whiskey and pleasure. Of danger and sex. I had to have more.

I was a mess, lost and without direction. I had no idea what I was doing with my life, but I knew one thing.

I wanted more of this man. And I'd do whatever I had to do to get him.

Chapter Two

Lucas

I was going to push her away. That was the plan. I've lived a wild life at times, but I didn't go around kissing women I'd barely met. Especially not my neighbor. Hooking up with a neighbor had *complicated* written all over it.

I didn't do complicated.

But shit, this girl could kiss. I put my hands on her shoulders, thinking to push her back, when her tongue slid across my lower lip and reason flew straight out of my brain.

Instead, I pulled her closer and sealed my mouth over hers, figuring I'd be too aggressive and scare her off.

I was wrong. Her mouth matched mine, her tongue stroking, her teeth nipping, sucking my lip inside before diving back into the kiss.

When I hauled her onto my lap, pulling her hips into mine and pinning the hard length of my cock between us, I expected her to back off, not arch into me, pressing those round tits into my chest.

God damn.

I was in over my fucking head. Most of my brain was

focused on my dick and the lush armful of woman on my lap, but I had just enough good sense to realize that:

#1 - I didn't know this chick. She could be a total nutcase. Trouble.

#2 - She'd been drinking.

Whiskey, by the taste of her, and whatever it was, it was the good stuff. For all I knew, she could be wasted. I didn't fuck drunk women. I had one hand up the back of her sweater, my palm splayed over warm silky skin, fingers reaching for the clasp of her bra.

So close.

So close and so fucking ready.

I kept kissing her, well past when I'd decided this had to stop. The taste of her, whiskey and sweet woman, the little noises she was making in her throat, the electric feel of her weight in my lap, and the raw desire in her kiss.

I should have stood up and dumped her on her ass, then run as fast as I could in the other direction.

Don't stick your dick in crazy.

The immortal wisdom of my asshole stepfather. No less true, even considering its source. It was one of the only pieces of advice I'd ever taken from Dale.

I'd seen this woman before, felt her eyes on me when I mowed the lawn, and even exchanged a neighborly wave once or twice. Nothing had indicated she'd ever end up here, straddling my lap, her tongue in my mouth.

No, every time I'd seen her, she was buttoned up tight, pearls, expensive suit, and a line between her eyebrows that said she was always stressed. And now, she was drinking and about thirty seconds from getting fucked on her back porch.

It was possible she wasn't crazy, but this was definitely out of character. Whatever was going on with her, I was too smart to jump in the middle of it without doing a little recon first.

It almost killed me, but I managed to stand up. When her legs wrapped around my waist, I groaned. So fucking close, and she was so goddamned sweet.

"Princess," I managed to say, "give me a minute here."

At the sound of my voice, her legs dropped from my waist and she pulled away. If I hadn't steadied her, she would have fallen right off the porch steps.

Yep, she might not be drunk, but she definitely wasn't sober.

Fuck.

Somewhere in the back of my mind, I'd been hoping she was completely clearheaded and just really, really turned on. Looked like it was more complicated than that.

Have I mentioned I didn't do complicated?

She wiped the back of her hand across her mouth, straightened her shoulders, and met my eyes with defiance. "Don't call me Princess. My name is Charlie."

"Your name," I said, "is Charlotte Winters. I'm Lucas Jackson." I held out my hand and she took it, her grip firm and brisk.

"How do you know who I am?" she asked, eyeing me with suspicion.

After the way she'd jumped me, I was relieved to see she had the good sense to be suspicious. I shrugged. "I checked into you when you bought the house," I said. "Wanted to know who was living next door."

She returned my shrug and sat back down on the top step. She refilled the glass of whiskey before she spoke again. "I don't go by Charlotte. Everyone calls me Charlie."

"Okay, Charlie. So what has you sitting alone out here drinking whiskey in the middle of the day?"

Charlie took a healthy slug of the whiskey. "Do you really want to know? Or are you just asking to be polite? Because I'm not in the mood for polite today."

The perfect opening to get the hell out of there. I opened my mouth to say something like *you look like you need to be alone.* Instead, I said, "Yeah, I do. I'm curious. I've seen you before. You've never struck me as the 'drunk in the afternoon' type."

"I'm not," she said, holding out the glass and offering me some of her whiskey.

I took it from her and sipped. Holy Christ. I like whiskey. I've had some pretty good stuff, but nothing that tasted like this. I took a second sip before handing the glass back.

"I don't know what that is, but I don't think you're supposed to drink the whole bottle in one sitting."

I leaned against the porch railing and looked down at her, irrationally turned on by the spark of irritation in her aqua blue eyes.

"You're not," she agreed. "At 15K a bottle, you're probably supposed to take a decade to drink the whole thing. But this isn't about getting drunk. This is revenge."

"Only a Winters would get revenge by drinking a bottle of whiskey that costs more than most people's cars," I said, crossing my arms over my chest.

Charlotte flushed. Her eyes narrowed. She should have looked petulant and childish as she took an angry sip of the whiskey. Maybe it was her kiss-swollen lips or the faint pink of beard burn on her cheeks, but she didn't look petulant. She looked fuckable.

Every time I'd seen her before, her hair had been tightly bound in a bun-like thing that looked elegant and restrained. It was still in a bun, kind of, but strands were falling out loosely around her face.

With her messy hair, bright eyes, and worn jeans, she looked years younger.

It was a reminder that she *was* years younger, twenty-four to my thirty-two. Yeah, I'd already told her I knew who she was. I was way too nosy and too much a hacker at heart not to pull up every detail on my neighbors.

None of them were remotely interesting. Until this morning, I'd lumped Charlotte Winters into the not remotely interesting category.

Clearly, I'd been wrong.

"I thought about murder," Charlotte said after taking another healthy gulp of the whiskey. "But my family has had enough of scandal, and I'd probably regret it later."

Taking the glass from her before she could guzzle the rest of it, I asked, "Who were you planning to murder?"

"My oldest brother, Aiden," she said, her eyes grim and dark.

"What did he do?" I asked. "Cut off your allowance?"

At the furious look she threw me, I was suddenly grateful both the glass and the decanter were out of her reach.

"Fuck you," she said, all trace of the passionate, reckless woman who'd kissed me gone. Her eyes narrowed on my face, coldly furious.

I held my hands up in front of me, palms out, to appease her. "What happened?"

She studied my face for a long moment as if weighing her options before she said, "You investigated me?" I nodded. "So you know who I am, who my family is?"

I nodded again. Everyone knew who her family was. The

notorious Winters clan of Atlanta. They'd been a power in this country before my grandfather was born. Charlotte's father and her uncle had taken charge of the family company, Winters Inc., and made it even more of a force than it had been before.

They had their fingers in everything—manufacturing, technology, healthcare. You name it and Winters Inc. had a subsidiary making cash hand over fist.

Her older brother Aiden ran the company. Surprisingly, given how many of them there were, Charlotte was the only other Winters actively involved.

The company and their wealth would have been enough to put them on the map, but the murder/suicide of her aunt and uncle, when Charlotte had been an infant, followed by her parents' almost identical murder/suicide when she was a kid, had made them ripe targets for gossip.

All of them had grown up under the poisonous microscope of the media, and while they worked hard to live quietly these days, it didn't take much to stir up a little scandal.

Probably why Charlotte was drinking in her fenced-in backyard instead of at a bar.

"What do you know about me?" she asked, reaching out her hand for the glass.

I took a healthy sip of the whiskey, savoring the smoky fire of it as it ran across my tongue before I handed the glass back. I could blow her off, give her a bullshit answer. I decided not to.

"Charlotte Winters, twenty-four years old. You live with your brother, Aiden, in Winters House, in Buckhead, where you've lived your entire life. Undergrad in economics at Emory, MBA at Emory. You work as a Vice President at Winters Incorporated, reporting to your brother. No current relationships, but last year, you were photographed with James Conroy and there were rumors you were engaged."

"You're thorough," she said. "And what would I find out about you?"

I couldn't help my laugh. "If you looked? Nothing. You might be able to dig up that I graduated from high school fourteen years ago and joined the Army, but that's it. Unlike some people, I know how to keep a low profile."

Charlotte gave a laugh that was a bitter echo of my own. "Trust me, as these things go, I keep a very low profile. Any lower and I'd have to change my name and disappear. But your info is out of date."

I raised my eyebrows, waiting for her to explain.

"As of this afternoon, I no longer work at Winters Incorporated and I no longer live at Winters House."

"Your brother kicked you out?" I asked in surprise.

I hadn't bothered with deep research into Charlotte. As a Winters, most of what I wanted to know was right there in the archives of the paper. But everything I'd seen showed me a family that stuck together.

"He didn't kick me out of the house. He fired me." Her voice went hard as she said the last words, and her eyes narrowed. "That fucking, ungrateful, betraying bastard fired me. Do you have any idea how hard I've worked for that goddamned company? I got a degree in Economics. I hate Economics. I went to business school at night, while I worked during the day, did all those stupid projects and presentations.

"And I rocked that job. If you look at the reports after I took over, profits were up and we expanded. I was fucking awesome. Since I turned eighteen, I've given it everything I have."

Her eyes flooded with tears, the vivid, watery blue

reminding me of the ocean. My gut clenched, instinctively rejecting the idea of this woman crying.

Her even white teeth sank into her bottom lip so hard the flesh turned white. She tilted her head up and blinked away the tears.

As soon as she had herself under control, she raised the glass to her bruised lips and drank every drop of the whiskey. This time, I didn't comment on how much she was drinking.

I got the feeling Charlotte Winters would rather pass out drunk than cry in front of anyone, much less a virtual stranger.

Oddly, I knew exactly how she felt. I'd go through miles of hell before letting anyone see my pain.

Who was I to deny her the same right? Giving her another minute to get herself together, I picked up the decanter and refilled her glass.

"So what happened?" I asked when she looked ready to talk again.

"He said that leaving the company was what was best for me. That I was wasting my life on a job I hated and he wasn't going to let me do it anymore."

I knew better than to say what I was thinking. Firing her was a dick move, but never once when she'd described the job had she said she liked it, much less loved it. But that wasn't my business. That was between Charlotte and her brother.

None of this was my business. If I were smart I would hand her the decanter of whiskey, offer my apologies, and get the hell out of there.

I didn't do any of that. Instead, I took the glass from her, helped myself to another sip of the absurdly expensive alcohol, and said, "So, are you going to get another job?"

She let out another hard, bitter laugh. "I can't. Not unless I want to leave town. And even that might not work. Aiden fucking blackballed me."

"Shit, that's harsh."

"Yeah, right?" She took back the glass, brought it to her mouth, and swallowed twice. "He wants me to, I don't know, find myself. I'm twenty-four years old. If I'm not found now . . ."

"What are you going to do?" I asked, hoping I wasn't stepping on another landmine, but I wanted to get her thinking about action rather than dwelling on what had happened.

I didn't know her brother, but it didn't sound like he was going to change his mind.

No one got to his position in life, successfully running a multinational corporation—not just maintaining, but expanding—if he was indecisive and emotional. Whatever reasons Aiden Winters had for firing his sister, I'd bet he had no plans to hire her back.

One way or another, she was going to have to deal with that.

Charlotte let out a sigh, her eyes scanning the back porch of her house. I'd looked at it before I'd bought my own. It had been on the market for a few years, gradually falling apart while the owners ignored it and hoped it would sell.

Twice the size of my own bungalow, it was a rambling craftsman style structure that had great bones but was a total disaster. I'd considered it for myself—the front rooms had detailed woodwork that was hard to turn down, but it was way too big for me and too much of a project.

I'd had my hands full with my own mess next door, but

that was nothing compared to this place. "You're not going to live here, are you?"

"Of course I'm going to live here," she said.

"You're insane." I'd revised my assessment of her from crazy to just having a bad day, but now the pendulum was swinging back to totally fucking nuts. "You can't live here. This place is about to fall down on your head."

"Only parts of it," she protested. "Look, the foundation is solid and I had a new roof put on right after I took possession. A lot of the electrical has been shut off, and what's on is safe. Not entirely reliable, but safe. Same for the plumbing. There's no kitchen. That was gutted a few weeks ago. And the upstairs is basically a bunch of studs since the contractor re-did the layout of the rooms.

"But the front of the house—the hall, the stairs, the dining room, and the living room just need cosmetic work. And I did get the bathroom in the back of the house in working shape. I have a portable AC unit if I need it and a sleeping bag. So yeah, I *am* staying here."

She'd struck me dumb. Whatever I'd expected Charlotte Winters to say, it hadn't been a concise rundown of the rehab on her house. At best, I'd figured she'd hire a contractor, have him get the whole thing into *House & Garden* condition, and then she'd move in.

Living in a back room with no kitchen and barely a bathroom while she fixed up the house?

I hadn't seen that coming.

"Don't tell me you're going to do the work yourself," I said. She narrowed those blue eyes at me again and scowled.

"Why, because I'm a girl? Because I'm too spoiled to know how to work?"

"Settle down, Princess—" I started to say, but she cut me off.

"Don't call me Princess."

"Fine, Charlotte."

"Charlie. Don't call me Charlotte. Only people at the office and Elizabeth call me Charlotte."

Sidetracked, I asked, "Who's Elizabeth?"

Charlotte shook her head. "Aiden's ex-wife, and we are not talking about Elizabeth. We're talking about why you think I can't work on my own house."

"I'm not trying to be an asshole, but there's a lot of work to do here, and most of it requires some pretty technical experience. Please tell me you don't think you're going to do anything with the electrical or the plumbing."

"I'm not an idiot, Lucas," she said, and the sound of her saying my name in that annoyed voice went straight to my cock. It was the first time she'd said my name.

"I don't think you're an idiot, Charlie," I said gently. "A little crazy. Reckless, maybe, but not an idiot."

"I think you're the first person to call me crazy or reckless since I was a teenager. You're just seeing me on a bad day. Normally, I'm perfect Charlie Winters. I always do the right thing, say the right thing, wear the right thing. Or, at least, I used to. Now, I don't know what the hell I am."

Something inside me rebelled at the sound of defeat in her voice. I'd seen her passionate, pissed off, and definitely reckless, but I couldn't stand the thought of her defeated.

Trying to get her back on track, I asked, "If you're not going to work on the house, what are you going to do?"

"I *am* going to work on the house. I've got a contractor handling the stuff I can't do like reworking the second floor and coordinating the plumber and electrician. But there is stuff I can do—I've got to pull up these rotten floorboards on the porch, and that just takes a crowbar and some muscle. And all that wood work in the house has three coats of paint on it. There's gorgeous quarter-sawn oak underneath all that paint. I have no idea what they were thinking covering it up.

"I've got crown molding, wainscoting, paneling, and all of those railings on the staircase to strip and stain, not to mention all the hardwood floors have to be refinished. I was going to hire someone to do that, but now that I'm out of a job, it seems like a waste of money."

I was willing to bet my house this girl had never stripped paint before. It wasn't that it was technically difficult, so much as boring, repetitive, and time-consuming. I gave her a week, max, before she got tired of it and hired someone else to take over.

Not that I was going to voice that thought out loud. I did have some sense of self-preservation.

She could figure out on her own that she wasn't cut out for the hard, sweaty work of renovating an old house. I knew exactly what she was getting into. I'd done everything she'd listed next door in my bungalow. I'd loved every second of it, but it hadn't been easy.

"Okay," I said, not wanting to piss her off again. "And what about today? What's your plan for the rest of today?"

Charlie eyed me with suspicion, as if wondering what my angle was. Her probing look wouldn't get her anywhere. I didn't know what my angle was.

Unfortunately, sex was out of the question. She'd had way too much to drink. Charlotte Winters could hold her whiskey, but the slight slur in her words and glaze to her blue eyes told me she was more drunk than she seemed.

That was a damn shame.

Maybe another time. Normally, I'd close the door on any possibility of sex with a neighbor, but that kiss had been something else. If she wanted another shot at me when she was thinking straight, I wasn't going to turn her down. Then again, I'd had a few drinks myself.

Maybe the memory of her mouth on mine wouldn't seem so magnetic by the next day.

Finally, she answered my question, speaking in the slow, deliberate cadence of someone who knew they'd had too much to drink.

"I'm going to finish that whiskey. Then I'm going to walk —or crawl—into the back room and pass out in my sleeping bag. That's my plan."

"What about food? It's almost dinner time," I said. Charlotte shook her head, the loose strands of shiny auburn hair tangling in her eyelashes. She pushed them back with the heel of her hand.

"Not hungry," she said.

"When was the last time you ate?" I asked.

She peered into the air over my head as if her day's schedule was written in the blue sky. "Breakfast, I think. I had a conference call through lunch. I was going to get something after I met with Aiden. Then I forgot I was hungry."

"Fine, stay there." I stood, grabbing the decanter of whiskey, now considerably lighter than it had been when I'd hopped the fence. "Cold, leftover spaghetti it is. You're going to feel like shit tomorrow no matter what, but a little food will help. I'll be right back."

I was down the steps and headed to the fence when she yelled, "You can't leave with my whiskey."

I didn't look back when I said, "Sit your ass down. I'll be right back."

I heard the thump of that sweet rounded ass hitting the decrepit boards of her porch. I hopped the fence with her whiskey and headed for my fridge.

She'd drained her glass by the time I made my way back, still holding the whiskey, a plastic storage container filled with cold spaghetti, and two forks under my arm.

Typical of anyone at her stage of intoxication, drunk but not so drunk she was sick with it, at the first taste of the spaghetti, Charlotte discovered she was starving. We didn't talk much as we dug in.

Unlike her, I'd eaten lunch, but I'd spent the afternoon hauling brick pavers and wood around my yard and I'd worked up an appetite. Cold spaghetti for dinner was good enough.

She packed away more food than I would've expected. Charlotte wasn't a tiny thing. She was at least 5' 8" with a solid, medium-size frame. Her body, in my opinion, was just about perfect.

A nice, round ass and tits big enough to fill my hands. She looked like a girl who knew how to eat, but I was too used to women pretending they lived on lettuce and diet soda.

When she was sober, Charlotte might do the same, but when she had a little whiskey in her, she had an appetite and wasn't picky enough to turn down my leftover spaghetti.

It only took one more drink after that before Charlotte passed out. One second she was lying on her back on her porch, her eyes fixed on the peeling paint of the overhang and rambling about her plans for her derelict house, and the next, her eyes were closed, soft snores drifting from her half-open mouth.

Feeling like a saint, I carried her in the back door, through her kitchen, down the hall, and into the back of the house to the room where she'd camped out.

I lay her on top of an unrolled sleeping bag. She'd be

stiff and uncomfortable when she woke up. And hung over as hell.

Not my problem.

Still, I filled the crystal whiskey glass with water and placed it a few feet away so she'd see it as soon as she opened her eyes. She was on her stomach, curled around her pillow when I left. I found an extra key to the back door on the ring beside her purse and locked up before I went home.

I wasn't leaving her in an unsecured house. And returning her key would give me an excuse to check out my new neighbor when she was sober.

CHAPTER THREE
CHARLIE

There was something dead underneath my tongue. Gross, but there was no other explanation for the fuzzy, sour taste in my mouth. Also, I was pretty sure someone had beaten the hell out of me before I went to sleep.

I cracked one eye to see shiny navy blue fabric and a scarred wooden floor. Those weren't my Egyptian cotton sheets. And this was not my bedroom.

I went to sit up, and the throbbing in my head convinced me to stay where I was.

Out of the corner of my eye, I caught a glimpse of a distinctive crystal highball glass filled with water. The day before rushed back into my sluggish, hung-over brain.

Aiden.

Lawnmower hottie, a.k.a. Lucas Jackson.

And a very expensive bottle of whiskey.

Oh, my God, Aiden's going to kill me.

I remembered I didn't care if Aiden was angry and I wanted to weep. Always, when something went wrong, I turned to Aiden. I'd never, ever, imagined my big brother would be the one to stab me in the back.

I wished he had another absurdly expensive bottle of whiskey I could steal and waste, not that stealing his whiskey was going to fix anything. And if the pounding in my head was any indication, alcohol was not the way I wanted to solve my problems.

Carefully propping myself up on one elbow, I reached for the glass of water and sipped. It was room temperature and smelled faintly of whiskey, but it was delicious.

I drained every drop before flopping back down and staring at the ceiling. I'd need to replace the drywall up there, I noted absently, taking in the water stains from pipes that had leaked decades ago.

The offending pipes were gone. The second floor was as close as you could get to a blank canvas in a house this age. Everything looked like a mess, but when I was done it would be a home. *My* home now that I'd moved out of Winters House.

I needed more water and I needed food. Fortunately, while my head was filled with jackhammers, my stomach felt okay—empty, ravenous, but I wasn't going to get sick.

I needed a shower, a change of clothes, and food. I could handle the shower and the clean clothes, but I'd have to leave to get food.

In fact, if I really planned to live here, I was going to have to go on a little shopping trip. I wouldn't go crazy. Now that I was unemployed and had a money pit of a house to make livable, I couldn't go throwing money around left and right.

Not that I did that anyway. But I needed some basics, like a mini-fridge and something to sleep on. My Girl Scout sleeping bag was not going to cut it long-term. Shower first.

I dragged myself to my feet and stumbled into the tiny bathroom next to the room I was sleeping in. I thought the room might have originally been a maid's quarters, based on its proximity to the kitchen and the garage, but I was grateful it not only had a shower, but the plumbing had been an easy fix.

Eventually, I'd gut and redo this bathroom, but for now, I was grateful for hot water and a working toilet.

I showered quickly, my stomach urging me to fill it. I'd forgotten linens, so I had to use my dirty t-shirt as a makeshift towel. Skin still damp, I pulled on a fresh pair of jeans and a fitted T-shirt.

Out of habit, I went to the mirror to pin up my hair. I was halfway through twisting the long, wet mass into a bun when I froze.

Why was I doing this? I wasn't going to work. I didn't need professional hair. I didn't need professional anything. The only benefit of being unemployed was that I didn't have to do what was appropriate.

I could do whatever I wanted. After all, it wasn't like I could ruin my future chances for gainful employment. Not after Aiden had put out the word that no one should hire me.

I ignored the sting in my heart and reached for the phone in my back pocket. I was tired of perfect Charlotte and I was tired of perfect Charlotte's perfect hair. Before I could think better of it, I dialed the salon where I normally got my hair cut.

Fate must've been on my side because my stylist had a last-minute cancellation. She could take me in an hour and a half, plenty of time for me to get coffee and breakfast before I took one more step in ditching Charlotte for Charlie.

Might as well. I didn't have anything left to lose.

I could've walked to the small café for breakfast, but I didn't want to run late, and to be honest, I was feeling a little shy about running into Lucas.

I bundled my hair into a messy bun and slapped on the bare minimum of makeup. It wasn't so much that I was worried about how I looked as the memory of launching myself at him.

Had I seriously kissed a total stranger? I'd had a little bit of whiskey, but really?

Okay, he was lawnmower hottie. I'd been drooling over him for a while, but kissing random men on a whim was so not me. It wasn't Charlotte and it wasn't Charlie.

It was crazy.

I couldn't avoid him for long. For one thing, he lived next door. For another, I was pretty sure I wanted to kiss him again.

After a plate of scrambled eggs, bacon, hash browns, and a fluffy, steaming biscuit smothered in honey, plus a very large, very strong coffee, I was feeling mostly human again.

Aiden's ridiculously expensive whiskey had been beyond delicious, but I wouldn't be drinking again anytime soon. Even if I had another bottle of Macallan Select Reserve.

I didn't need alcohol, I needed a coffeemaker. A mini-fridge. Towels. And a whole bunch of other stuff. Keeping an eye on the time, I pulled out my phone and started making a list.

Twenty minutes before my hair appointment, I was in the car and my hair was on its way to its new destiny.

My stomach was in my throat as I watched Tracy snip

away what felt like yards of hair. We decided on an edgy, layered bob only a few inches longer than my chin.

With my hair's natural wave, I could let it air dry for a messy, unstructured look or I could use a flat iron for something sleeker and more grown-up. It sounded perfect, exactly what I wanted.

I loved it when I saw the picture in the book. I'll admit I felt a little queasy once her scissors started clicking away and I watched my hair falling to the floor.

It'll grow, I reminded myself. *If I don't like it, it'll grow.*

When Tracy was done, she gave the new style a quick hit with the blow dryer, twisting and messing it up with her fingertips to show me what it would look like when it air dried. She spun me around for the final reveal of my new look and I barely recognized myself.

My eyes were huge in my face, and the auburn of my hair seemed brighter, the shade more red than brown now that there was less of it and it wasn't tightly wound into a chignon.

It floated around my face in shiny waves, making me look younger. Carefree. Everything I hadn't felt in years.

I let out the breath I'd been holding, feeling something in my chest unwind and relax. I looked at the piles of dark hair on the floor and thought, *good riddance*. Charlie stared back at me in the mirror, imperfect and a little reckless, but far more willing to have fun than Charlotte had ever been.

I went just a tiny bit crazy after that. Just a tiny bit. Like I said, I needed to watch my budget if I was going to pull this off. No way in hell was I asking Aiden or my family for a penny. He probably thought he could fire me and just take care of me until I figured myself out. He probably thought that was sweet and protective.

And if I had run into a hard time on my own, it would have been, and I would've been grateful. But firing me from a job I'd worked my ass off for was bad enough. I didn't need Aiden to take care of me. I'd worked hard and saved money for years. I could take care of myself.

But I did need some basic necessities. And, unfortunately for my budget, my salon was across the street from a shopping center filled with big box stores. I could get everything I needed there, from the supplies to paint stripper, to a coffeemaker, to something to sleep on.

I was pretty responsible when it came to the mini-fridge and a set of sheets and towels. Everything I got was either the least expensive model or was on sale.

Ditto for the paint stripping supplies. From what I looked up on the Internet, it seemed like that job had more to do with elbow grease than expensive equipment anyway. But I did go a little overboard on the coffeemaker and the futon.

I tried to get the least expensive coffeemaker. I really did. The one I ended up with was not the top-of-the-line. It was somewhere in the middle and about twice what I'd planned on spending. But coffee was an essential ingredient to a happy Charlie. I figured that was an investment in my future.

The futon?

Okay, here's the thing. I was going to buy an air mattress. I was.

I had it in the shopping cart. And then I thought about Lucas and that kiss and how much I'd wanted him to roll me over onto my back, strip my clothes off, and fuck me.

A very un-Charlotte-like thought. If I were being honest with myself, and I was trying to be, I had definite thoughts about finding myself naked with Lucas Jackson, at some point in the future.

I didn't want a relationship.

I was not looking for a boyfriend.

The last thing I needed was to get mixed up with some guy. Sex was another story. I didn't want to try to remember the last time I'd had sex.

Counting back that far would just be depressing. And I definitely couldn't remember the last time anyone had kissed me the way Lucas had.

Charlotte would never have an affair. But maybe Charlie would.

Who knew if Lucas was even interested? Once I got the thought of an affair with Lucas stuck in my head, I couldn't make myself buy that air bed.

I couldn't have sex with Lucas Jackson on an air bed. For one thing, he was huge—six and a half feet tall and packed with muscle. He'd probably roll over and the thing would explode.

I wasn't buying a real bed. That would be an irresponsible waste of money. Eventually, that room was going to be my office so it didn't need a bed.

But a futon . . . a futon was perfect for an office, especially one with a full bath right next door. It could be an extra guest room, I reasoned, ignoring the fact that there were plenty of bedrooms on the second floor of the house and any family guests would just stay with Aiden, at Winters House.

Never mind that. A futon was practical.

That was my story and I was sticking with it, especially since there happened to be a futon store on the other side of the shopping center and for an extra fee, they did same-day delivery.

Fate had wanted me to cut my hair, and now it seemed that fate wanted me to buy a futon.

So I did.

See? Just a little bit crazy.

CHAPTER FOUR

CHARLIE

P rying the rotten boards off the front porch was both easier and more difficult than I'd anticipated. The wood was in such bad shape that it came up without too much effort, which was a good thing.

I wasn't exactly muscle girl.

Unfortunately, once I'd gotten the boards up, they left rusted, bent nails behind, each of which I'd have to remove before we could lay a new floor.

I could pry some of them out with the hammer. On a few, the heads popped off, leaving me with only a spike of rusty nail to work with. Also, as I removed the rotten boards, I started running out of places to stand.

The ground beneath the front porch was uneven and littered with decades of trash. On top of that, every time I managed to pull up a board, I had to lug it to the front yard for the contractor's crew to haul off later.

It was messy, slow, and frustrating. Seeing the change to the front of the house made it all worthwhile. It looked raw and unfinished without the decking there, but my imagination filled in the blanks and I could envision how it would look when it was done.

In a way, I was working on the house to fill time. I needed something to do. I was used to work. I'd been working since I was eighteen. A part of my mind couldn't help worrying over the job I'd left at Winters Inc.

It's not that I thought I was irreplaceable, but I'd been in the middle of so many projects. Who was taking over for me? Did they know all the details? I'd had an assistant, and the people who worked with me were all very good at their jobs, but in the past, every time I left the office during the day, my phone rang nonstop.

Today, my phone was silent.

I won't deny that the silent phone was a relief. And that relief was annoying since it seemed to prove Aiden right.

Even if he *was* right, even if I was happier out of the office than in it, it hadn't been his place to make that decision for me. I was a grown woman and I'd been working my ass off for him for years.

I'd earned that job, and taking it from me on a whim based on some paternalistic impulse to do what was best for me, without asking me what I wanted for myself—it was bullshit.

I was caught between relief that I didn't have to deal with work and frustration that Aiden had yanked me out of everything I've been working on and kicked me out of my own life.

I wasn't sure how I was supposed to handle this. I knew I'd make up with Aiden eventually. He was my brother, the closest thing to a father figure I'd had since I was a child, the glue that held our shattered family together.

No question he was being an ass. I was completely justified in being pissed at him. But I wouldn't be able to hold onto my anger for long. Our family had been through too much to let a grudge drive us apart now.

I'd forgive him. But not yet. Not when I still wanted to punch him in his arrogant, controlling face.

I was adrift without my job, but was I really going to fix this place up on my own? I remembered telling Lucas that I was. And in truth, it wasn't entirely on my own. I did have a contractor, and he was coordinating the aspects of the job I couldn't handle, which was most of it.

So far, he'd overseen the new roof, moved around the walls on the second floor, and was in the process of overseeing the new plumbing and electrical work.

All of which was way above my pay grade. He had a crew showing up in a few days to lay fresh planking on my front porch, and drywall for the upstairs was already on the schedule.

But I was going to do what I could. This was my house, and if I couldn't do my real job anymore, I had to do something productive, even if that meant hauling wood and stripping paint.

When I had most of the rotten boards pulled off the front porch, I decided to take a break. I was soaked with sweat and needed a shower. Before I could clean up, I still had a few things from my shopping trip stuffed into my car that I needed to bring in.

I took a long look at the decade-old sedan in my driveway. It was still in good shape, though it had well over 100,000 miles on it. The car had only been a few years old when Aiden had given it to me on my sixteenth birthday.

I don't think either of us expected me to still be driving it at twenty-four. I just wasn't that into cars. I'd thought about replacing it here and there, but picking out a new one, registering it, changing my insurance . . . it seemed like a huge pain in the rear-end when the car I had was nice and still ran perfectly well.

The sedan was a great car for an executive but not so practical for a woman rehabbing an old house.

As I'd walked through the home improvement store grabbing what I'd need to strip paint, I found myself eyeballing all sorts of tools and gear for other projects, most of which would not fit in my car.

What I needed was a truck. Nothing new or fancy. My budget didn't have room for either. But I'd bet I could trade my sedan for a good truck with some miles on it that would serve me much better than leather upholstery and a ten-speaker sound system.

I'd have to think about that. The hassle of organizing a new vehicle wasn't as big a deal when I didn't have my busy work schedule holding me back. But for now, I had to get the rest of my stuff out of the car and jump in the shower.

I was wrestling the mini-fridge out of the backseat when I heard an annoyed voice say, "What the hell are you doing?"

I jumped in surprise and almost lost my grip on the box. The small refrigerator wasn't heavy so much as bulky and awkward. I'd barely managed to get it *in* the back of the car.

Getting it back out was proving tricky. Settling its weight on the seat, I turned around to glare at Lucas Jackson.

"I'm getting a manicure," I said. "What does it look like I'm doing?"

"It looks like you're going to hurt yourself. Is that a refrigerator?"

He planted his hands on his hips and scowled at me, those clear green eyes gleaming with annoyance. For a second, I was grateful I'd grown up surrounded by over-bearing men.

Lucas Jackson was intimidating, but he didn't scare me. I planted my hands on my own hips and scowled back.

"It's a mini-fridge. It's not that heavy."

"Get out of the way," Lucas ordered.

I thought about telling him to shove off, and then I looked at the mini-fridge again. I could get it in the house by myself, but it would be a whole lot easier if Lucas did it for me.

Lately, I was proving that I could be a little reckless, but I was no fool.

Stepping back, I gave an exaggerated wave toward the backseat of my car and said, "Be my guest."

Lucas let out a huff of irritation and shouldered me out of the way. He picked up the big box like it was nothing, extracting it from its tight position in the car with ease. "Where to?"

"Follow me," I said, grabbing a few bags from the backseat before shutting the car door and locking it. I led Lucas past the half-demolished front porch, around the side of the house, and through the gate to the back entrance where we'd sat the night before drinking whiskey.

And kissing.

The heat of a blush hit my cheeks when I saw the steps and remembered the way I'd jumped him. I should probably regret it. It had been impulsive and a little nuts.

Glancing behind me and watching Lucas carry the heavy box, his muscles bulging, his dark hair sliding into his eyes, I couldn't find even the tiniest bit of remorse. It would've been foolish *not* to kiss that man.

He followed me into the house saying, "You shouldn't leave your door unlocked."

I didn't answer. He was right. I shouldn't have left the door unlocked. I was used to living behind walls and gates.

This house had deadbolts on the doors but no security system. Definitely no walls or gates.

I had to remember to be more careful. I'd never been a woman living alone before.

Lucas put the box down in the middle of the empty kitchen. "This where you want it?"

"This is good," I said. "The outlets next to the back door still work. I can plug it in there."

I took off my baseball cap and shook out my sweaty hair, running my fingers through it to cool my scalp. At the sight of me, Lucas's eyes widened.

"What did you do to your hair?" he asked.

"I had it cut," I said slowly. "Why? Is it awful?"

His green eyes studied me and I looked away.

I wasn't vain most of the time. I was too busy to spend a lot of energy on the way I looked. And based on the way Lucas had kissed me last night, it hadn't occurred to me that the attraction between us was ephemeral enough to disappear after a haircut.

But what did I know? Maybe he was really into long hair.

Or maybe I looked horrible with my hair short. My shoulders slumped. I'd thought I looked pretty cute when my stylist was done with me. Then again, I'd spent the last few hours sweating, my hair jammed under a faded baseball cap.

I doubted there was any makeup left on my face, not that I'd been wearing a lot to begin with, and I already knew I needed a shower.

Shit.

So much for my plan to have an affair with Lucas Jackson.

"It looks fine," Lucas finally said. "I was just surprised."

"Oh." I shrugged. "Well, thanks for your help with the fridge."

"I'll get it set up for you." He started to tear open the cardboard box, his strong fingers making quick work of the job.

"You don't have to," I protested.

Lucas didn't answer. He just finished unwrapping the refrigerator, lifting it out of the box and plugging it in. It kicked on with a low hum. It was pretty small, but I didn't need much room—just enough to hold leftover take-out, yogurt for granola, and half-and-half for my coffee.

I took advantage of Lucas's distraction with the refrigerator to step into the bathroom and splash water on my face. It felt good against my hot cheeks. A shower would feel even better. Soon.

I came back into the kitchen to find Lucas standing in the middle of the empty room, arms crossed over his chest. I tried not to notice the way his shoulders stretched the worn fabric of his T-shirt. Or the lush curve of his lower lip.

Looking everywhere but at him, I said, "Well, thanks."

"I have your key," he said.

"Oh. Why do you have my key?"

I pulled my keys from my back pocket and belatedly noticed that only one house key was on the ring.

"I locked up after you passed out last night."

I hated blushing. I didn't do it very often, but when I did, I turned bright red. Looking everywhere but at Lucas, I held out my hand and said, "Thank you. I'm sorry about that. It was a bad day."

"Yeah, no shit. Any day your brother fires you from the family company is a bad day. You were due a little whiskey. Though your brother may kill you when he finds out what you were drinking."

"He's not going to be happy," I agreed. "And I regretted it when I woke up this morning."

"Hung over?" Lucas asked, one dark eyebrow raised.

"Not now, but I was earlier. I don't think I'll be drinking for a while."

"Do you regret everything you did last night?" Lucas asked, those vivid green eyes locked on mine.

A bolt of awareness shot through me at the neutral yet flirtatious question.

He was giving me an out.

I could laugh and shrug and blame the whiskey. He'd give me my key and walk out the door, and we'd both be off the hook.

I'd assumed he didn't want me, but maybe Lucas Jackson liked to play his cards close to the vest. He wasn't going to put himself out there, but he wouldn't have opened the door for me if he wasn't interested in walking through.

I held his eyes, seeing the intensity behind his casual question. Lucas wasn't an easy man. He'd probably be a nightmare as a boyfriend.

Calling Lucas Jackson a boy-anything felt wrong. He was all man, more than a little dangerous, and probably too much for me to handle. The men I was used to dating were nothing like Lucas. Refined, clean-cut, and appropriate.

None of those men had ever kissed me like Lucas.

I wasn't looking for a relationship. I didn't want Lucas to be my new boyfriend. I had to figure out what the hell I was doing with my life, and I didn't need the complication of a new man added into the mix.

Why did it have to be complicated?

I'd never had an affair before. I'd had sex, of course, but always with someone I was dating. Someone I'd been dating for a while before we got to the naked parts. I didn't know if I had the guts to tell Lucas what I really wanted.

There was only one way to find out.

Before I could lose my nerve, I smiled and said, "No. The only thing I regret from last night is finishing that bottle of whiskey."

"You sure about that?" Lucas asked, dropping his arms to his sides and taking a step closer.

I hooked my thumbs in the back pocket of my jeans and took a step toward him myself.

Now only a few feet apart, we eyed each other. I was reminded of shows I'd seen on the Nature Channel—two wild animals, cautiously circling, looking for an opening.

After the way I'd jumped Lucas the day before, the comparison wasn't too far off.

"I'm sure," I said, taking another step closer.

Cocking my head to the side, I reconsidered my words. "On second thought, I take that back."

Triumph surged through me at the flash of disappointment in Lucas's eyes.

Before he could move away, I said, "The only thing I really regret from last night is that I had too much to drink and ended up sleeping alone."

"You're not drunk now," Lucas said.

"No, I'm not."

Anticipation fizzed in my stomach. I was standing on the edge of a cliff, one foot hovering in midair, just about to fall over the edge. The feeling faded when Lucas crossed his arms back over his chest and shook his head.

"This is a bad idea," he said. "We're neighbors. And you're not my type."

"Not your type as in not the kind of woman you usually

fuck? Or not your type as in you're not attracted to me?" I asked, raising my chin.

It's hard to look down your nose at someone almost a foot taller, but I did my best. Lucas laughed, the sound a low rumble in his chest that turned me on despite my irritation.

"Oh, I'm attracted," he said. "I thought that was obvious. But you don't strike me as the kind of woman who says *fuck*, much less does it with a guy she just met, Princess."

"Don't call me Princess," I shot back. "You don't know anything about me. You know about my family, you know my resume, but you don't know me. For your information, I say *fuck* all the time. And no, I don't usually sleep with men I've just met. I was interested in making an exception for you, but if you're going to be an ass about it, then never mind—"

I was working up a good head of steam when Lucas reached out, closed his big hand over my wrist, and tugged. Off-balance, I fell into his arms, too surprised to continue my tirade.

This time, *he* kissed *me*.

Kissing Lucas Jackson was even better sober.

His lips were soft and full against mine, but his kiss was hard. The way he used his mouth was all about possession and control.

The contrast made my head spin. I closed my hands over those strong shoulders and held on for dear life, kissing him back with everything I had. He tasted of coffee and something indefinably male that was just Lucas.

His hands skimmed down my back, closing over my ass and lifting me as he turned and pressed me to the wall, pinning me with his hips. I wrapped my legs around his waist, arching into him.

I forgot all of my uncertainty, forgot that I needed a shower and that I didn't think he liked my haircut. None of that mattered.

The only thing I cared about was Lucas's body against mine, the thrust of his erection pinned between us, his hands on my ass, my breasts pressing against his chest, and his mouth moving on mine over and over.

I wanted more. I dropped my hands from his shoulders, sliding them to his waist until I found the hem of his T-shirt. His skin beneath was warm and smooth.

That was what I wanted. His skin against mine.

I ran my hands up his chest, lingering over every groove of muscle, scraping my fingertips over his nipples as I pulled the fabric up and out of the way.

Lucas let out a groan and stepped back, setting me on my feet. His voice was rough when he said, "I don't have a condom. Do you?"

I shook my head. Shit. Clearly, I was unprepared for this spur of the moment affair with the neighbor thing. I must have looked as disappointed as I felt because Lucas dropped his head and pressed a kiss to the corner of my mouth.

"I'll be back in a few hours with pizza," he said. "And condoms."

"Sounds like a plan," I said, surprised by the husky undertone to my voice. *Was that me?* I sounded different, aroused and awake in an entirely new way. I liked it.

"I'm keeping your key," Lucas said. "Lock the door behind me." A second later, he was gone.

Distracted, I did as he'd ordered, flipping the deadbolt on the kitchen door as I watched him hop the fence between our backyards.

I might have stood there for a while, staring after him

with kiss-swollen lips and a silly smile on my face, if the doorbell hadn't rung.

I hurried to the front of the house and saw a van with the logo of the futon company in my driveway. Knowing Lucas would be back for dinner armed with pizza and condoms, splurging on the futon didn't seem quite so reckless.

I had plans for that futon.

Chapter Five

Lucas

This time, I didn't jump the fence. I had my hands full with an extra-large pizza, a six-pack of beer, and a brown paper bag hiding a box of condoms. No flowers. No bottle of wine.

That's not what this was. If Charlotte was looking for a date, she was out of luck. I wasn't that kind of guy.

I'd thought about trying for romance, but I tossed that idea out before it could fully form. Flowers and wine were asking for trouble. If we were going to do this thing, we weren't going to dress it up as something else.

I knocked on the back door and waited. As much as it was going to kill me to do it, we were going to have to talk first.

I was fully aware that the outcome of that talk could be me, with a painful set of blue balls, and Charlotte, swearing she'd never speak to me again.

I hated that idea. My cock was definitely not in favor.

Sleeping with my neighbor was already a bad idea. Going into it without setting some ground rules would be a disaster.

I hadn't gotten to where I was in life by listening to my cock. I caught a flash of movement on the other side of the door just before I heard the lock turn. Again, I shook my head at the state of her house.

Aside from the fact that it looked like it might fall down around her ears, it wasn't safe. I could kick the door in without breaking a sweat and the locks on the windows were a joke.

Not my business, I reminded myself.

This was what happened when you saw too much of the dark side of life. You imagined danger around every corner. Charlotte didn't like it when I called her Princess, but I knew where she'd grown up. She had no idea what was out there.

The door swung open. The sight of her was a punch to the gut.

She'd taken a shower since I'd left, and her new haircut had dried in a mess of waves and loose curls that made her look years younger than the woman I'd first seen when she bought the house.

With her hair short, her ocean blue eyes were huge in her face, her cheekbones more defined. That pink mouth was a flower against all her creamy skin.

Fuck, she was beautiful.

Before, in her suits and with her hair in a bun, she'd been cold and unapproachable. A statue of a woman. Beautiful but untouchable.

The woman standing before me needed to be touched. Deserved it.

I'd told her the new haircut was *fine*. I'd known it was wrong the second the word left my mouth. I hadn't needed to see the disappointment in her eyes.

You never told a woman her new haircut was *fine*. Even

if you hated it, you lied and said it looked great. But Charlotte had looked so different—younger, happier, and so fucking sexy.

I'd been struck speechless.

All I could see were those big blue eyes and that lush pink mouth.

Fuck.

She stepped back to let me in the kitchen and I realized I was staring again. "Hungry?" I asked.

"Starving," she said, closing and locking the door behind me.

She wore a faded pair of cut-offs and a cotton T-shirt. No bra. My mouth watered at the visible points of her nipples and the shift of her breasts beneath the thin fabric.

"I don't have a table or anything," she started to say.

I set the pizza box on top of the mini-fridge, bending to stow the six-pack inside, and straightened.

"That's okay, I'm not picky. But we have to talk."

She crossed her arms over her chest and raised one eyebrow. "What are we talking about?"

Charlotte Winters was feisty. I shouldn't have liked it. It should have been annoying. Feisty women were work. Not my style.

But I did like it.

I liked the way she didn't let me steamroll her. I liked the way she matched me, the way she wasn't afraid of me. Let's face it, I'm a big guy. Most people get a good look at me and exercise a healthy sense of caution.

They should. Between my career in the military and the things I'd done since then, I was a dangerous guy. When Charlotte looked at me, she saw something else.

Whatever it was she saw, I didn't want her to look away.

"Don't get your panties in a bunch, Princess," I said,

crossing my own arms over my chest and raising an eyebrow back at her.

To my surprise, she laughed and said, "I'm not wearing any panties."

I squeezed my eyes shut tight.

Fuck.

We had to talk. Then, I'd find out if she was telling the truth about what she had on under those cut-offs.

My eyes on the ceiling, I said, "We need to lay some ground rules, that's all. I'm not planning on selling my house anytime soon, so we're going to be stuck with each other. I don't want things to be weird when this runs its course."

She surprised me again. "It's probably going to be weird for a while," she said with a shrug. "But we'll deal. Neither of us is looking for a relationship, right? Just sex."

"Basically, yeah," I said carefully, looking for the trap.

There had to be a trap. I'd never had a woman agree to casual sex so easily. "We have nothing in common, and even if we did, I'm not looking for a girlfriend. But I want you."

"Good," she said. "I've got enough going on in my life right now. I don't want to date. I don't even want friends with benefits. I just want the benefits."

"Works for me," I said.

I stalked toward her, crossing the room in two long steps. Charlotte's eyes flared, and she took a half-step back before holding her ground and reaching for me.

God damn, I liked this girl.

No, I didn't like her. I wanted to fuck her.

I can't remember the last time I wanted to fuck a woman this badly. It didn't matter. I was done with waiting. It was time.

The second I was close enough, Charlotte grabbed my arm and pulled me out of the kitchen and down the hall. I followed, already imagining where I was going to start with her.

Two kisses. We'd shared two kisses, and I was half-desperate for her.

Having an affair with my neighbor was stupid. Hooking up with Charlotte Winters, the crown princess of the Winters clan, was insanity.

I was a logical guy. You didn't stay alive in my business if you acted on impulse. I thought things through. I was careful. Measured. I weighed my options, and I was always, always smart.

So what the fuck was I doing?

Mesmerized by the sway of Charlotte's ass in those worn cutoffs, I didn't bother to answer my own question. I knew exactly what I was doing, and for the first time, I didn't care if it was stupid.

I didn't care if I was going to regret it. All I cared about was stripping her naked and fucking her until we both got this out of our systems.

She pulled me into the room at the end of the hall, the one just past the bathroom. There wasn't much in there aside from a duffel bag on the floor and a futon folded out into a bed.

Jackpot.

I'd been more than willing to take Charlotte on her sleeping bag on the hard wooden floor. I could get creative, and a little discomfort wasn't going to stop me. But I could work with the futon.

Tossing the paper bag holding the box of condoms onto the futon, I pulled my hand from hers and turned to face her. Her eyes caught mine, wide, blue, and torn between desire and alarm.

She tucked her hands in her back pockets and looked away, clearing her throat.

"I don't do this—"

I pressed my index finger to the pink curve of her lower lip, stopping her words. "I know you don't, Charlotte," I said.

And I did know it. I don't know how or why I was so certain that inviting me to her bed was completely out of character for Charlotte Winters.

I'd grown up thinking rich girls like her didn't have to worry about keeping their legs together. She had the world at her feet. She didn't need to care about things like good behavior.

Except everything I'd seen of Charlotte so far told me she didn't cut loose very often. I couldn't imagine her picking up some random guy at a bar and bringing him home to fuck.

So why me? How did I get so lucky? I wasn't going to waste any more time wondering.

I didn't want to, but I had to ask, "Do you want to call this off?"

I rubbed the tip of my finger along the curve of her full lip, my gut tight at the thought that she might send me away. Silent, Charlotte shook her head.

Those petal pink lips parted and her tongue darted out to flick over my finger before she sucked the tip inside. My cock went rock hard in a heartbeat.

Holy fucking God. This woman was going to kill me.

She nipped my finger, just a pinch of pain, and soothed it with her tongue before she stepped back and said, "I don't want to call this off. But you're going to have to be patient with me. It's been a while and I'm not sure I remember how to do this."

"How long?" I asked.

Charlotte made a face.

"A while," she repeated. I traced my finger across her collarbone, savoring the silky skin revealed by the loose neckline of her thin T-shirt. She leaned into my hand as I slid my fingers up her neck to bury them in her hair, cupping the back of her head.

"Just in case you forgot," I said, tilting her face to mine, "it usually starts like this."

I planned to kiss her slowly, to seduce her with my mouth and my hands, to chase away all of her doubts. The second our lips touched, slow went out the window.

Her mouth opened to mine, her breath hitching in her chest as my tongue stroked her lips. I wanted to taste her. I wanted to absorb her. Her hands snaked under my shirt, fingers splayed over my back, arms pulling me into her body.

Too many clothes. I wanted her skin bared to me. I wanted to see everything.

Dragging my mouth from hers was a struggle. I could kiss this woman all day. Stepping back, I tugged my shirt over my head and tossed it on the floor.

Hers was next. Obedient, for once, she lifted her arms for me and let me strip off her shirt. Bare to the waist, she was so perfect my mouth watered for a taste of her.

Her breasts weren't big, not more than a handful, capped with tight pink nipples the exact shade of her lips. Was her pussy the same? I had to know.

Nodding to her cutoffs, I said, "Drop them."

Her cheeks flushed, but she unfastened the button and slowly lowered the zipper. With a shimmy of her hips that I felt in my cock, she shoved the denim shorts down her legs.

"Liar," I said, my eyes locked on the tiny lace thong hiding her pussy.

She shrugged.

"Now you," she said, her gaze locked on the tent of my hard cock in my jeans.

I had them on the floor beside her shorts in a second. Closing my hands around her waist, I lifted her off her feet, grinning at her gasp of surprise.

Tossing her on the futon, I pulled her to the edge and knelt between her legs.

"I thought you were a good girl, Charlotte. But good girls don't lie."

"I am a good girl," she protested.

"Then what's this?" I asked, sliding my finger beneath the lace of her thong and dragging it down from the edge of her hipbone to just above her pussy.

Her breath caught in her chest, and she let out a whimper.

"Don't you wish you'd been telling the truth?" I asked, tugging at the lace thong.

Charlotte nodded, reaching down to slide the thong over her hips. Grabbing her hands, I stopped her.

"Nope. Keep those there. Liars get punished."

"What are you going to do?" she asked, her voice thin and strained.

"Exactly what I was going to do when I thought you were naked under those cutoffs. Only now, this will be in the way."

To illustrate, I leaned down and licked her through the lace.

Charlotte let out a long moan, her thighs trembling on either side of my shoulders. Holding her hands in mine to keep them still, I licked again, tasting her through the lace.

She'd showered, but she still smelled of woman, musky and sweet.

"Lift your legs," I said, nudging her thigh with one shoulder.

She raised them, bracing her feet on my arms. Fucking perfect. Spread like that, the thong hid nothing.

Now I was the liar. Eating her through the thong wasn't a punishment. The lace was so thin it was barely there, almost transparent now that it was soaked from my mouth and her own arousal.

I circled my tongue around her clit, and she shivered at the scrape of the lace combined with the heat of my mouth.

Moving lower, I nudged aside the narrow strip of fabric over her entrance and dove in.

Hot and sweet and so, so slick. I had to get my cock inside her. Right after she came on my face. I needed to hear Charlotte come for me. I had to feel it with my lips before I felt it again on my cock.

Squeezing my hands on hers, my chest gave an odd jolt when she twined her fingers through mine and held on tight, tilting her hips to my mouth and whispering, "Lucas. Please."

My restraint broke.

I gave her everything I had, sucking her clit through the lace until she squirmed and gasped, licking her under and through the fabric, and fucking her with my tongue until she was on the edge of orgasm before I released her hands, tore off the thong, and sucked her clit. Hard.

Charlotte buried her hands in my hair, holding me to her as she came, calling my name on a long moan that was so hot I was on the edge of coming myself.

God damn, it was like being a teenager again. I hate to admit that, as much as I wanted to feel her come on my cock, I wasn't sure I'd last that long.

Climbing up on the futon, I looked down at Charlotte,

her eyes half-closed, a smile on her pink lips. She spread her legs to make room for me and pulled me down on top of her. The silky heat of her skin on mine was heaven. My eyes locked to hers, I reached out, fumbling for the bag with the condoms.

I had to get inside her. Now.

"So that was my punishment? I'll have to try being bad again," she said, sounding so satisfied with herself I didn't think before I answered.

"Only with me."

My fingers touched the paper bag and I hid my face from hers as I tore at the packaging.

Who the fuck thought it was a good idea to wrap so much plastic around a box of condoms? And what the fuck had I just said?

Only with me.

We'd never talked about this being exclusive. I'd just assumed Charlotte wouldn't be fucking another guy if she was fucking me. I shoved that idea right out of my head. We could talk about it later. After.

I managed to get the box open and the condom on, my hands shaking the whole time. Had I ever needed to fuck a woman this badly? If I had, I couldn't remember.

Charlotte's eyes met mine when I rose over her, her gaze direct and completely without artifice.

No teasing. No games. Just Charlotte.

I kissed her, closing my mouth over hers as the head of my cock touched the gate of her pussy and I pushed my way inside.

CHAPTER SIX
CHARLIE

My head was spinning. I'd come harder with Lucas than I'd ever come in my entire life. Then the way he'd looked at me afterward—possessive and hungry, like he was ready to eat me alive.

Sign me up.

After the way he'd made me come, I'd do anything he wanted.

His cock pressed into me and he kissed me. I was drowning in Lucas, swept under by the passion in his kiss, the need, and the way he took over, his mouth owning mine like it had owned my pussy.

Not even the bite of pain as he pressed inside was enough to turn me off. It made me hotter.

I wasn't a virgin, but it had been a long time and Lucas was big. He went slowly, though I could tell it cost him.

We could go slow later. It mattered that he was trying to take his time with me. It mattered more than it should. I didn't have a lot of experience with considerate lovers. But consideration went both ways.

I didn't want to make Lucas wait. Raising my legs, I

wrapped them around his hips and tilted mine up, taking him another inch deeper.

"Charlotte," he groaned, pulling back a fraction.

He didn't need to. It hurt, but I wanted him. I wanted all of him. Every inch. Another orgasm was building, the tension coiling in my nerves and muscles.

I was going to come, and he was going to fuck me blind while I did so. Tightening my legs, I drove my body onto his, taking him to the root in a flash of pain and hot pleasure.

"Lucas," I gasped. "So good. You feel so good."

He froze above me, his body still, letting me get used to his size.

Oh, God. He was almost too much.

Lucas shuddered and dropped his forehead to my shoulder.

"Charlotte. Fuck, Charlotte," he whispered, his breath hot on my skin, the rasp of his chin prickly.

I wasn't sure if I could move, but I had to. I had to feel more, feel him moving in me. Fucking me.

I dug my heels into the backs of his legs and squeezed, sucking in a breath at the sharp pleasure. Lucas let out a groan and thrust hard, drawing back a second later and doing it again, filling me with his cock.

I sank my fingers into his shoulders and held on, my mind and body focused on one thing.

Lucas fucking me.

He wasn't holding back anymore. I didn't want him to. There was something about Lucas unleashed, knowing he'd lost control, that pushed me closer to the edge.

We moved together, our bodies straining, until the coiling tension inside me broke free into an orgasm that made the first into a shadow of pleasure. I don't remember anything clearly after it hit.

I moved in desperate jerks beneath Lucas, gasping for air and feeling him pound into me faster, then letting loose a shout as he followed me into orgasm.

He sagged onto his elbows, almost crushing me for a second before he rolled to the side and stood unsteadily. I lay on my back, blind eyes staring at the ceiling. I caught a glimpse of his tight ass and tattooed back as he left the room.

Yum.

Cool air drifted over my skin from the portable air conditioner. I thought about reaching for the sheet. In the end, I couldn't be bothered. Lucas had seen everything. There was no point in being shy now.

Water ran in the bathroom. Footsteps echoed down the hall. I thought about sitting up, maybe going to the bathroom myself. Every muscle in my body was limp, echoes of that last orgasm cascading through my nerves. I'd get up later.

Lucas appeared in the doorway, holding the pizza box, a six-pack of beer balanced on top. "Do you have a problem with eating in bed?"

I propped myself up on my elbows and took him in—six and a half feet of gorgeously naked man, holding pizza and beer.

Maybe that orgasm had killed me and I was in heaven.

"Only if it's crackers," I said. "Pizza in bed is a great idea."

I sat up, peering over the edge of the futon for my t-shirt. Snagging it, I dragged it on and pulled the sheet up to cover my naked lower half. I had no idea what had happened to my thong. I had a feeling it was in shreds, and I didn't care.

The pizza was cold by now, and I didn't have a way to

heat it up. That didn't matter. It smelled delicious, spicy and garlicky and cheesy. Food.

Lucas set the box down on top of the sheet and flipped it open to free a piece. He handed it to me and I dove in, too hungry to be polite.

I'd been right. The pizza was cold, and it was delicious. Lucas took his own piece and held up a bottle of beer, already open. "Beer?"

I thought about it. I wasn't hung over anymore, and we only had a six-pack. It wasn't like I was going to get drunk again.

"Sure," I said, taking the cold beer from his hand. I took an experimental sip.

Beer was always a crapshoot. I liked wine, most wines. But I was picky when it came to beer. I wasn't a Pilsner girl. I favored IPAs and stouts. Atlanta had some great breweries and I'd turned into a little bit of a beer snob. Lucas didn't strike me as a microbrew kind of guy and I wasn't sure what to expect.

It was a Pilsner. I must have made a face, because Lucas said, "Not a beer drinker?"

"I am, but I like IPAs better," I admitted.

"Fancy," he said with a raised eyebrow.

"Not really. Lots of people drink IPAs these days." I took a long sip to prove it wasn't a problem. The beer wasn't that bad. Not my first choice, but not awful.

"I meant what I said before," Lucas said cryptically.

"Which part?" I asked, my hand over my mouth to cover my obvious chewing.

"You don't fuck anyone else while we're fucking."

I bit my lip to cover the laugh that wanted to bubble out. If he had any idea how long it had been since I'd slept with anyone, he wouldn't have worried about warning me off other men.

"So you want monogamy, but not a relationship," I said.

"I don't share," he said, his eyes meeting mine with a straightforward gaze that offered no excuses. He'd said what he wanted, and it was up to me to agree or walk away from the deal.

Like I was going to do that. I'd never had an orgasm like that in my entire life, and now lawnmower hottie was offering me the security of monogamy without the responsibility of a relationship. I was in.

"I can do that," I said, "as long as the same applies to you. When either of us is ready to move on, we have to let the other know and it'll end."

"I think you just described the perfect relationship."

"I do have a condition," I said.

"Strings already? That didn't take long."

I couldn't tell if he was messing with me. It didn't matter. I was serious about my condition. If he couldn't do this one small thing for me, we'd have a problem.

"Stop calling me Charlotte," I said. His eyebrows raised. "Outside of the office, everyone calls me Charlie. The only two people who've ever called me Charlotte are Elizabeth and my father. Elizabeth is a raging bitch, and I really don't want you to remind me of my father."

"Elizabeth, your brother's ex-wife?" Lucas asked, taking another piece of pizza.

I nodded. I didn't want to talk about Elizabeth, but I was the one who'd brought her up.

"We don't get along. She's a bitch and she doesn't like me. I think she resented being stuck with the rebellious teenager when she married Aiden. Aiden thought she could help him raise me, but Elizabeth isn't the maternal type. I always liked being called Charlotte before Elizabeth. Only my dad called me Charlotte, and it was special, but after years of hearing Elizabeth shriek at me, it just gives me the shivers. And not in a good way."

Lucas chewed his pizza and appeared to be thinking over what I'd said. He swallowed and took a sip of beer before he spoke.

"I can call you Charlie. But if there were ever a woman who shouldn't be called by a man's name, it's you."

"I think that's a compliment," I said. I hoped it was a compliment. Lucas didn't answer, just grinned at me with a hungry look in his eyes. "Well, consider me a study in contradiction, because I only answer to Charlie."

"Charlie it is," he agreed. "Do you want any more pizza?"

I shook my head. I had a moment to wonder if he was going to leave before he tossed the pizza box on the floor, set his empty beer bottle beside it, and pulled mine from my fingers to do the same.

Then I was flat on my back, his long body looming over mine, a devilish grin on his face. He had my shirt off in a whisk of fabric, his eyes scanning my bare body as if he was trying to decide where he wanted to start.

I was open to suggestion. So far, he hadn't done a single thing I didn't love. While he was thinking, I ran my hands down his chest, tracing the ridges of his muscles until I reached his hipbones.

Lucas Jackson was built on a large scale, every inch of him beautifully formed. Even his scars. Both of my hands moved in from his hips, following the lines of that oh, so sexy V that pointed straight down to his thick, hard cock.

I wasn't completely sure what I was doing with Lucas. I'd done some reckless things lately, but getting involved with my unknown tattooed neighbor was at the top of the list.

All I knew for sure was that I wanted more of him. I definitely wanted more of that cock. Lucas shuddered in my grip. Bracing his weight on one arm, he reached down to pull my hands off him.

"This time, we're going slower," he said. "If you keep doing that, I won't last five minutes."

"A big guy like you?" I teased. "Are you trying to say you don't have any stamina?"

He pinned my hands over my head.

"I've got plenty of stamina. I'll fuck you all night if you think you can take it."

"I can take it," I said, lying. I wanted to take it, but if I planned to walk the next day, going all night would leave me too sore to move.

It would be worth it.

We didn't go all night. Only half of it.

We took a break to finish off the pizza, had sex again, then passed out.

Sometime after that, Lucas woke me with his hands on my breasts, his lips tugging on my nipple, then his body moving over mine. I drifted back to sleep after we finished.

The next time I woke, I was alone.

I lay flat on my back on the futon, letting my brain slowly come back online, random thoughts filtering through, one by one. I was cold, the chilly air from the portable air conditioner too much without Lucas's body heat beside me.

It was late. Well past midnight, but too dark to be near dawn. I was sore. Not just between my legs, though I could feel the tenderness there and knew it would be worse once I stood up.

No, I was sore all over. I wasn't in bad shape, but

hauling around lumber was a different kind of workout than sitting at my desk and hitting the gym a few times a week.

More importantly, why was I awake? I sat up carefully, mindful of my sore muscles and tender body. Now that I was alone, it felt weird to be sleeping naked.

I was too exposed, though there was no one here to see. Feeling my way in the dark, I found the nightshirt I'd left at the top of my duffel bag and pulled it over my head.

Wood creaked, then a thump. I froze, listening. Was that a shuffle? A foot on the floorboards? Or on the back porch?

My heart thumped faster in my chest, tingles of nerves tightening my stomach.

I was being ridiculous. There was no one here.

I just wasn't used to living by myself, that was all. I sat on the floor, torn between trying to go back to sleep and admitting I was too on edge for slumber.

The house was silent around me, dark and empty. I stood up, deciding to go to the bathroom and drink a glass of water, maybe take a walk through the house to reassure myself that all was well.

I'd only taken three steps across the room when I heard it. Another thump and the creak of wood.

I knew that creak.

It was the exact sound the middle step made on the back porch when someone set their foot on it. My heart pounded harder, stealing my breath. I bit my lip, using the pain to push back fear.

I was overreacting. I had to be.

My trip to the bathroom forgotten, I pulled on a pair of underwear and silently searched the floor for my phone. There was no one out there, but on the off chance there was, I didn't want to be caught without underwear.

The stupid things that shoot through my brain in a crisis.

Except that this was not a crisis.

You're overreacting, I told myself firmly. *Go check it out, and you'll see that there's nothing to worry about.*

I straightened my spine, raised my chin, and crossed the room to the door, thinking quickly. If—and it was a big if—there was someone out there, was it smarter to hide or turn on the lights?

Turn on the lights, I decided. If I were Lucas, one of my brothers, or the Sinclairs, I might've left the lights off and tried to sneak up on whoever might be out there.

Unlike them, I didn't have a gun and I wasn't trained in self-defense or any of the other sneaky stuff they knew. Also, there was no one out there, so creeping around in the dark was just foolish, right?

With more confidence than I felt, I flicked on the hall light, jumping a little at the bright glare. The hallway was empty, and I was alone.

Of course.

I strode toward the kitchen, rounded the corner, and reached for the light switch.

I screamed. Loudly.

There was someone on the porch. A dark, narrow shadow filled the glass panes of the back door. It was too dark to identify whoever it was. At the sound of my startled scream, the dark figure whirled and disappeared into the night.

My breath strangled in my chest, I flicked on the kitchen light, rushed to the back door, and turned on the porch light.

A sickly yellow glow illuminated the space outside the back door.

There was no one there.

From what I could see of the yard, there was no one back there either.

Peering through the window, I saw no evidence that anything had been disturbed on the porch. My flip-flops sat at the top of the stairs exactly as they'd been when I'd kicked them off. My painter's tarps were still neatly folded to the right of the door.

Dragging air into my tight lungs, I tried to think. Had I really seen someone at the back door? I thought I had. I'd heard noises. But it was dark, a moonless night, and my eyes had been adjusting to the light from the hallway.

Every nerve in my body strung tight with tension, I reached out to touch the knob of the back door. My fingers closed around the cool metal and I turned my hand.

The knob moved a millimeter before stopping. It was locked. I gave it a tug. The door didn't move. In the bright light of the kitchen, I could clearly see the gleam of the deadbolt crossing from the door into the doorframe.

I dropped the doorknob and stepped back to the center of the kitchen, studying the windows. All closed, all undamaged. Mostly to prove to myself that everything was fine, I made my way down the hallway from the kitchen to the front door, passing the dining room on my right and the living room on my left.

Both were quiet and dark. The front door was locked, just as I'd left it. When I peered through the bay window of the dining room, the front porch, yard, and street were as quiet and dark as everything else.

Just as I had thought, I was overreacting. I made my way back to my temporary bedroom, with a quick stop in the bathroom, and sat on the side of the futon, staring at the dimmed screen of my phone.

When I'd thought there was someone at the back door, it had occurred to me to call Lucas, but I didn't have his number. I could call Aiden.

For that matter, if I was going to be such a scaredy-cat, I could just go home.

This was what happened when you never moved out of your childhood home. I'd traveled all over the world, been a vice president of a major corporation, and I'd never spent the night in a house by myself.

Even when Aiden was traveling, Mrs. Williamson was always home and there was security on the property. I didn't go on vacations often, but when I did, I was with family or friends.

It was only to be expected that I'd feel a little jumpy and off-balance my first night sleeping in the house by myself. The night before didn't count, considering that I'd been insulated by half a bottle of whiskey.

A herd of elephants could've come through and I doubt I would've cracked an eye.

If I was going to do this, live here, renovate this house, and everything else I'd been thinking about, I was going to have to learn to be on my own.

And I would. But for tonight, I was going to compromise. I wasn't calling anyone, and I wasn't running home to Aiden. There'd been no one outside the door and no one trying to break into my house.

Still, I was too nerve-wracked to fall back asleep. But that's what books were for. My tablet was tucked into the side of my duffel bag. I pulled it out, got back in bed, and opened the book I'd been reading.

I was still a little freaked out. Every time the house creaked, I flinched. I'd half convinced myself that I'd imagined the shadowy figure outside my back door.

But what if I hadn't imagined it?

There was nothing I could do about it in the middle of the night. I'd think it over in the morning. And in the meantime, I was going to power through it, Goddammit.

I was an intelligent, capable woman, and I did not need someone else in the house to make me feel safe.

Though maybe it was time to buy better locks. Or have the Sinclairs install some basic security.

Just in case.

At that thought, I relaxed enough to fall into my book, if not to sleep.

Chapter Seven

Charlie

Finally, dawn pearled the overcast sky a luminous gray. The soft light chased away the last of my fear and I pushed my tablet aside. Closing my eyes, I drifted into an uneasy sleep.

It didn't last long. I'm one of those people who wakes up at the same time every day, no matter when I go to sleep. Even missing half a night's rest, my eyes popped open before eight a.m.

That was about the best I could do when it came to sleeping in, but it was better than nothing.

I dragged myself off the futon and pulled up the sheet and blanket, folding them over neatly. I'd grown up with a housekeeper, but the Winters children made their own beds. Every day.

My mother always said it was enough of a job to beat back the dirt, fingerprints, and crumbs we left all over the house. Mrs. Williamson didn't need to deal with making our beds or cleaning our rooms.

Coffee. I needed a cup of coffee. Preferably many cups of coffee. Standing in my bathroom, I reached for a hairbrush, planning to tie my hair back in a messy ponytail when I caught sight of my face in the mirror.

I grinned at my reflection. My new haircut looked pretty damn good first thing in the morning. Messy, wavy curls framed my face, needing only a swipe with wet fingers to tame them.

I pulled on a pair of jeans and another T-shirt before stumbling down the hall into the kitchen, headed straight for my new coffeemaker.

In the light of day, my panic from the night before seemed childish. Sipping from my mug, I approached the back door, my shoulders tight. Boldly, I flipped the deadbolt, turned the handle, and swung the door open.

As I'd suspected, everything looked normal. There was no sign that anyone had been on the porch the night before. I stood in the open door, both hands wrapped around the warm mug, breathing in the fresh morning air and listening to the sounds of the neighborhood.

Voices. A car starting. The beep of a truck backing up. My little street was removed from the main drag, but all in all, it was a much livelier neighborhood than what I was used to.

I liked it.

I let out a breath, the tension in my shoulders unknotting, when I saw it—a cigarette butt crushed into the grass at the bottom of the steps.

It doesn't mean anything, I reassured myself.

Just because I hadn't seen it the day before, just because I didn't smoke and Lucas didn't smoke, didn't mean it wasn't from one of the contractors or workmen who'd been in and out of the house over the last month.

Just because I hadn't seen it yet, didn't mean it had been

dropped the night before by the mysterious shadow at the back door.

I wasn't going to jump to conclusions. The last thing I needed was to go rushing off to my brothers or my cousins, panicking about someone trying to break in.

Before I could insist I was fine, they'd bundle me up and drag me home. Or worse, move in with me.

I stared at that cigarette butt for a very long minute.

Refusing to consider the reasoning behind my actions, I picked it up by the charred end, carried it into the kitchen, wrapped it in a paper towel, and carefully placed it in an envelope of papers I had propped up against the wall of the kitchen.

Checking my phone for the time, I decided it wasn't too early to call Sinclair Security. I dialed Evers's direct line, hoping he was in the office.

He wasn't. I left a message explaining that I needed an upgrade on the security at my new house and asked him to call me back.

I'd get faster service if I went through the front desk, but then everyone—everyone meaning both my family and the Sinclairs—would know I needed fast service and they'd want to know why, what was wrong, and try to talk me into moving home.

It was easier to play it casual.

Fatigue weighed on me. My early morning nap didn't make up for the hours I'd missed when I should've been sleeping. I longed for my bed, but just like I couldn't sleep in, I was not a good napper.

If I got back in bed, I would lay there, fighting to keep my eyes shut, my mind and body too awake to find sleep. My best bet was to exhaust myself with work so that I would sleep deeply that night.

My plan set, I pulled on a pair of scuffed work boots, grabbed my crowbar and hammer from where I'd left them next to the front door, and went back to work on the front porch.

The muscles in my arms and shoulders wailed with affront as I pried free the first board of the day. By the third, I was sweating, but the activity had loosened up my muscles and my arms didn't hate me anymore. A few more hours, and I might have the front porch ready for the contractors.

Every time I wanted to take a break, I pictured what the front porch would look like with fresh, straight boards in place of the rotted wood I was tearing out.

I still needed to redo the pillars and repaint the siding and the front door, but fresh planking on the front porch would make a huge difference. It was the first step in making the neglected house look like a home again.

I needed that, to see it begin to shine the way it was meant to. Bringing the house back to life was worth the hard work. I could take a break later, when the job was done.

The smack of my crowbar and the creak of wood were loud enough to cover the rumble of an engine in my driveway. I turned in time to see Aiden's car come to a stop.

Dammit.

I wasn't ready to talk to Aiden. Not yet.

He emerged from his sleek, low-slung car, his eyes locked on me over the roof, face carefully neutral. I couldn't tell if he approved, disapproved, or was braced for a fight.

It was hard to figure out what tactic to take with him when he gave me nothing to work with.

He bent back into the car and straightened, shutting the door before coming around to walk through my yard. He was carrying, in one hand, a white cardboard cup that looked like it was from my favorite coffee shop.

"I come bearing hot chocolate from Annabelle's, but I'm not going to give it to you if you're going to throw it in my face," he said, holding out the white cup.

I put my crowbar and hammer down before I climbed over the framing of what was left of the front porch and approached Aiden. He stood in the scrubby grass of my front yard, surveying the house, one eyebrow slightly raised.

I wanted to be mad at him. I *was* mad at him. Furious. On the other hand, this was Aiden. My big brother. And he'd brought me cocoa.

When I was a little girl, Aiden hadn't known what to do with me when I was upset. Our parents' death had thrown him headfirst into fatherhood when he was barely out of his teens.

We'd been close when we were just brother and sister, but once our parents had died and he'd had to fill their shoes, he'd been at a loss.

Typical of Aiden, he'd approached the challenge of raising me like a problem to be solved. If something didn't work, he took a new tack and tried again.

Aiden refused to give up on me. He could've hired a nanny and gone on with his life. Instead, he worked his way through every hurdle and he never let me down.

Early on, he'd discovered that a mug of hot cocoa was the fastest way to stop my tears, whether they came from a nightmare or a fight at school.

Even once I grew up, it hadn't been unusual for him to pop into my office at Winters Inc. with a cup of Annabelle's hot chocolate when he knew I was having a stressful day.

I sighed.

This would be easier if I could just be pissed at him.

"Is that a peace offering?" I asked, stopping a few feet away, my hands braced on my hips.

"Maybe. Or maybe it's just hot chocolate."

I took it, bringing the white paper cup to my nose for a long sniff. Annabelle made the best hot chocolate. Her shop also had amazing coffee and pastries I couldn't resist, but her hot cocoa was the best, rich and not too sweet. Heaven.

"So this is the house, huh?" Aiden asked.

"Yep, this is it."

"Based on what Vance said, I thought it would be falling apart," Aiden said, his eyes scanning every inch of my beloved, but somewhat decrepit, new house.

I kept my mouth shut and waited. Finally, he spoke again.

"It's got good bones. And this neighborhood has solid investment value. How was the inspection?"

"It was fine," I said tightly. Was he just going to pretend everything was okay? He had to know I was still furious with him.

"Fine meaning it's not going to fall down on your head? Or fine meaning the foundation is in decent shape?"

I crossed my arms over my chest, pressing the warm hot chocolate against my collarbone, savoring the bittersweet scent.

Trying to control my frustration, I said, "Fine meaning the foundation is in great shape, and the rest of it isn't as bad as it looks."

"Are you going to show me around?" Aiden asked.

"Are you going to apologize for firing me?" I demanded.

Aiden let out a short laugh and shoved his hands in his pockets, shaking his head. His brown eyes met mine long enough for me to recognize his innate stubbornness was at play.

Damnit. The only person I knew more stubborn than me was Aiden.

"No," he said without remorse. "I'm sorry the situation ended up with me having to fire you. And I'm sorry that you're angry. But I'm not sorry I did it."

"Then I don't think I have anything to say to you right now." I sipped at my cocoa to cover the quaver in my voice.

"I'm really pissed at you," I went on once I had my emotions under control. "I know you're used to having the whole world fall at your feet like you're the king of the universe, but that was my job you took away. I've been working my ass off for that company, our family's company, my entire adult life, and you just yanked it out from under me because you thought you knew what was best. Now, you think you can stroll back in here, and I'm just supposed to let it go? It's not that easy, Aiden."

Aiden looked away, seemingly very interested in the missing decking on my front porch. He let out a sigh, his shoulders slumping just a little.

"I don't want you to be mad at me, Charlie," he said.

"Tough luck. You don't get to choose when I'm mad at you. And you don't get to completely screw me over and then expect me to forget about it a few days later."

"Then I guess you won't agree to move home?"

"No," I shouted. "No, I'm not moving home. This is *my* house, and I'm living in it."

"It's not safe," Aiden said.

"What *would* be safe enough? Jacob's building? Winters House?" I asked, fighting the urge to either walk away or pitch my hot chocolate at Aiden.

I stayed put. Walking away was too childish, and I wasn't going to waste Annabelle's hot chocolate on a tantrum.

"Either of those," Aiden retorted. "Do you even have a security system here? Have you changed the locks?"

Evading his question about the locks, I said, "I left Evers a message this morning about putting in a system."

"That's a start."

"Do you have any specific reason to think I'm not safe here?" I asked, suddenly worried that Aiden knew something I didn't.

He shook his head and shrugged one shoulder.

"No. But you're my baby sister, and you've never lived on your own before. I don't like it."

"Well, deal with it." Not the most mature response, but it was the best I had to offer.

"Charlie," he said in that gentle tone I knew so well, "I am sorry. This is my fault. If I'd handled you right in the first place, you never would've ended up working so much and being so stressed out. Firing you was an extreme solution, but at this point, I didn't feel like I had another option. I'm asking you to forgive me."

I stared at the blue sky over Aiden's head, tears filling my eyes at his apology. Goddamn him for making me cry.

This was one of the things I'd always admired about Aiden. He was bullheaded and thought he had the right to tell everyone what to do, but he was never afraid to apologize when he knew he was wrong.

I knew he meant it. He was sorry. But that wasn't enough. Not this time.

Trying to make him understand, I said, "Aiden, do you even hear yourself? You have a complex. Seriously. *If you'd handled me right in the first place?* What does that even mean? You're not God. You can't control everything around you. I'm an adult woman who's made my own choices. Some of them are good and some of them are bad. None of them are your fault or your responsibility."

"Charlie, you were a little kid when mom and dad died. Don't tell me I'm not responsible for you."

"But you were, Aiden. You were responsible for all of that parent stuff. You took me to doctor appointments, you made sure I had my homework done, applied to college, and got home by curfew. But you aren't responsible for every small decision I make. Not for me, not for any of us. You take every-thing on your shoulders and you never pay attention to *you*."

I cut off when my voice cracked and a tear rolled down my cheek. I hadn't realized how much this bothered me.

I'll admit—though not to Aiden—that he was probably right in firing me. Not the way he did it, but I was wasting my life at Winters Inc. I was shocked at how easy it was to walk away. I was worried about my projects, but I didn't want to go back. Not really.

So I'd been wasting my life. But so was he, in a different way. Aiden loved the company and he loved his job.

He didn't need a career change, but he needed to refocus his priorities.

"We're all grown up now, Aiden. When does your life get to be about you? You deserve better than working all the time and worrying about your family. When was the last time you went on a date?"

"I went out on a date Saturday night, Charlie, not that it's any of your business," Aiden said, giving me the big brother glare.

"I meant with a woman you're planning to take out on a second date and possibly bring home to Sunday dinner."

"We don't have Sunday dinner."

"Not the point. And maybe we should. I'm aware you have an active social life."

I framed the words *social life* with air quotes. I wasn't

squeamish, but I couldn't say the words *sex life* to my brother.

"But you haven't gone out with anyone seriously since Elizabeth. And I think you only married her because you thought you were making a family. I know you didn't like her."

"This is none of your business, Charlie."

"Oh, so you get to rearrange my life to fit what you think is best for me, but I don't even get to comment when I think you're making a mistake? This is what I mean when I say you have a complex, Aiden."

"I don't have a complex," he interrupted. I wanted to laugh, but I was too worked up.

"You think you're the only one capable of being in charge. You think you have the right and the obligation to tell everybody what to do, but the second we try to help you, you shut us down. Well, I'm done listening."

"Charlie, I'm not that bad."

Aiden tried for a sheepish expression but it didn't work on his face. His bone structure was too austere, too sharply handsome to pull off sheepish.

"You are *exactly* that bad. But I'll make a deal with you. You let me interfere in your life, and I'll move back home."

It was a safe bet to make. There was no way in hell Aiden was going to let me, his baby sister, start telling him what to do.

As expected, he said, "Charlie, be realistic."

"I am being realistic. I'm an adult now. Even you can't argue that. Until you're willing to treat me like an adult, then I'm not coming home and I don't really want to talk to you. I need some time. And if I'm being completely honest, even if you do start treating me like an adult, I doubt I'm coming home."

Aiden let out a gust of air, deflating a little. My heart squeezed in my chest. I didn't want to hurt my brother's feelings, but he'd been an asshole and I wasn't ready to let him off the hook.

Just because I didn't miss my job didn't mean it was okay that he fired me. I couldn't resist asking, "How's work? How's my department?"

"They're fine. They're muddling along without you. And every single one of them is pissed at me, which probably makes you happy."

I wasn't going to deny it. "Yes, yes it does. Tell them I say hi."

"I will," Aiden said in a tight voice. "So you're really not going to give me a tour?"

"Fine," I said. "But we have to go around back. It'll be a few more days before we can use the front porch again."

I led Aiden to the backdoor, ignoring the way he gingerly climbed the steps as if afraid they'd collapse beneath his weight. The tour didn't take very long.

There wasn't much to see downstairs with the kitchen stripped bare and all of the rooms but my office empty.

Aiden's jaw tightened when he saw my futon and open duffel bag on the floor. I ignored it. I wasn't moving home. He'd have to get used to it.

Showing him the upstairs was more interesting. I'd worked with an architect to redesign the existing layout. We'd combined some of the smaller bedrooms to create a master suite, complete with a spacious bedroom, his and hers dressing rooms, a sitting area, and an enormous bathroom.

It was too much for me on my own, but a renovation like that was excellent for resale. I had no plans to sell my house. I was too in love with it.

Still, I'm a Winters. I have business on the brain. Especially since I'd sunk a ton of my hard-earned money into the place.

The contractor had already overseen rerouting the plumbing and electrical. The studs for the walls were in. Drywall was scheduled for the next week.

Walking through the space with Aiden gave me a tingle of excitement. I'd imagined what this house could be when I'd bought it, but seeing the fresh wood framing the new rooms, I knew the home I'd dreamed of was within reach. So close.

Just some drywall, trim, paint, new floors . . . okay, not that close. It was still the most exciting thing I'd done in ages. At that thought, I stopped, frozen, as I watched Aiden study the layout of the master bath.

It *was* the most exciting thing I'd ever done, more than any challenge I'd ever taken on at work or in school. My work for Winters Inc. never sparked my imagination. It never made my heart beat faster in anticipation. It never made me fall in love.

Was this how Aiden felt when he was working a deal for the company? This exhilaration? The sheer thrill of seeing a dream come to life?

I'd worked hard for Aiden. For the family. Aiden said he loved the company, and if he felt this way about it, maybe he really did.

Something to think about.

I wasn't ready to forgive him, but possibly, maybe, I was starting to understand.

Aiden didn't stay long after the tour. He had to get back to the office. I had no doubt he'd be researching my contractor as soon as he hit his desk.

After he called Sinclair Security and lit a fire under

their asses. No question, as soon as Aiden got a Sinclair on the phone, my security system would shoot to the top of their list.

I watched Aiden drive away with an odd mix of pride and homesickness. I was still angry with him. Angry, frustrated, and not ready to let it go.

I loved my brother.

I wanted to run after him and beg him to take me home.

I wanted him to tell me he was proud of me.

I wanted him to leave work at a reasonable hour and maybe even find a girlfriend so he could have a life.

My feelings for Aiden would've been simpler if he'd just been my brother, if he hadn't raised me after our parents died. There was nothing I could do about that. The past was our history. It couldn't be changed.

We had to find a way to deal with our tangled relationship. I hoped we'd emerge on the other side as adults with mutual respect.

If we didn't, if he kept trying to organize my life, I really would throw hot chocolate at him.

Or worse.

The encounter with Aiden had distracted me so much, I almost didn't hear the knock at my back door. With no car in the driveway, there was only one person it could be.

Lucas.

The shiver of anticipation went all the way to my toes.

CHAPTER EIGHT

CHARLIE

I tried to play it cool as I unlocked the door and swung it open.

"You remembered to lock your door," he said, his deep voice a low rumble in his chest. My mouth went dry at the sight of him filling the doorway. He was just so big—tall and broad and very, very fit.

"I did," I agreed. "I'm even having a security system installed soon."

Lucas stepped inside, his big body crowding mine until I took a step back.

Then another.

And another.

My shoulders bumped into the kitchen wall and Lucas's arms came up, his hands flattening on either side of my head until he had me penned in.

"Who's doing the work?" he asked, lowering his head so that his breath brushed my temple.

"Huh?"

What were we talking about? Wasn't he going to kiss me? It seemed like he was going to kiss me.

"Your security system," Lucas clarified, his lips brushing my cheekbone as he spoke.

"Sinclair." I let out on a breath. "Sinclair Security is doing it."

"Sinclair is good. They'll set you up."

His hands left the wall to frame my face, tilting my head up. The lust simmering in his hot, green eyes turned my knees to water.

Lucas was done talking.

His mouth took mine, his lips urging mine apart, his tongue tasting me.

God, this man could kiss.

He pinned me to the wall, one hand coming behind my ass, lifting me. Out of instinct, my legs wrapped around him, and the firm pressure of his hard cock against my soft heat drove me wild.

I sank my fingers into his thick, silky hair, pulling his mouth down, tilting my head to fit us together. He squeezed my ass, rocking into me. I arched my back, pressing my breasts into his chest, my body needy and restless for more.

Too soon, it was over.

I would've been perfectly fine if Lucas had carried me straight to the futon. Instead, he set me gently on my feet and leaned back, my mouth following his as if I needed just one more taste.

"Got a job," Lucas rasped in my ear, sounding out of breath. "I won't be back till later. You around?"

At his question, my frustrated desire flipped into anticipation. Going for casual, I said, "I'll be here. I'm going to work on the house and maybe get takeout."

"I'll be back when I'm done," he said.

Before I could get my bearings, he was out the door, his boots thumping on the steps as he left.

Fucking Lucas Jackson.

Damn, but I'd never met a man who could have me so spun after five minutes.

He walked in my house, kissed me senseless, arranged a booty call, and was gone. I raised a hand and touched my finger to my lower lip, the flesh swollen and sensitized by Lucas's kiss.

I could kiss him all day. And all night. I was beginning to think I could kiss Lucas Jackson forever.

At that thought, I shook my head.

This is sex, I reminded myself. *Friends with benefits, without the friends part.* There would be no forever for Lucas and me.

We had nothing in common and neither of us wanted more than sex. Since sex would have to wait until later, I might as well get my work done.

I was not going to sit around doing nothing and mooning over Lucas.

With the help of some YouTube videos and the directions on the supplies I'd bought, I went to work stripping the paint from the mantle in the living room.

It was a gross, smelly, time-consuming job. I had enjoyed ripping the boards off the front porch. I was not enjoying stripping paint.

Every time I got frustrated, I closed my eyes and envisioned the woodwork cleaned of decades of paint, the grain of the wood brought to life by a warm stain. Between the hardwood floors and all the trim, the house would glow.

It was just going to take work. Based on how slow the paint was coming off the mantle, a lot of work.

A few hours after I'd started, my stomach was rumbling and I had a headache from the paint fumes. The glare of the work light aimed at the fireplace mantle wasn't helping.

The sun had long since gone down. If I was going to work in the evenings, I was going to have to get more work lights.

I put away my equipment and jumped in the shower, the fruity floral body wash delicious after the caustic scent of paint stripper.

I was starving, but I took the time to smooth on lotion that went with the body wash and put on just a little makeup. I didn't know when Lucas was coming back, but I knew he *was* coming back.

Getting dressed in jeans and a T-shirt, I shoved my feet into my flip-flops, grabbed my purse, and headed out. One of my favorite things about living in the Highlands—I could walk to all sorts of fun places like shopping, cafes, and most importantly, food.

Good food.

My street was dark. There were streetlights, but not as many as there were on the main road. A spot between my shoulder blades tingled.

I couldn't help looking behind me. There was no one in the street. The houses around me had their lights on and cars in the driveway, and up ahead, I could hear people talking.

I was only jumpy because of what had happened the night before.

Which was nothing. Nothing happened the night before.

I'd gotten spooked. I bet everyone got a little spooked the first time they lived on their own. It was just that I was doing this later than most people, that was all.

My stomach was tight until I reached the end of the block and turned right onto Virginia Avenue. Here, the sidewalk was well-lit and there were people around.

Most of the retail shops were closed for the night, but the bars and restaurants were doing a brisk business. I fit right in with the crowd, though in my jeans and T-shirt, I was a little more dressed down than everyone else.

I'd planned to eat out, but everywhere was crowded and loud. If I hadn't been alone, it would've been fun, but I found I wasn't in the mood for people.

I wanted food and the quiet peace of my house. Fortunately, my favorite burger place was not only a few blocks away, but the line for takeout was blessedly short.

I got my favorite, a luscious concoction of greasy meat, three different cheeses, avocados, bacon, and onion strings on a brioche bun with a generous side of hand-cut fries and a lemonade.

I placed my order and leaned against the tile wall of the restaurant, flicking through YouTube videos on paint stripping while I waited.

It wasn't long before I was collecting my meal, packaged neatly in a brown shopping bag with twine handles. I headed back out the door, sipping my lemonade.

My mind was mostly on my dinner as I walked home. Since I'd been working on the house, my appetite had increased. I guess it was the difference between sitting at a desk all day and spending hours using my muscles, small though they were.

I was going to have to stock up on more than yogurt and coffee. Idly, I wondered what Mrs. Williamson had made Aiden for dinner. My chest hollowed at the thought of him eating alone.

Not my problem.

Except that it was my problem. Aiden was my brother. I loved him. But there was nothing I could do about it.

He needed a girlfriend, someone good enough for him

whom he could take care of and watch over, maybe make babies with so he could drive them nuts and give the rest of us a break.

If only I had someone to fix him up with, I—

The attack came out of nowhere.

My only warning was the slide of a shoe on the concrete sidewalk before a body hit me from the side and I went flying, losing my grip on my purse and my dinner, but not fast enough to catch my fall. A hand latched onto my hair, my scalp burning with a fiery pain as a chunk of hair tore free.

I came down hard on the side of my face, twisting into my shoulder and slamming into the scrubby grass of my front yard.

I rolled and tried to come to my feet, looking around frantically to get my bearings. My yard was dark, shadows everywhere, and one of them was coming straight for me.

I couldn't make out much. My attacker could have been a man or a woman, taller than me but not as tall as Aiden. Definitely not as tall as Lucas.

Its hands stretched toward me, the shadow came closer. I scuttled back, thinking fast. I had no idea who it was or what they wanted, but I knew this was not a mugging.

My purse had flown out of my hands, but whoever jumped me wasn't going for my wallet.

They were coming straight for me.

My mind raced over my options as I slowly backed up on the uneven grass.

My phone was in my purse, which was somewhere in the dark yard. Or the street, or the sidewalk, or the bushes. I couldn't call for help.

Lucas wasn't home.

And the locks on my doors weren't enough to keep out a determined intruder.

I could run for it—I was fast—but I was wearing flip-flops and the sidewalk was too uneven to run barefoot.

I was totally screwed, and the dark shadow of my attacker was coming closer with every second that passed.

I thought about the sledgehammer I'd neatly put away when I'd finished with the front porch, cursing my own tidiness.

A sledgehammer would've come in handy.

Risking a quick look over my shoulder, I caught sight of a light at my neighbor's back door and more lights in the front of their house.

I didn't know them, but it looked like they were home.

I was forming a vague plan of running next door and pounding on their door when a second shadow emerged from the darkness and launched itself at my attacker.

What the hell was going on?

I teetered on the balls of my feet, ready to run but needing to know if I was going to be followed before I realized I should take advantage of my attacker's distraction and run.

I spun and took off toward my neighbor's house.

It was a great plan right up until I stepped into a hole in the grass and pitched forward.

A scream tore from me as I tumbled head over heels, landing on my back, the breath knocked out of my lungs.

Somewhere in the dark, I heard my name. I didn't answer, desperate to get my breath back, wishing I could sink into the grass and cursing myself for wearing a white T-shirt instead of something dark.

I was rolling over onto my side, propping myself up on my elbows, when I heard it again.

"Charlie!" And then, "Goddammit."

A dark figure loomed out of the darkness, towering above me, dressed all in black except for the gleam of a white shirt.

Was that a bowtie?

What the ever-loving hell was going on?

"Just tell me if you're okay," a familiar voice demanded.

Lucas?

"I think I'm good," I said, my voice weaker than I would've liked.

I couldn't seem to get a deep breath, though that was probably less having the wind knocked out of me and more sheer terror.

"Lucas?" I asked, praying I wasn't imagining him.

"It's me."

In the dim light, I could barely see him striding across the yard, moving to the corner of the house, then back to the sidewalk, then toward me.

"God fucking dammit. He's gone."

Even though I knew it would've been better if my attacker weren't gone, the muscles in my chest relaxed. Finally, I drew a deep breath.

"What the fuck is going on, Charlie?"

Lucas turned and crossed into his own yard, opened the door of his car, and rooted around in the front seat. A second later, a flashlight switched on, the beam swinging back-and-forth over the ground between us until it stopped on my purse.

Stating what had already occurred to me, Lucas said, "A mugger would've gone for that."

I didn't say anything. Coming slowly to my feet, I realized I was shaking and cold. It wasn't hot outside, but it definitely wasn't cold.

Shock.

My thoughts sluggish, I watched the bobbing beam of the flashlight as Lucas collected my purse and picked up the brown shopping bag that had held my dinner.

I had a fleeting sense of regret for my cheeseburger, surely destroyed after flying across the yard.

Then Lucas was at my side, holding the beam of the flashlight down so as not to blind me. He wrapped his arm around me, pulling me into his side and taking my weight.

"You hurt? Can you walk?" He asked gently.

"I think I'm okay," I said.

"Let's get you inside."

As I shuffled beside Lucas over the uneven ground and through the gate into the backyard, aches bloomed all over my body. My hip, shoulder, and the side of my face were sore. A patch of scalp near my temple burned. I thought I felt the sticky heat of blood on my cheek.

Lucas led me up my back steps and into the kitchen. Depositing me next to the back door, he left me leaning against the wall and said, "Don't move."

He shut the back door and turned the deadbolt. Handing me the flashlight, he took off. Moving through each room in the house, upstairs and down, he checked every door and window before returning to the kitchen and flipping on the light.

At the sight of my face, his eyes narrowed and he swore.

He disappeared again, this time into the bathroom, and returned with a wet washcloth.

"Did he hit you?"

"No," I said carefully, wincing as Lucas cleaned the side of my face. The cold washcloth stung on my raw, scraped skin. "He knocked me down and I fell in the grass. I think he pulled out a chunk of my hair."

I stepped back and finally got a good look at Lucas.

My brain slid off the rails.

Lucas Jackson was wearing a tuxedo. His thick, dark hair hung in his face and his bowtie was slightly askew, but otherwise, he looked as if he'd stepped right off the ballroom floor.

With his tattoos covered up, he looked almost respectable.

Almost.

There was a hardness to his face, something in his eyes that was too alert, too on edge.

Respectable was safe. Lucas Jackson radiated danger.

But I was ignoring the most obvious point. Lucas Jackson in a tuxedo was the hottest thing I'd ever seen in my entire life.

The tux must've been custom tailored because it fit his broad muscular frame to perfection, showing off his lean waist and his long legs beautifully.

It was enough to distract me from the throbbing pain in my body.

I wondered if he'd let me unwrap him like a present after he was done yelling at me.

I hoped so.

CHAPTER NINE

LUCAS

C harlie was staring at me like she wanted to lick me from head to toe.

This was not the time.

It wasn't easy, but I tried to ignore the heat in her blue eyes and focus on cleaning her face. Blood dripped from a raw patch on her temple where the attacker had ripped out more than a few strands of hair.

She'd hit the ground hard, leaving an ugly, raw scrape on her cheek, tearing the shoulder of her T-shirt, and probably bruising the fuck out of her hip and shoulder.

Goddammit.

I didn't get scared. I'd learned a long time ago that fear is the enemy of rational thought. In my line of work, I had to think clearly and make smart decisions.

I did not get scared. Not for me. Not for anyone. Ever.

So I didn't know how to explain the ice in my gut when I'd seen Charlie go down.

One second, I was sitting in the cab of my dark truck, texting the client for the night's job before I went in and watching Charlie walk down the street, her bag of take-out swinging from one hand.

I got distracted from my text at the thought of all the things I was going to do to her after I changed and knocked on her back door, when out of nowhere, a figure erupted from the trees and launched itself at Charlie, taking her to the ground in a hit so hard I imagined I could feel it from twenty feet away.

Rage had flooded my brain.

Rage and fear.

Images kaleidoscoped through my head—all the things the attacker could be doing to Charlie.

Did he have a knife? A gun?

I couldn't see them anymore from my position in the truck, but I was moving before the thought was complete.

Diving out of the truck, I raced around the back to see indistinct dark figures rolling in the scrubby grass.

Charlie somehow broke free and stood frozen for a heartbeat before taking off toward the neighbor's front door.

Smart girl.

I went after her attacker. I was on him, had a grip on his neck with one hand, when I heard her scream.

If it had been a job, I might've handled it differently. But Charlie wasn't a job. I called her name. No answer. Her attacker struggled beneath me, grunting and kicking. I called Charlie's name again. Still no answer.

"Goddammit," I'd shouted, pissed at the asshole trying to get away and at Charlie for disappearing. I didn't have any restraints in my tux, no way to secure the attacker and still go after Charlie.

"Goddammit," I repeated under my breath.

I should have been calm. Deliberate. Calculating.

An hour before, I'd been at a benefit ball in a Buckhead

mansion, had made small talk, disappeared, disabled the security system, hacked into the owner's computer, downloaded his protected files, and strolled out.

My heart rate had never risen above normal. Now, it raced in my chest.

I let go of the attacker and surged to my feet, striding across the yard to where I'd seen Charlie go down. I almost tripped in a hole in the grass when I saw her white shirt.

All white. No blood. That was a good sign.

She said my name, her voice weak and shaking. I needed to get her in the house and figure out how badly she was injured.

I got her inside, cleared the house, and went to work on her face. At the sight of her smooth skin scraped raw, I wanted to find the asshole who'd jumped her and beat the shit out of him.

Why the fuck would someone be after Charlie?

Her eyes cleared gradually, shock from the attack wearing off as she took in the sight of me in my tux.

At the look on her face, I wanted to strip her naked and take her to bed, but that would have to wait till later.

"Why are you dressed like that?" she asked.

I thought about messing with her, telling her I'd been at the party for fun, but I found myself saying, "I had a job."

"What kind of job?"

"Maître d'?" I said, unable to resist teasing her just a little.

She didn't buy it, raising one eyebrow and waiting patiently for the truth. I shrugged one shoulder.

"A confidential kind of job."

"A confidential job for a client who required you to wear a tux?" she probed.

"Exactly. Almost all of my work is confidential," I said.

"You sound like the Sinclairs," she said. "They never tell any of the good stuff."

"Same line of work, but I freelance. Still, same principles. You don't get a lot of repeat clients if you talk about the job."

"I get that. Is it dangerous?"

"Sometimes. Tonight, not as dangerous as your walk home."

"I guess not."

Keeping my voice carefully neutral, I asked, "Any idea who it was?"

"I don't know for sure," she said slowly. "I couldn't see them in the dark. But there's been some stuff going on . . ."

She trailed off, either not sure how to explain or uncertain if she wanted to.

Tough luck. I wanted answers and I was going to get them.

"What kind of stuff?" I asked.

She shrugged one shoulder—the one she hadn't landed on—and said, "Well, for the last few months, some nut bag has been sending pictures of my aunt and uncle's deaths to different people in the family. Not to me . . . yet."

"Anyone attacked? Anything direct, like this? Or just leaving pictures?"

"Just pictures," she said. "So far, only for Jacob and Vance."

"Anything else?" I asked.

"A former client of Winters Inc. threatened me a few weeks ago," she admitted, squeezing her eyes shut as I went to work on the raw spot at her temple.

"Sorry," I said, hating that I was hurting her. "You got dirt in here."

"It's okay," she whispered. "Thank you."

I ignored her thanks and said, "What kind of threats?"

"Nothing specific," she said. "I was responsible for reporting his company to the FBI for fraud and he was pretty pissed off about it."

"Is that why Aiden fired you?"

"He says not. But I don't know. Maybe he thought if he fired me, Hayward would think I'd been punished."

"Could this have been him? Hayward?" I asked, lowering the washcloth.

"It could," she said. "It was dark and it happened so fast. I didn't really see him after I hit the ground, and then you were there . . ."

"If this guy is after you, what the fuck are you doing living in this house by yourself with no security? You barely even have working locks, for Christ's sake."

I tossed the washcloth on the floor and glared at her. She looked away for a second before her spine stiffened and she glared back.

Why did I like it so much when she went head to head with me? I should have been annoyed. Instead, I didn't know if I wanted to kiss her or keep arguing with her.

"I do have locks on the doors," she said. "And I didn't know anyone was after me. A few weeks ago, Hayward said he was going to 'get me'. But he's been busy with the FBI and he hasn't done anything. He hasn't called. He hasn't come by. Nothing. We don't even know that this was him."

"Is there anyone else who might want to attack you in the dark?" I demanded.

"No, of course not. I don't know what's going on, okay? Maybe it was Hayward, maybe not. I don't know."

I was too pissed at her to respond. Some guy was threatening her and she thought the best response was to move out of her fortress of a home into this completely unsecured, barely habitable house?

Life is dangerous enough without throwing yourself in the path of trouble. What would've happened to her if I hadn't been there?

I didn't want to think about it.

Didn't want to consider what her attacker's plan had been. She was lucky the worst of it was a scraped cheek, some missing hair, and a handful of bruises.

Charlie might not be so lucky the next time.

"You realize we have to call the police," I said, waiting for her to argue. She didn't disappoint.

"We can't call the police." Her jaw set, she crossed her arms tightly over her chest.

"Why the fuck not?" I demanded.

"Because it would be all over the news in about five seconds," she said. "I'm not doing that. I'm not going to be their bug under a microscope. Nothing happened. I'm fine. I'm getting a security system tomorrow, and everything will be all right."

"You're deluded," I said, facing her down. "For one thing, if it *is* this guy who threatened you, he'll come back for more. You need to establish a pattern of attacks at the beginning so you can press charges and we can make it stick when we catch the guy."

"No."

She wouldn't meet my eyes. Probably because I was glaring at her and she knew I was right.

"What if I can promise you it won't get out?" I asked.

"You can't promise me that, Lucas," she said, sounding exhausted.

Charlie was being obstinate, but she wasn't wrong. At least not about the press. If we called 911, the press would be all over her and the attention would be relentless.

She might be pretending she was a normal girl with a normal life, but she wasn't. She was Charlotte Winters, the crown princess of the Winters clan.

Her departure from Winters Inc. hadn't hit the news yet, but it would, eventually.

Even sooner if the attack got out.

It was too juicy a story, and we both knew the media would gnaw on it for weeks.

She wouldn't be able to walk down the street.

She wouldn't be able to leave her house.

She'd have to move home, a prisoner in Winters House, until the attention died down.

"I promise you it'll be quiet. Will you trust me?"

"Are you going to call my brother? Or one of the Sinclairs?" she asked, not trying to hide the hope in her voice.

"No. I'm going to call a detective I've worked with on another case. He can keep his mouth shut, and he'll take your statement and get the attack on record, but do it under the radar."

"And he won't call my brother?"

Charlie stared me down, raising an eyebrow. I might've thought she was being paranoid, but I knew how these things worked.

Aiden Winters had his finger on the pulse of Atlanta, at almost every level. There was no cop in town who would process a police report involving Charlotte Winters and not call Aiden.

Except, possibly, Detective Ryan Brennan.

"Brennan won't rat you out," I promised, "but we'll have to tell Sinclair Security before they put in your system."

Charlie opened her mouth to speak, but I raised a finger and pointed it at her face. Her eyes narrowed. I didn't care.

I was done arguing about this.

"Charlie, they have to know what kind of threat you're under so they can design the system to handle it. I know why you want to hide this from the press, but you can't hide this from your security team. It's idiotic. Do you have any idea what could've happened to you if I hadn't been sitting in my driveway when you got jumped?"

Charlotte's eyes went dark and she looked away.

Shit.

I didn't want her to start shaking again. I needed to get some food in her, and maybe a beer, before Brennan showed up.

Pulling my phone out of my back pocket, I flipped it open and dialed. Brennan answered on the second ring.

"Jackson. What is it?"

"I have a situation. I have a friend who needs to make a police report, but it has to stay quiet. She can't come into the precinct and she can't have a black-and-white in her driveway. Completely under the radar."

There was a long silence.

"Are you going to tell me who we're talking about?" Brennan asked carefully.

I gave him Charlie's address in answer.

"Be there in ten," he said.

That was why I liked working with Brennan. He was always calm, collected, and on the ball. I shoved my phone back in my pocket and glanced at Charlie, now leaning against the wall of her kitchen, hands hanging loose at her sides, staring at the floor.

She looked beat to shit and so tired she could pass out

right where she was. She couldn't go to sleep, not until she talked to Brennan, but a little food would steady her.

Grabbing her bag of take-out, I opened the container inside. Her burger was all over the place, avocado and onion strings and melted cheese mixed in with her fries. It looked a hell of a lot better than the dry chicken and finger food I'd had at the party. I did my best to reassemble it and handed the box to her.

"If you don't want furniture, you need to at least get some folding chairs and a table. For now, sit down on your futon and eat."

"Bossy," she said under her breath as she took the container and turned her back on me to walk down the hall to her makeshift bedroom.

I didn't give a shit if she thought I was bossy. Charlotte Winters needed to get her fucking head on straight. She wasn't going to like it, but she was going to goddamn listen to me.

I waited until she was settled on her futon and had a mouthful of food before I laid down the law.

"You need looking after," I said. As expected, her blue eyes flared with aggravation. It shouldn't have turned me on.

Since when did I like argumentative women?

Since never.

Charlie started chewing faster so she could swallow and start yelling at me.

I pointed a finger at her and said, "Can it. I know you're a smart, responsible, adult woman. Do you have any self-defense training?"

I could tell she was surprised by the question. Her reluctance was so obvious I had to fight a grin. She shook her head 'no'.

"Can you handle a gun?"

Another reluctant shake of her head.

"Do you have any of the skills you need to defend yourself if you're attacked or spot someone following you?"

This time, she didn't bother to shake her head, just gritted her teeth and swallowed, getting ready to argue back.

"You need looking after," I repeated.

Charlie took a huge bite of her burger and began to chew, her mutinous glare adorable.

"Does Sinclair have you on the schedule for your security system?"

She nodded.

"Tell me it's tomorrow."

Another nod.

That was something. They'd put in a solid system, and if they missed anything, I could upgrade it.

"Tell them you need a panic button. I could get you one, but I don't do a lot of personal security and I don't think I have any in stock. Sinclair will have them."

She swallowed her burger and asked, "What's a panic button?"

"It's a device you keep on you at all times. If anything happens, you hit it and it alerts your security team, and the police, that you need help immediately. I'll have them wire it to my phone, too, since I'm right next door. I can get here faster than they can."

"That sounds like a good idea," she said.

"Charlie, you need to be careful. That wasn't a mugger. A mugger would've knocked you down and taken off with your purse. Whoever that was, they wanted to hurt you. That's a hell of a lot more dangerous than someone who's out to steal something. Hopefully, it's this Hayward guy."

"Why are you hoping it's Hayward?" she asked.

"Because we *know* he's a threat. This crackpot who's

targeting your family is a complete unknown. I take it the Sinclairs have been trying to track down the source of the pictures?"

"Yeah. Since Jacob got the first one a few months ago. They haven't found anything. No fingerprints, and they said that whoever dropped the pictures off seems to know where the security cameras are, at least the cameras in Jacob's building, because we have them on video but they couldn't identify who it was. We don't even know if it's a man or a woman."

"There's no one you can think of with a grudge against your family?" I asked, not surprised when Charlie rolled her eyes at me.

It was a loaded question when talking about the Winters family.

"No one specific I can think of," she said. "But between people who have a problem with Winters Inc. and the way my cousins and brothers have slept their way through the state of Georgia, you could probably put together a very long list of people who don't like us."

"True. But sending pictures of the crime scenes is unusual. That's going back decades. Both cases are closed. Why bring them up now?"

"To mess with us?" Charlie asked. "I can't think of another reason."

I turned the problem over in my mind. I doubted it was about money. Normally, when a wealthy family was targeted like this, money would be my first thought.

But there was no blackmail here. Crime scene photos of the deaths weren't a secret. Someone who wanted money would be better off getting pictures of an affair or the company doing something underhanded.

The only reason I could think of to send the crime scene

pictures was to cause emotional upset. Someone wanted to scare them or hurt them.

"We've been hoping they'd make a mistake," Charlie said, "but so far, we haven't gotten another picture since Vance's. Maybe they gave up."

"Maybe. And there's no one other than Hayward who might have a grudge against you? An ex-boyfriend? One of those fiancés you didn't marry?"

Charlie's eyes flew wide. "How did you know about them?"

"You're a Winters," I reminded her. "It's common knowledge that you've been engaged four times and dumped all of them. Are you sure one of those guys isn't out for revenge?"

"Pretty sure." Charlie took another bite of her burger and studied the takeout container on her lap, rearranging what was left of her French fries as she chewed.

Pink flags of color stood out on her cheeks. She was embarrassed. I was curious.

"Really? Getting dumped by his fiancée is one of those things that can push a guy over the edge."

"Not these guys," she said after she swallowed. "Maybe if I'd messed with their golf clubs."

She shrugged one shoulder and took another bite.

"What does that mean?" I pushed.

I should've let it go, but someone had attacked her and it had been personal. A discarded lover was at the top of the list in this kind of crime.

I wanted to know why she was so sure not a single one of her four fiancés would be hurt or angry enough to come after her.

There was no future for me and Charlie, no engagement waiting around the corner, no white wedding followed by the pitter-patter of little feet.

We were the world's worst fit, but I knew if I'd been in love with a woman like her, if I'd had that face and that body and that attitude, and it was all mine and then she walked away . . . I could imagine that kind of loss breaking a man.

"So?"

"None of them loved me, okay?"

Charlie put the takeout container on the floor and pulled her feet up on the futon, propping her chin on her knees and wrapping her arms around her shins. Sitting like that, she looked about sixteen.

"Every single one wanted to marry me because I'm a Winters. None of them wanted *me*. With the first two, it took me a while to catch on.

"Number one was cheating, which was a pretty good giveaway. Number two kept asking me to spend money on him. Number three interrupted his proposal to take a phone call from a client. And I was never really engaged to number four. He just told everyone we were engaged."

"Why would he do that? He had to know you wouldn't go along with it."

"He did. But he was trying to impress a prospective employer. We'd been dating, so people knew we were together, and by the time I spread the word that we'd broken up, he had the job so it didn't matter."

"That sucks," I said.

It did. I'd assumed Charlie would be a target because she was gorgeous and sexy. How would it feel to realize the person you thought you'd spend your life with was only interested in your family and your bank account?

She deserved better than that. I was unreasonably grateful that she hadn't married any of those assholes.

"Yeah. It wasn't fun. So you know you can believe me

when I tell you I don't want a relationship. I'm kind of burned out on the whole *Where is this going? Let's get married.* thing. I'm tired of trying and being let down. I'd rather be on my own. I watched Aiden with Elizabeth for years. I always swore I'd never get married if I wasn't really in love, and then—"

Charlie let out a long sigh.

"You didn't love the guys you got engaged to?"

I couldn't imagine Charlie agreeing to marry someone she didn't love. She was too headstrong, too focused. She'd never commit the rest of her life to someone she didn't really want to be with.

She'd be tired of him before the ink was dry on the marriage license.

"Well, technically, number four wasn't an engagement. Neither was number three. If he hadn't taken the call in the middle of proposing, I still wouldn't have said yes. He was fun and a nice guy, but I didn't love him.

"But the first two guys . . . I did think I was in love with them. I was too young, I think. Looking back, I cared about them and they were important to me, but I don't think it was really love. Not the kind that lasts."

"You want a beer?" I asked, changing the subject.

At her nod, I snagged the discarded takeout box and went to go get us two beers. Charlie's answer to my questions left me feeling oddly deflated. I don't know what I wanted to hear, but her lack of hope was depressing.

It wasn't that I thought marriage was the pot of gold at the end of the rainbow. I hadn't seen a single example worth repeating when I was growing up.

Watching my mother with my stepfather was enough to sour me on the idea of marriage for life. I had no intention of ever finding a wife.

But Charlie . . . the idea of Charlie turning her back on marriage, on family—it just felt wrong. I toyed with the idea of looking up those first two fiancés, the ones who really hurt her.

I knew she wouldn't thank me if I did, but I was keeping the idea on the back burner. I didn't like the idea of some golf-playing dickhead breaking Charlie's heart.

I went back into the room to find Charlie curled up exactly as I'd left her, her un-scraped cheek resting on her knees, arms wrapped around her shins.

Handing her a beer, I set mine on the floor unopened and said,

"I need to run next door and change and grab a few things. I'll be right back."

"K."

I didn't like leaving her alone in her house, even behind locked doors. If she'd had a first-aid kit, I wouldn't have bothered going home, but she needed some ointment on that cheek and the raw spot where her hair had been yanked out.

I'd done my best to clean her wounds, but she'd hit the dirt hard, grinding soil into her opened skin. She'd heal better if I took care of it the right way.

I was back a few minutes later, staying next door only long enough to trade my tuxedo for gym shorts and a T-shirt and grab my first aid kit. I let myself back into Charlie's house, locked the door behind me, and rechecked the windows and doors on the first floor to make sure the house was secure.

I'd feel better when she had that security system in.

"Stay just like that," I said when I found her sitting in the same position. "I need to clean your face again."

Unzipping my first aid kit, I grabbed the disinfectant spray, antibacterial ointment, and a band-aid for her temple.

"What the hell do you have in there?" Charlie asked.

I followed her glance to my kit. I was so used to it that the size didn't seem weird. To a civilian, it must've looked like serious overkill.

The size of a small duffel bag, it had everything I needed to handle almost any injury. I'd trained in the Army as a field medic, among other things, and my skills had grown out of necessity in the years since.

I tried to answer her question without freaking her out.

"Just stuff. Band-aids, antibacterial spray, ointment, butterfly bandages, sutures. Stuff."

I could tell by the piercing look she gave me that Charlie wasn't buying my explanation, but she didn't push.

Quietly, she let me spread ointment on her cheek and temple, then pull down the shoulder of her T-shirt to check for bruising.

Her eyelids drooped. Between the adrenaline crash after the attack and her full stomach, I knew she was ready to pass out.

I got two ibuprofens out of the kit and handed them to her. The low hum of a car engine pulled up to the house.

"Take these and meet me in the kitchen," I said. "Brennan is here."

CHAPTER TEN
LUCAS

Brennan had his hand raised to knock on the door when I swung it open. He looked the same as always—button-down shirt, blazer, tie a little loose. His dark brown hair hung a fraction too long and always slightly out of place.

Friendly brown eyes disguised a sharp brain. I'd seen Detective Ryan Brennan at five a.m., five p.m., and every time in between. He was always the same.

I could've pulled him from his desk or from his bed and it wouldn't matter. I didn't trust many people, but Ryan Brennan was on my short list.

"You gonna tell me what's going on?" he asked in a low tone. Charlie stepped out of the hall and into the kitchen, the overhead light harsh, glaring down on the raw wounds on the side of her face.

"Holy shit," Brennan said. "You're in it this time, Jackson."

"Charlie Winters," I said, crossing the room to stand beside Charlie. "This is Detective Ryan Brennan. You tell him what happened, and he'll get it on record."

Charlie looked up at me with startled eyes. I couldn't stop myself from tucking a loose strand of hair behind her ear so it didn't get caught in the ointment on her cheek.

"You're sure I can trust him?" She whispered.

"I'm sure."

Charlie shoved her hands in the pockets of her jeans and told Brennan everything that had happened, including the cigarette butt she'd found by the back door and the intruder she'd thought she'd imagined.

That revelation had me fighting for control of my temper, but I managed to keep my mouth shut. She was under enough stress as it was. I wasn't going to make it worse.

As she spoke, she leaned into me, letting me support her weight. I wrapped an arm around her, ignoring Brennan's curious eyes.

He took notes and assured Charlie no one would find out anything unless it became unavoidable. As soon as they were done, I sent Charlie to get ready for bed and walked Brennan out.

"So, is she a job?" Brennan asked before he left.

"Next-door neighbor," I answered, deliberately leaving out the details.

Brennan met my eyes with a knowing look and stared me down.

"Next-door neighbor and a friend," I clarified.

That was all he was getting. Anything else was between Charlie and me. I wasn't going to make her a target of gossip, even with a man I trusted.

Knowing I was full of shit, Brennan shook his head, but he let me get away with it. Before he left, he said in a low voice that wouldn't carry down the hall, "Keep sharp. The Winters family are good people, but they're trouble, and that girl is way above your pay grade. Don't let whatever mess is swirling around her take you down with it."

"I've got this," I lied as I locked the door behind him.

It was only half a lie. As far as Charlie's safety was concerned, I did have it under control. I'd talk to whichever Sinclair showed up to put in her system, and we'd get her security settled.

If she was smart and used her head, I could keep her safe.

The rest of it?

Brennan was right.

She was way fucking out of my league. I had no business being friends with a woman like Charlotte Winters, much less claiming a place in her bed.

Too fucking bad. Now that I'd had a taste of Charlie, I wasn't giving her up. Not until I had to.

Charlie was in bed when I got back, wearing some kind of strappy sleep top. I couldn't miss the blooming bruise on her shoulder. If I looked, I knew I'd find another on her hip. They matched the skin on her cheek that hadn't been scraped raw.

If I'd had a target to punish for touching her, they'd be dead.

I stripped off my shorts and T-shirt, leaving them on the floor beside the futon, and slid in beside her. My ego loved the regret in her eyes as she took in my mostly exposed body then realized she was too sore for sex.

Wrapping one arm around her waist, I said, "Maybe in the morning, Princess. I'm exhausted and you're too beat up to do all the work."

As I'd meant her to, she smiled.

The smile drooped, her lips wobbled, and she looked away, saying in a thin, nervous voice, "I'm okay. You don't have to stay since we're not . . . you know. You can go home. I don't want you to feel like—"

Her unease was cute, but I put her out of her misery.

"I'm not going anywhere. I'm not leaving you to sleep here alone after you got jumped. Just close your eyes and go to sleep. We'll see about fucking in the morning."

I tried not to like the way her cheeks went pink when I said 'fucking'.

"I usually sleep on the outside," she said, rolling onto her un-bruised side and trying to get comfortable with the wall blocking her in.

"I'll move the futon away from the wall tomorrow," I said, "but for now, I stay between you and that door."

"Okay," she whispered.

A slow blink, then another, and she was asleep.

I lay beside her, listening to the house settle, alert for any creak, any thump, anything that sounded out of the ordinary.

I was more comfortable than I wanted to be with her warm body tucked up against mine, smelling of fruit and flowers and Charlie.

I never spent the night with women.

Ever.

I liked having a bed to myself. I didn't like clinging or the kind of expectations you created when you were there for breakfast.

I liked to fuck and go.

Tonight, I didn't even get a fuck, and there I was falling asleep with a woman for the first time in my life. After all these years, the surprise wasn't that I was sleeping with a woman, but how right she felt in my arms.

I woke before dawn to find myself wrapped around

Charlie, one leg between her thighs, my arm over her waist, my hand under her sleep shirt, holding her bare breast.

I was already hard, my cock pressing into her soft ass. I wanted Charlie, but I was going to wait. She needed sleep, not for some horny asshole to wake her up before sunrise for a fuck.

I had a thousand things I should do. Get up and get in a workout. Run next door to grab my laptop and see what was in my queue.

A lot of my jobs were in the field, but more of them used my strongest skill set, one that only needed a computer and a connection to the Internet.

I didn't move. I wasn't ready to wake Charlie, but that was only part of it. As much as I tried to think of reasons to get up, I couldn't seem to drag myself from her bed.

She shifted in her sleep, grinding her soft ass into my cock. I pushed back, just a little, the heat between her legs so enticing my head spun.

I could be patient. I'd learned how to wait a long time ago. Nothing worth having came easy, anyway. I closed my eyes. The sun would be up soon enough.

Reaching behind me, I felt for the box on the floor beside the futon. My fingers tagged the lid and I snagged a condom, sliding it under my pillow before I let myself fall into a light doze.

I didn't make my move until I felt Charlie shift against me, her body slowly coming awake.

My turn.

My fingers, still wrapped around her breast, tightened and slid to her nipple, squeezing and rolling with a firm pressure that had her squirming that soft ass against my rock hard cock.

It was a simple matter to push up her flimsy nightshirt, pull her top leg over mine, and tug her thong out of the way.

In this position, her pussy was completely open to me. I took full advantage, skating my fingertips over her, circling lightly.

I let out a groan when I discovered she was ready for me. I pressed one finger inside, my cock surging in demand as her slick heat closed around me.

Patience, motherfucker, I reminded myself, working the condom on my cock. She was bruised and battered, and when she got out of bed, she'd realize how stiff she was.

She didn't need me slamming into her. A second finger joined my first, dipping in and out, my thumb teasing her clit. Holding her open, I nudged my cock forward until just the head was inside. My breath caught in my chest at the tight clasp of her body on mine.

Nothing felt like fucking Charlie.

So sweet.

I buried my face in her hair and rocked deeper, filling her in degrees, our bodies barely moving.

"Touch your pussy for me," I whispered against her neck, taking her hand and leading it between her legs, pressing her fingers to her clit and rolling them in a circle.

I could feel the heat of her blush, but she did it. I slid my hand up her body, tracing a circle around her belly-button and along her ribs until I reached her breasts.

Her nipples were tight and hard. I plucked at them, teasing and pulling, loving the way her body clamped down on my hard length as I fucked her, deep and slow. She ground back into me, gasping my name.

"Lucas, oh my God, Lucas."

"Shh, baby. Just let it come. I'm going to take care of you. Just let it come."

Instinct told me to roll her onto her stomach, lift her by her hips until she was on her knees, and pound into her until we both exploded.

Another day, I would. Not this time. This time, she needed gentle. Charlie moved against me restlessly, pushing back into my cock, trying to take me deeper.

"Be still," I said, pulling her leg high and back, opening her body wide to mine. I moved her hand from her pussy and slid mine in its place, whispering, "Just let me. I've got you, Charlie."

I was fucking ready to come, the slide and clasp of her hot pussy driving me out of my mind. I pressed and rolled my fingers into her clit over and over until her body went stiff, her back arching, her hips thrusting into mine in one long surge as her muscles tightened in orgasm.

Finally, I let go, filling her in a release that left me drained and oddly weak.

I stayed there, holding her, breathing in the fruity floral scent of her hair and skin as her body relaxed around mine.

"Good morning," she said, sounding only half-awake, her voice husky and low.

"Morning."

"What time is it?" she asked.

"Probably a little after seven," I answered. I hadn't looked at my phone or my watch, but I didn't need to. I could tell by the light outside the window. "What time is the security team getting here?"

"Shit, seven thirty or eight," she said, starting to pull away from me. I didn't want to let her go, but we both needed to get up.

"Stay there. Don't move."

I rolled out of the bed and walked naked to the bathroom. Taking a washcloth from the pile on the back of the sink, I wet it with warm water and brought it to her, saying, "I'm gonna jump in the shower, won't take me a minute."

It would've been more gentlemanly to let her have the bathroom first, but I knew from experience that I'd take less than five minutes in the shower and she would undoubtedly take a lot longer. This way, I could get dressed and start making coffee while she took her time getting ready.

With her bruises, she'd need a long, hot shower far more than I did.

Charlie stood outside the bathroom door when I opened it. I started to apologize for making her wait when she reached up to place a palm on either side of my face and pulled my mouth down to hers.

The kiss was long, slow, and sweet. Her fingers slid into my hair, tugging me closer, her lips feeding from mine in delicate sips, tasting my lower lip, then the top before fitting her mouth to mine and driving her tongue deep. It was all I could do to let her take the lead when every instinct drove me to wrap her in my arms and devour her.

She pulled back, grinned up at me, and said, "Thanks for the wake-up fuck. Will you make coffee while I'm in the shower?"

"I'm on it," I said, a little thrown by her grin and the tender kiss.

She's not your girlfriend, I reminded myself. *I know. I know she's not my girlfriend.*

But that was not a fuck buddies kiss.

That was something else.

I put the kiss out of my mind. I had other things to focus on than kissing Charlie. My cock didn't agree, but that fucker was going to have to wait his turn. He'd gotten first dibs today, and now his needs were at the bottom of the list.

Aware that the security team was going to be all over

the house, I pulled the sheet up on the futon and straightened the pillows, hiding the box of condoms behind one leg of the frame.

I wasn't ashamed of fucking Charlie, and I didn't think she was embarrassed about me, but I didn't want her exposed to gossip. I got dressed in the shorts and T-shirt I'd put on the night before and went to make coffee.

Evers Sinclair was early. I should have expected it. Charlie Winters was as good as family.

I opened the door when he knocked, fighting amusement as he eyed me up and down, scowled, and said, "Lucas fucking Jackson. What the hell are you doing in Charlie's house?"

"I live next-door, asshole," I said, stepping back to let him in. And because I knew it would irritate him, "Coffee?"

"Yeah. Where's Charlie?" he demanded, following me down the hall into the kitchen, his eyes sweeping every inch of the foyer and what was visible of the dining room and living room. "What the hell is up with this house? Is it going to fall down on her head?"

"Hey, Evers," Charlie said, coming down the hall and walking into the kitchen. "You're early."

"What the fuck happened to your face?" The bruise beneath the red scrape on Charlie's cheek had bloomed into an ugly blue-purple overnight and a bright white bandage covered the raw spot on her temple where the asshole had pulled out her hair.

Evers whirled to face me. "What the fuck did you do to her?"

His arm flew back, ready to strike. Before he could swing, Charlie jumped between us. I slung an arm around her waist and shoved her behind me, catching Evers's arm in one hand.

"He didn't do this, Evers," Charlie said from behind me. "Back off."

Evers wrenched his arm from my hand and dropped it to his side, eyeing me like he was still thinking about hitting me.

"Step out from behind Jackson and look me in the eye while you tell me he had nothing to do with this."

Charlie tried to move away from me. I wound my arm around her shoulders, tucking her into my side. She'd known Evers her entire life, but he was a little too volatile right now.

I wasn't letting Charlie get between us. I could feel her thinking, then she settled into my side. Smart girl.

"I was walking home last night a little after eight thirty and someone jumped me in my front yard," she said.

Her delivery was emotionless, as if she were describing something that had happened to someone else.

"He knocked me down and I hit on my side, face first. My shoulder and hip are bruised up, and he tore out a chunk of hair, but otherwise, I'm fine."

Evers stared at her for a long moment, considering, before he turned to me. "Where the fuck were you?"

Charlie cut in. "Fortunately for me, Lucas was sitting in his truck in his driveway. He saw the whole thing, and if I hadn't tripped in the front yard, he would've had the guy."

"I had him on the ground," I explained. "Charlie took off for the neighbor's house, but she went down and I couldn't see her. I didn't hear a shot, but I couldn't be sure. He could have had backup."

Charlie's cheeks were pink and her eyes on the floor when she said, "I tripped in a hole in the lawn. Stupid. It knocked the wind out of me so I couldn't tell Lucas I was okay. If I hadn't tripped, whoever jumped me wouldn't have gotten away."

"But they did," Evers concluded. "And now we don't know if you have a stalker or if that was just a random attack."

"Whoever it was, he had no interest in her purse or getting in the house. Her locks are shit, not that there's anything to steal," I said. "She needs motion sensor lights, sensors on all the basement and first-floor windows and doors, and a panic button, to start."

"I know my job, Jackson." Evers sent me a scowl.

"Just helping out," I said with a grin. Unlike Charlie, Evers knew exactly who I was. He wouldn't fuck with me unless he had to. It probably wasn't smart to poke at him, but it was fun.

"Do you want coffee, Evers?" Charlie offered.

"Yeah, I'll take some coffee. And while we're getting it, you can explain why Lucas Jackson is in your house at the crack of dawn, Charlotte."

Charlie's spine went straight and her hands landed on her hips. She raised her chin and narrowed her ocean blue eyes on Evers.

"Don't you 'Charlotte' me, Evers Sinclair. It is not the crack of dawn. And I can have my neighbor over for coffee if I want to. It's none of your goddamn business. So fucking nosy."

Turning to me, she said, "They're the worst gossips. Tell one of these boys anything and the others know it five minutes later."

"Hey," Evers protested. "I know how to keep things confidential, Charlie. We've never had a client—"

"I wasn't talking about work, Evers, and you know it. I was talking about you Sinclair boys and the Winters boys and the way you all tell each other everything. Especially when things are none of your business."

I dropped my face to my coffee, hiding my amusement. Evers was honest enough not to argue with her.

"Evers," she said, the teasing tone gone, "you can't tell anybody about this."

"Charlie, you know that's not going to happen." He shook his head at her. "You really think I'd keep something like this from Aiden? Or Cooper? No fucking way."

"Sinclair," I started, and when his eyes swung to me, they were hard and calculating.

"What, Jackson? You don't want me to tell Aiden or Holden that you're banging their sister?"

"Fuck you, Evers," Charlie said without heat, handing him his coffee. "This isn't any of their business."

"You and Jackson? Debatable. You getting jumped in your yard? That's definitely their business, and you know it. I didn't hear about this, so I'm assuming you didn't make a police report."

"She made a report," I said.

"Brennan?" Evers asked, approval in his eyes for the first time.

Charlie looked between the two of us for a few seconds before awareness dawned.

"You two know each other," she said. "How do you two know each other?"

I cleared my throat, trying to think of the best way to explain who I was. Evers took care of the problem for me, the interfering bastard.

At least he told her the truth.

"You remember the president of the Raptors motorcycle club who killed Big John when he went after Abigail?" Evers asked Charlie.

Her eyes went comically wide. I would have laughed if my heart hadn't been trying to pound its way out of my chest.

Charlie wasn't mine, but I wasn't ready to give her up yet. And that Lucas Jackson, the Lucas Jackson who'd been president of one of the most notorious biker clubs around—he wasn't me. Not really.

"That was a temporary thing," I said. "I'm out of the Raptors. I have been for a while, and you fucking know it, Sinclair."

"You have a motorcycle?" Charlie asked, her head tilted to the side, curiosity alive in her sparkling blue eyes.

What?

Of all the things I'd imagined her saying after Evers's revelation, asking about my bike wasn't on the list.

"In the back of the house, under a cover. Actually, I have two. The Harley was my brother's. He's the reason I was working with the Raptors. The Triumph is mine."

"I'll do you a favor," Evers said to Charlie. "I'll wait until the end of the day to talk to Aiden. We need to get the security system up and running. My team should be here any second. Let's talk about what we're going to do."

Evers ran through a list that included everything we'd already discussed, plus a gate on the driveway, cameras inside and out, and a handful of other things that would guarantee no one would get to Charlie while she was in her house.

The Sinclair team arrived and got to work. Evers took charge of the installation, which kept him too busy to bother Charlie or me.

I thought about going home. I had plenty to do and no reason to stay. Charlie was safe. I had work piling up.

Instead, I found myself following her into the living

room where she was stripping paint from an old mantle. It was a beautiful piece, made of oak with intricate carving that had been all but ruined by multiple coats of paint.

"Are you stripping all the paint off the trim?" I asked, turning around to study the rooms in the front of the house.

All of them had wood trim that had been painted dark brown. Why you'd paint trim like that a dark brown instead of just staining it, I didn't know.

The trim in my house had been the same, and returning it to its natural state had been a bitch.

"I'm planning to," Charlie said. "This paint stripping stuff is awful though. It stinks and it takes forever."

I crouched in front of the fireplace mantle beside her and picked up the paint stripper and a rag.

"This isn't the best way to strip paint off wood. Not on the regular trim anyway. The way this mantle is carved, it's pretty much your only option."

"There's another way to do it?" Charlie asked.

"Yeah, heat. I've got a thing at my house. I'll lend it to you when you're done with the fireplace. You plug it in, hold it over the paint, and the paint bubbles up—practically lifts right off the wood. I'll show you how it works when you're ready to move on from the mantle."

"That sounds awesome," Charlie said. "I really wanted to stain all of this trim, but after working on the mantle yesterday . . . ugh."

Between the two of us, I figured we could have the mantle knocked off in an hour or two. We worked in silence for a while before Charlie got up to open the windows.

When she came back, she asked, "So why were you with the Raptors? Was it a job?"

"No. That wasn't a job. That was revenge."

"Will you tell me about it?" Charlie asked, sneaking a glance at my face.

I thought about it.

Why not?

I didn't have anything to hide, and her brothers or the Sinclairs would probably tell her if I didn't. But not now. Not with the Sinclair team and Evers in the next room.

Glancing over my shoulder, then back at Charlie, I said, "I will. Another time."

A thud and curse sounded from the kitchen and Charlie nodded. "Later," she agreed.

I wondered if she'd still welcome me into her bed after she knew the whole truth. I was going to find out. The truth was ugly, but I wouldn't lie to Charlie. She'd have to take me as I was, scars and all.

Chapter Eleven
Charlie

I left the Sinclair team at work securing my house. Lucas went home to check in on a new job, and I was headed to Winters House to ransack my storage bins in the attic.

We'd finished with the fireplace mantle, and it was as gorgeous as I thought it would be, but I'd underestimated exactly how messy stripping paint could be.

I'd spent the last few years wearing mostly suits and dresses. I didn't have a large collection of clothes I was happy ruining while I worked. I was pretty sure that after college, I'd thrown a bunch of old jeans and T-shirts into a storage bin and hauled them up to the attic.

Assuming they still fit, they'd be exactly what I needed. I'd already dropped a bunch of money on the futon, the mini-fridge and the coffeemaker. The idea of a newish truck to replace my ancient sedan hovered in the back of my mind.

If I decided to trade my car for a truck, I didn't want to have wasted money on new clothes I was just going to end up ruining.

I let myself in the front door and locked it behind me. Footsteps echoed through the front hall, too heavy to be Mrs. Williamson. Still edgy after being jumped the night before, I spun around and froze.

Aiden loomed in front of me. When his eyes landed on my bruised, scraped face, they went white-hot with rage.

"What the fuck happened?"

Aiden took my face in his hands, his touch gentle in contrast to his furious voice. He tilted my cheek to the light and gritted his teeth.

"Are you okay? Did Lucas Jackson do this?"

"Why does everyone think Lucas would hurt me?" I asked, stepping back and jerking my face out of Aiden's hold.

A thought occurred to me. "How do you know about Lucas? Did Evers call you?"

"How does Evers know about Lucas?" Aiden asked with a raised eyebrow. "To answer your question, I know about Lucas Jackson because my sister bought the house next door to his and I make it my business to know who her neighbors are. He helped out Jacob with Big John, but that doesn't mean he isn't a dangerous man, Charlie."

"Well, he didn't do this. I got jumped in my front yard last night and Lucas happened to be sitting in his truck next door. He ran the guy off. Lucas would've had him but I tripped and he let the guy go so he could make sure I was okay."

"Fuck," Aiden ground out.

"He called a police detective he knows so I could make a statement without it getting out to the media. He may be dangerous, Aiden, but he took care of me."

Aiden's jaw clenched.

"And how does Evers know about Lucas?"

I shrugged one shoulder and studied the crown molding in the entrance hall, suddenly feeling like a teenager getting the third degree after missing curfew.

"Lucas was at my house this morning when Evers got there to start working on my security system," I said, trying to sound innocent.

Aiden let out a harrumph that let me know he wasn't buying it.

"Charlie," he said on a growl.

I pinned him with a glare.

"Not your business, Aiden."

Aiden matched my glare for a long moment before he let out a long, resigned sigh.

"You're right, it's not my business," he said, the growl still in his voice. "And you're wrong because everything about my baby sister is my business."

I let out a growl of my own and started past Aiden toward the stairs, saying over my shoulder, "You're annoying. I'm going up into the attic to grab some stuff. You're working from home?"

"Just for a little while," he called after me. "Stop into my office before you leave. And give a shout if you have anything heavy to bring down. I'll get it."

I shook my head at him as I climbed the second flight of stairs up to the attic. Aiden, for all of his alpha-male bossiness, had his mother-hen act down to an art.

The attic was not as creepy as it sounded. Our house was old, but not ancient. It'd been built at the end of an era in which families like ours had live-in staff. What we now used as the attic used to be staff quarters and the nursery.

These days, the only live-in staff were Mrs. Williamson and the gardener, both of whom had small private cottages on the grounds.

In the years since we'd downsized, these rooms had been taken over by a disorganized array of old furniture, unused artwork, unlabeled boxes, and plastic storage bins.

At some point in the last five or six years, Mrs. Williamson had taken a stab at bringing order to the chaos, but she didn't get very far before deciding it was a waste of time. Running Winters House was a full-time job and organizing the attic was a massive project.

She'd settled for making sense of a single room, the one that used to be the nursery. Now, it was lined with custom-built shelves filled with neatly stacked bins, all meticulously labeled.

This was where Mrs. Williamson stored holiday decorations, extra linens, and anything else she deemed important for the proper management of Winters House and the Winters family members in her charge.

The other rooms remained a mess. I picked my way through the room where I thought I'd dumped my stuff from college.

Hands on my hips, I surveyed the hodgepodge of boxes, bins, and loose junk strewn around the room. We really needed to do something about this. The problem was that sorting through old dusty boxes of stuff wasn't anyone's idea of fun. It definitely wasn't mine.

I opened the first bin that looked like it could've been a few years old. Baby clothes, whose I don't know. Maybe mine or Annalise's based on all the pink. I refastened the lid and shoved it aside, reaching for a dusty green plastic bin.

Papers and manila envelopes. A quick glance through the contents told me this was decades worth of report cards. I was not going through those.

The next bin had clothes, but not mine. These were for a boy, bigger than baby but not an adult.

Why did we save all the stuff?

As I realized the answer, tears filled my eyes. My mother had been a packrat. I'd forgotten that.

Surrounded by storage bins she'd probably packed herself, I remembered my father teasing her about her need to hold on to every scrap of our childhoods.

She always smiled at him and said, "Someday, you'll thank me." I rested my forehead on the side of the bin and let out a sigh.

I wished I had more of her than this. We had pictures, and somewhere up here, someone had probably packed up their clothes and things for us to deal with later. I wasn't sure if I wanted to find them or not.

Either way, they were both gone. Both my parents and my aunt and uncle. All of them gone. I dragged in a ragged breath, scrubbing my wet cheeks with the heel of my hand.

Crying about it wasn't going to do anyone any good.

I stood up and picked my way through the stacks of bins on the floor, looking for a new section to try out. I saw a bin that looked newer than the others, closer to the door. That could be it.

Peeling back the lid, I spotted a faded Emory Athletics T-shirt I remembered caging off an old boyfriend.

Jackpot.

I tossed the lid on the floor and rummaged through the neatly folded clothes. Jeans, cut off shorts, piles of T-shirts. Exactly what I was looking for.

I checked the sizes on the jeans and was relieved to see most of them would still fit. That was something, but I'd thought there was more than one bin.

Putting the top back on, I shoved it through the door and out into the hall. There'd been another bin next to it. Same color, looked to be the same relative age. I was pretty sure I'd filled one with sandals and sneakers and a few sweatshirts.

I tugged at the lid and pulled it back to find a pile of papers. I almost closed it up and moved on but my aunt's name on the label of a file folder, yellowed and curled with age, caught my eye. Why were my aunt's papers in one of the newer storage bins?

I pulled out the file folder and flipped it open. Medical bills. Not that interesting. The folder beneath had the record of her stay in the hospital when Tate had been born. The one under that was from Vance and Annalise, the next from Gage.

I gathered the files together and moved to put them back in the bin when I realized there was one more folder like the others.

Older. Opening it, I looked for the date. July 6, 1981. Before Gage was born. Before she married Uncle James.

A fine tremor shook my hand as I reached for the sealed manila envelope that had been beneath the mysterious hospital bill in the folder. I worked one finger beneath the seal and carefully opened the envelope.

What the hell?

Adoption papers?

Aunt Anna had a baby she gave up for adoption? I had a cousin—my cousins had a sibling—that none of us knew about. Unless they did know and just hadn't told me.

I knew Aiden didn't tell me everything, but this was too big to keep a secret, wasn't it? I stacked the folders with the hospital records in the envelope with the adoption papers and shot to my feet, running for the stairs.

I had to know.

The tread of my sneakers skidded across the polished hardwood floors as I raced down the staircase and took a hard right down the hall to Aiden's office. I screeched to a halt in his doorway, the stack of papers clutched to my chest, to find him on the phone.

One look at me and Aiden ended his call, setting his phone down on his desk.

"What is it?" he asked.

All my earlier haste had fled. The carpeted floor between the door and Aiden's desk was a mile wide. I trudged across it, suddenly afraid of what he would say when he saw the papers in my hands.

I couldn't imagine he'd shrug and dismiss them. He couldn't know about this. He couldn't. We'd lost enough family. Aiden wouldn't hide something like this from the rest of us.

Unless they were all hiding it from me. That sounds paranoid, but the boys—the older ones—have always had a tendency to try to keep things from Annalise and me, as if we were too innocent and delicate to handle the uglier aspects of life.

Absurd, because we'd all seen too much ugliness before we were old enough to drive. We didn't need to be shielded. Try telling that to Aiden, Gage, and the rest of them.

I thrust the stack of files and the envelope at Aiden. He carefully took them and asked, "Where do I start?"

"Three of the folders are from when Aunt Anna was in the hospital with Gage, Vance and Annalise, and then Tate." Aiden opened the folders one by one and scanned their contents, nodding in agreement. "But the fourth," I went on, my voice shaking. "The fourth is from July of 1981. Before she married Uncle James. The hospital was in Virginia, not Atlanta. In the envelope . . . those look like adoption papers, Aiden. Is that what they are?"

Aiden turned the stiff manila envelope over in his hands.

"Did you open this? Or did you find it this way?"

He raised the ragged flap I'd torn a few minutes before and eased out the stack of papers.

"It was sealed. I opened it. But Aiden, all of this was in a new bin. Wouldn't this stuff have been put away years ago?"

His eyes flicking back and forth across the papers, absorbing every word, Aiden said absently, "There was a leak in the attic a few years ago. Must have been while you were in Texas for that internship after you graduated. Mrs. Williamson re-packed some of the damaged boxes in new bins. But none of us went through any of it."

We fell silent as Aiden reviewed each sheet of paper from the envelope. A stapled stack of legal size documents and something that looked like an official certificate, gilt gleaming from the border and a round seal in the corner.

I paced in front of his desk until he shot me a quelling glance over the papers. I sat, obedient for once, in one of the big leather chairs opposite Aiden's desk, wishing I hadn't drunk all of Aiden's whiskey.

That Macallan would've come in handy.

After what felt like hours, Aiden swept the papers back into a neat pile and slid them into the envelope, carefully sealing it shut. He lay his palms flat on the surface of his desk and let out a long breath.

"It looks like Aunt Anna gave birth to a baby boy July 6, 1981, and put him up for adoption. There's no information in that file on the family who adopted him or what his name might be. Or who the father is. I'm making two guesses—that Uncle James knew about this, or Anna never would've brought these papers to the house, and that he wasn't the father."

"So you didn't know?" I asked. It didn't seem like Aiden knew, but I had to be sure. He shook his head.

"Of course not. I may not tell you everything, Charlie, but I'd never keep a secret like this."

"But wasn't Aunt Anna already with Uncle James in July of 1981?" I asked, trying to piece the timeline together in my mind.

"It's hard to say. They all knew each other back then, Uncle James, Dad, Mom, Aunt Anna, William—hell, half of their friends were from college.

I know James and Anna knew each other, and they started dating some time around then because they got married a year later. But the only one who would know the exact timeline is William."

"We're not going to talk to William about this, are we?" I asked.

I loved William. I called him Uncle William most of my childhood, even though he wasn't a relative, and he'd done his best since our parents had died to step in and speak for them the way he thought they would've wanted him to.

He loved us, and we loved him. Lately, though, we'd been clashing. I wasn't there, but I'd heard from Vance, Emily, and Jo that he'd been awful about Abigail when she first got together with Jacob.

I was dreading talking to him about Aiden firing me. I knew he'd say something archaic like, "Now you can focus on finding a husband," or something stupid like that.

William was all about proper behavior. He was on the board of the country club and expected all of us to behave in a manner befitting the Winters name.

He'd been disappointed a lot in the past fifteen years. I knew there was no way he would support our attempt to find an illegitimate child our aunt had given up for adoption.

"Talking to William would certainly clear things up," Aiden said. "But I think we need to have a family meeting and then bring the Sinclairs in. If anyone can find Anna's son, they can. Once we find him, we can decide what we want to do."

"Do you want me to stay quiet about this?" I asked.

"Not for long. Vance and Magnolia get home in a few days. I don't want to tell everyone else without them."

That made sense. A few more days wouldn't change anything. Still, this was huge. It felt weird to just sit on the information. We should be trying to find this mysterious missing Winters child.

"Okay," I reluctantly agreed. "We can wait."

"You look like you need a drink," Aiden said. "I'd offer you one, but someone seems to have absconded with my best whiskey."

"That's terrible," I said, trying not to smile. "What kind of fiend would do such a thing?"

"Are you still mad at me?" Aiden asked.

"I'm too busy to be mad at you," I said.

I wasn't ready to admit that I forgave him. He didn't deserve to be let off the hook that easily.

He stood up from behind his desk and said, "Did you find what you were looking for upstairs? Before this?" He gestured at the papers on his desk.

"I found enough." I'd lost interest in looking through any more of the bins.

Aiden rounded his desk and I stood. Slinging one arm around my shoulder, he tugged me into his side, dropping his head to kiss my hair.

"Come on, show me which one it is and I'll carry it down for you."

I rose up on my toes to kiss his cheek. "You're a pain in the ass, Aiden, but I love you."

I didn't forgive him. But it didn't matter. I loved him anyway and I always would.

Chapter Twelve

Charlie

I was distracted when I got home. I didn't like having a secret. It made me feel like I was lying to everyone I saw.

Evers could tell something was off, but he probably thought it had to do with the attack the night before and didn't push. He walked me through the security system, which seemed overly complicated. I was one woman, not Fort Knox.

If anything moved in my yard, lights would go on and the system would send an alert to my phone and Sinclair Security. If I hit the panic button, the police, the Sinclair team, and Lucas would know in an instant. And all the time, the cameras would be recording.

If anyone touched the windows or tried to break open the door, the wrath of hell would descend upon them in the form of a screeching alarm that rendered me temporarily deaf when Evers tested it.

I didn't like the idea that there were cameras inside my house, even though I trusted the team at Sinclair Security not to spy on me without reason. It just made me uneasy to know people could be watching anything I did.

After I'd convinced him I understood how to work the system, Evers left with a hug, a kiss on my cheek, and a warning to be careful.

He'd been relieved to find out that Aiden knew about the attack, but I was absolutely positive he'd be calling my brother anyway. Oh well. I was used to it. Aiden had probably called one of them the second I left the house, demanding to know all about the security system. And as soon as he pried Detective Brennan's name out of Evers, Brennan would get a call of his own.

I threw the clothes from the storage bin in the washing machine in the mudroom and tried to figure out what to do next. We'd finished with the mantle that morning, and I wasn't ready to tackle the paint on the rest of the trim until Lucas showed me the easier way to strip it.

I'd pulled all the rotten boards off the porch, and it was ready for the contractors to show up the next day to start putting it back together.

I was about to go upstairs to make notes for my meeting with the contractor in the morning when there was a knock on the kitchen door. I tried to ignore the giddy feeling in my chest at the thought of seeing Lucas.

It's just Lucas, I told myself. *Nothing to get giddy over.*

Ha.

If there were ever a man worth getting giddy over, Lucas Jackson was at the top of the list. But giddy was an emotion reserved for the heart. What we had going on was focused a little lower than that.

I unlocked the door and turned the handle before I remembered the alarm. Holding up one finger to tell him I'd be right back, I went to the keypad in the hallway off the kitchen and stared at it for a second before punching the buttons to disarm the system.

The screen flashed green, indicating the alarm was off. Sweet. I was sure I'd eventually manage to set the thing off by accident, but not yet. I went back and finished opening the door, letting Lucas into the kitchen.

"You remembered to turn on the alarm," he said with approval. "A lot of people only turn them on when they're out, but you need to use it all the time."

"I know, I know," I said, interrupting him. "Evers gave me the lecture. Seriously, I don't want anyone getting in here and coming after me. I won't forget to use the alarm."

"What about the work on the house?" Lucas asked. "You're exposed while workmen are going in and out. Even if we vet everyone, they're not going to set the alarm every time they open and close the door."

"Then I'm just going to have to take a risk," I said, "because I'm not stopping work on the house."

Lucas crossed his arms over his chest, preparing to argue, and I rushed on. "Lucas, I can't. My contractor has me on his schedule. If I pause the job, he'll move his crews on to his next client and who knows when I'll get them back. I like this guy. He doesn't talk down to me and he does good work. He shows up when he says he's going to show up, and so far, every project has been completed almost on time. We don't even know that whoever came after me last night is going to come back."

"Is there any point in arguing with you about this?" Lucas asked.

He uncrossed his arms, letting them fall to his sides, hooking his thumbs in the pockets of his army green cargo pants. His T-shirt had been washed so many times it was a mottled gray, the fabric stretched tight over his biceps and across his chest.

Lucas was used to using his size to intimidate. I'll admit, with his eyes narrowed and all those muscles showing in stark relief, he *was* intimidating, even a little scary.

I wasn't afraid of Lucas. No, when he towered over me, looking pissed off and dangerous, all I wanted to do was touch him, to peel up that tight T-shirt and lick my way across the ridges of his abs. To unsnap his cargoes and shove them down over his lean hips and tight ass.

I shook my head, chasing off my lustful thoughts. It was the middle of the day, for God's sake.

What had we been talking about?

The side of Lucas's mouth quirked up in a half-smile and he said, "Are we going to fight or do you want me to fuck you?"

Well, if those were my only choices . . . no contest.

Lucas's smile grew into a full-blown grin. "I brought the equipment to start stripping the paint off that trim in the front hall, but if you'd rather fuck, we can do that instead."

I bit my lip in indecision. I really, really wanted to have sex with Lucas again. I couldn't imagine ever not wanting to have sex with Lucas.

I also wanted to get that paint off the trim, especially without using that smelly paint stripper. He laughed at the look on my face and said, "Or, we could work on the house for an hour, and then I'll fuck you."

He walked past me to the back door, pausing to drop a kiss on my lips before he disappeared onto the porch, reappearing a few seconds later with a cardboard box in his arms, a power cord spilling over the edge.

"Do you want to start in the front hall or the living room?"

I thought about it. It would be nice to have the front hall finished so when I walked in the door, I could see a clear sign of progress. On the other hand, we'd already started the mantle in the living room, so it felt like we should finish the rest.

"The living room," I said, making my choice.

Lucas led the way and set his box down in front of the mantle. Taking out the equipment, he lay it on the floor in a neat row.

"We're going to use this," he said, pointing to a rectangular metal box with a handle and a power cord, "to heat up the paint. Just hot enough so it bubbles up off the wood. Then we'll scrape it off and move on to the next section. It's still a pain in the ass, but it's much easier than using that paint stripper."

It didn't take long to work out a system, Lucas heating the paint and me coming behind him to scrape it off. The sight of raw wood emerging from beneath the paint scraper, inch after inch, thrilled me.

The house was shedding its past like an old skin, and I was making it happen. Well, I was part of making it happen. The first time I'd seen it, I'd known this place could be beautiful.

It could be a home, filled with warmth and love, despite its state of disrepair and neglect. A few feet of baseboard weren't much, but it was one more step to bringing the home back to itself.

Maybe, in the process, I was bringing me back to myself, too. I must have been more quiet than I realized as we worked because Lucas sensed something was off.

"Did you have a fight with your brother when you went home?" he asked.

"No," I said slowly.

"Worried about what happened last night?"

I could take the easy way out and just say yes, but I wasn't really worried about the attack. If I hadn't had so much else on my mind, I probably would've been freaking out, but Lucas was right to sense my distraction.

I hadn't known him very long, but I got the sense he wouldn't bother to ask what I was thinking if he didn't really want to know. And if he really wanted to know, he wasn't going to take a vague answer.

"Can I trust you?" I asked.

Typically, Lucas's answer was honest, if not reassuring. "That depends. What do you want to trust me with?"

"A secret."

"About you? Or about someone else?"

"Both," I said. "I found something when I was at home. Aiden asked me not to tell anyone, but it's making me a little crazy. You're in the same line of work as Evers, right? You know how to keep your mouth shut."

Lucas laughed. "Yeah, I know how to keep my mouth shut. And I'll keep your secret. What's going on?"

I told him about the records I'd found, the adoption papers, the possibility that I had a cousin out there somewhere who didn't know he had a family.

When I was done, Lucas said, "You know, whoever he is, this guy might not want to be found. Or, he could already know who he is. He could already know who you are."

"What are you saying?" I asked, afraid I knew exactly what he was getting at.

"The pictures? Someone jumping you in your front yard? I know you want to swoop in and find this guy and bring him into the fold. You're imagining a joyous reunion, and maybe that's what's going to happen, but just because the lot of you Winters are nice people doesn't mean this guy is. You don't know who raised him or what his life has been like."

"But that's why we have to find him," I said. "What if he needs a family and he doesn't know we're here?"

Lucas shook his head at me and put down the heater, flicking it off. He sat back on his heels and said gently, "Princess, you lost a big chunk of your family at a young age. It's natural to want to fill in the gaps. Maybe this guy is a good guy. I hope to hell he is when you find him. I'm just saying, be careful."

His words left me deflated. Lucas was right, and I was being naïve. I absolutely did not want to believe that my long-lost cousin had anything to do with the pictures being delivered or whoever jumped me in my yard. That would be too depressing for words.

We fell silent again, working in harmony for another few feet of baseboard before I gave into my curiosity and said, "Will you tell me about the Raptors now?"

Lucas blew out a breath. "If you really want to know. It's not a pretty story."

"Tell me."

I wanted to know more about this man who had quickly become a part of my life. So much of him was a secret, and too many people knew who he was while I knew next to nothing.

"I left home at eighteen," he said. "My stepdad was an asshole. He married my mom when I was ten and Gunner was seven, and from what I could see, he didn't do a whole lot except drink beer and order the rest of us around.

"I hated him, and he hated me. The second I could leave, I did. I joined the Army right out of high school. I stayed in touch with my brother and my mom, but I never went back. Dale was a Raptor, a foot soldier—no one important, but he loved that club.

"The only work I ever saw him do when I was growing up was running errands for the club. When he wasn't half-drunk on an easy chair in our trailer, he was at the club-house, kissing Raptor ass. He brought Gunner in when he was just a teenager. By the time my mom died, Gunner had worked his way up in the club."

"What does that mean, that he worked his way up in the club?" I asked. What I knew about biker clubs could fit on my thumbnail with space left over.

"The Raptors were into a lot of shit, mostly protection—helping drug dealers move their product from one place to another. They didn't deal themselves, but there were other things . . ."

Lucas gave me a long look, then shook his head and fell silent. When he spoke again, it was clear he wouldn't be explaining what 'other things' meant.

"Gunner was always a smart kid, less rebellious than I was. He thought Dale was an asshole too, but he played along and kept from getting his ass kicked."

"You didn't?" I asked. It wasn't hard to imagine a teenage Lucas mouthing off to his stepdad.

True to my vision, he said, "Never could keep my mouth shut. Which is funny because I loved the Army, and they don't appreciate smart asses. But it was different, because even at eighteen, I recognized the Army's authority. I chose them. Dale was just some dickhead who talked my mom into marrying him, and she was so tired from working two jobs, she didn't realize that he was going to be one more burden."

"I can't see you taking orders from anyone," I said.

"Neither could I," he admitted. "But I had to get out of

that house. Out of that town. I was done with everyone looking at me, at Gunner, like we were trash.

"I played football in high school once I filled out. Could've gotten a scholarship. I wanted to go to college, but I was too angry. Restless. The Army seemed like a good compromise. I'd have opportunities, and I could work out some of my aggression without getting thrown in jail."

"And you liked it?" I asked.

I was surprised he was telling me so much, and I wanted to hear more. I wanted every crumb of Lucas Jackson I could get. He fascinated me.

Gorgeous, amazing body, fantastic in bed. But beyond that he was a mystery, one I wanted to solve. It occurred to me that I wasn't supposed to want to know the life story of a fuck buddy. Asking personal questions kind of defeated the purpose of keeping things casual.

"I fucking loved it," he answered. "Shocked the hell out of me, but the Army and I were a perfect fit. I went to college while I was in, got an IT degree, and got to do some really cool shit with it. I ended up in Spec-Ops for a few years before I got out and started freelancing."

"Is Spec-Ops what I think it is?" I wasn't exactly sure, but I was imagining something like the Rangers or the Seals. Or one of those teams you hear about that doesn't exactly have a name.

Semi-confirming my suspicions, Lucas said, "Probably. And if it's not, I can't tell you what it is."

After years of knowing the Sinclairs, and with my cousin Gage doing something equally secretive in the Army himself, I knew better than to press further. When they said they couldn't tell me, it meant they *really* couldn't tell me.

"So how did you go from freelancing to the Raptors?"

"My brother," Lucas said.

The words had weight, dragging the smile from his face. I knew grief. I'd lived with grief for years. I didn't need Lucas to tell me that Gunner was dead.

I kept my mouth shut and waited. We moved a little further down the baseboard, stuck in a corner for a few minutes where the paint in the cracks wouldn't heat up enough for me to scrape it off. Finally, Lucas started speaking again.

"The Raptors had a president with ambition. He wanted to expand the club, which ended up in a turf war. Gunner took his back and got promoted to lieutenant, then VP. Around that time, Dale got himself killed and I came home for the funeral. Mostly to see Gunner. I didn't give a shit about Dale, but I needed to make sure Gunner was all right.

"He was like a different guy. Serious. Had his shit together. We hadn't been close for a while, but after that, we stayed in touch. I didn't like what he was into. Not that my hands were always clean, but I fought for our country. And even freelancing—let's just say I have a well-defined line I won't cross."

"The Raptors were on the other side of that line?" I asked.

"Yeah. Way on the other side. But he was my brother. The only family I had left. We got a lot closer those last few years. I was traveling all over, almost never stateside, but when I was, we'd hang out. Then the president of the Raptors decided to get in bed with Big John. You know who Big John is, right?"

I did. Vaguely. I knew he was dead and that before he'd died, he'd run his own criminal enterprise, based mostly outside of Atlanta, and Abigail's first husband had been his son.

After the son died—according to the story, Big John had him assassinated—Big John had tried to kidnap Abigail. I also knew Lucas had killed Big John in Jacob's penthouse.

I didn't think Lucas needed a recap, so I just said, "Pretty much, yeah, I know who he is. Or was."

"The Raptors hooked up with Big John, and a month later, the president died in an accident—that I doubt was an accident—and Gunner took his spot. I was overseas under a blackout, so I didn't know any of this until it was way too late. A few months after Gunner became Prez, Big John had two people killed the same day . . . his son and my brother."

"That's why you shot him," I whispered, mostly to myself.

"It was a long time coming. He was an evil bastard. As soon as I got the message that Gunner was dead, I finished my job and came back. I made a deal with the Raptors. I took Gunner's position long enough to take down Big John's organization. Once that was done, I was out.

"That's how I got to know Brennan. We got a lot of pushback on all sides. Nobody liked my working with the Raptors, including most of the Raptors. But they wanted revenge and the territory they could grab with Big John out of the way. The police think I'm a wildcard, but we got the job done."

"That's why you trust Brennan?" I asked.

"Yeah. Too many times, everything seemed like it would go sideways and Brennan always had my back."

"So you're not with the Raptors anymore?"

"No. I dealt with Big John, we took out the rest of his organization, and I handed my kutte to the real Prez and walked away. I'm not a cop, and I'm not on a crusade, but their thing is not my thing. And their bullshit got my brother killed. He made his own decisions. I know that. He didn't see the line between right and wrong the same way I do. I couldn't have saved him. He didn't want to be saved."

"But at least you got revenge," I said. "Does it help?"

Lucas gave me a long, measuring look before he said, "Not really."

I stared down at the bubbled scraps of paint I was scraping off the baseboard. The police reports said my aunt and uncle's and my parents' deaths were both murder-suicides. Both cases were closed.

But I knew, all of us knew, that there was no way my uncle would've killed my aunt or my father my mother.

No way.

They'd been murdered.

After all this time, we still had no idea who had done it or why. Their deaths had left a wound that wouldn't heal. Not just grief, but a rage that had no target.

Someone had stolen them from us.

Someone needed to pay.

I'd always thought revenge would help that wound to heal. According to Lucas, I was wrong.

Lucas switched off the portable heater and set it down on the floor, upside down so the heating element could cool. Pulling the scraper out of my hand, he set it aside and stood, bringing me to my feet along with him.

"Come on," he said. "Let's go get a beer and some food. Then we'll come back here and I'll fuck you until you beg me to stop."

At that absurd thought, I busted out laughing. "Good luck," I said when I got my breath back. "That's not gonna happen. You can fuck me all night and I'll still ask for more. You'll be begging me to leave you alone and let you sleep."

"You want to bet?" Lucas asked with a chuckle. "First person to beg has to mow the other one's yard. You spent enough time watching me behind the mower. Now it's my turn. I can see you now, nothing but the mower and you, in a bright red bikini."

"Cocky much?" I asked as we went down the back steps —after I set the alarm and locked the door. "No bet. I don't mow lawns. And I don't own a red bikini."

"'That's a crime. Your body in a red bikini?" Lucas shook his head and looked at the sky, the anticipation in his eyes so hot I immediately considered some emergency online shopping. Though I still wasn't mowing the lawn.

It was only a few blocks to a neighborhood bar that had a great beer selection and a fantastic bar menu. We dropped the bet, which was a good thing because a few minutes after we hit the futon, I was naked with Lucas's mouth between my legs, begging desperately for him to stop teasing and start fucking me.

Which he did.

All night.

CHAPTER THIRTEEN
LUCAS

I slept late, waking with the glare of sunlight in my eyes. Charlotte Winters was a bad influence. After our unexpectedly heavy conversation while I helped her strip paint, I planned to get something to eat, fuck her senseless, and leave her safely tucked into bed, protected by solid locks and a secure alarm system.

My plan had gone to hell the first time she came on my tongue.

I loved making that woman come, the way she fought it at first, embarrassed she got so hot for me so fast. The way she squirmed, then rocked up into me—my mouth, my cock, my fingers—it didn't matter.

As soon as she decided she wanted it, Charlie went after her pleasure with a hunger and a heat that turned me on like no woman ever had. And then after, the way she collapsed into me, defenseless and sated and so fucking gorgeous.

Knowing that I did that to her, that I gave her that pleasure, that her beautifully relaxed face was mine, was a rush like nothing I'd ever known.

No fucking way I could leave that. I went back for more, again and again. We slept a little, here and there. Not enough.

I needed coffee. So did Charlie. And if the light streaming through the window was any indication, we both needed to get up.

She had a crew coming to rebuild the front porch and I had a job I needed to finish before afternoon. I caught a quick glimpse of her face, eyes closed in sleep, her dark lashes feathery half-moons against her creamy cheeks.

I tried not to think about her naked body beneath the sheet.

Get up. Get up, you horny bastard, and get in the shower before the construction crew catches you balls deep in Charlie's sweet little body.

Without looking at her again, I dragged my ass out of bed and jumped in the shower. I was going to smell like Charlie's flowery, fruity body wash all day, a constant reminder of a woman I didn't need to be thinking about when we weren't fucking.

This whole thing with her was going sideways.

I knew it and I didn't seem to be able to stop it.

It's safe to say Charlotte Winters was not what I expected. I knew from experience that the rich were different from the rest of us, but the truly, obscenely wealthy were a completely different breed of human.

I worked with enough of them to know how set apart they were. I had money. Hell, after the jobs I'd been doing the last few years, I had the kind of cash in the bank I'd never dreamed of, growing up in a rundown trailer. In a few years, I'd be able to retire and never have to worry about money again. But the Winters family probably had that kind of cash rattling around in their couch cushions.

I'd expected Charlie to see my tattoos and my truck and dismiss me as beneath her.

Instead, she was Charlie. Sexy, funny, adventurous, smart, sweet, and fucking gorgeous as hell.

The second I laid eyes on her, weeks ago, as she strode up the cracked driveway of her house beside a pretty, curvy redhead, I'd known I wanted to see what was beneath her perfectly tailored gray suit.

Any man would. There was no denying the suit was professional, but it didn't hide her body.

I'd never expected to like her, to look forward to seeing her. To need her.

I was going to have to get this shit under control. Charlie Winters was not for me. I was a rebound guy. An experiment. An adventure.

She was not, and she never would be, a girlfriend. I needed to remember that.

I didn't even want a girlfriend. Been there, done that.

I needed to stay focused. My goals were to build my client list, finish my house, and maybe look for another one to rehab and flip.

That was it. I didn't have room for a relationship, especially not one destined to fail.

I jumped out of the shower, drying off with a quick swipe of the towel, and steeled myself before I walked back into Charlie's bedroom.

Steeling myself didn't work.

Propped up on one elbow, the sheet barely covering her breasts, her mass of wavy auburn hair tangled in her blue eyes, still half-asleep, she was a siren.

Without saying a word, she called me back to bed. It took everything I had not to drop the towel and join her.

Focus, I reminded myself. Also, the construction crew.

We wouldn't be alone for much longer. Pulling on my clothes, I snagged my phone and my keys before heading to the kitchen, saying over my shoulder, "I'll make coffee, but you'd better get up. Your guys are going to be here in ten minutes."

Behind me, I heard Charlie scramble and I grinned to myself. She shuffled into the kitchen a few minutes later wearing an ancient pair of jeans with holes in the knees and an equally threadbare T-shirt, her hair pinned back from her face with matching butterfly barrettes.

"You look fifteen," I said. She grunted and held out a hand.

"Coffee," she demanded. Then, after taking a long sip, "What time is it?"

"7:57," I said, laughing a little as her eyes flew comically wide.

"Oh, my God! I never sleep this late."

"Neither do I," I said. "That's what happens when you stay up all night fucking instead of sleeping."

A faint blush colored the apples of her cheeks. She slanted me a sideways look from beneath her lashes and said, "I'm really tired, but it was worth it."

We heard the sounds of doors slamming outside. The alarm panel beeped, as did Charlie's phone, letting her know there was motion on the property.

After a glance at her phone, Charlie said, "The crew's here. Should I turn the alarm off?"

"You can turn it off when I leave, but unless they're going in and out of the house today, you should leave it on while you're inside."

"I think I'm going to work on stripping more paint. And they're scheduled to stay outside, working on the front porch. Can I hang on to the heater for a while? I can go get my own if you need it."

I shook my head. "No, it's yours as long as you want it. I won't need it again for a while."

"Okay, thanks—"

Charlie cut off at the sound of a knock at the back door. With the front door unreachable until the workmen replaced the decking, the back door was the only entrance to the house.

I turned to see a man in a suit at the door, average height, medium brown hair, and one of those patrician faces that made me think he'd been born in a country club. I didn't recognize him, but Charlie obviously did.

Crossing the room, she reached for the back door, flipping the lock before I interrupted to remind her, "Alarm, Charlie."

"Oh crap, I forgot already."

She held up one finger, telling the man on the other side of the glass to wait and turned for the alarm panel, missing the expression of disdainful annoyance that crossed his face.

The muscles in my shoulders tensed, and I shifted my weight to the balls of my feet. No one looked at Charlie like that.

She wasn't mine to protect, but I couldn't help myself.

This stranger's arrival was the perfect excuse to go back home and get started on the work I had to finish by the end of the day, but I wasn't leaving Charlie alone with this guy.

Successfully deactivating the alarm, she finished opening the door, swinging it wide. "Uncle William," she said in an easy, relaxed tone that told me she thought this man was no threat.

As he took in the bruising on her face and wounds on her cheek and temple, his eyes narrowed, then flicked to me.

"Charlotte, Charlie, sweetheart, what happened?"

He raised a hand as if to touch her, but dropped it before he made contact.

Charlie shrugged. "It looks worse than it feels. Someone jumped me when I was walking home the other night. But I'm okay, and Sinclair put in a security system yesterday."

He frowned, studying her face, then turned to stare me down. Well, he tried to stare me down. I was immune to stare downs from stuck-up old men in suits. I crossed my arms over my chest and returned his measuring look.

There were times when my size was a liability. It came in handy when I wanted to intimidate someone. As I'd expected, he looked away, breaking our eye contact.

Knowing it would annoy him, I stuck out my hand and said, "Lucas Jackson. And you are?"

He took my hand in a firm grip and shook. "William Davis. Are you Charlie's security?"

Charlie let out a high-pitched nervous laugh. Reaching out, she lay a hand on William Davis's arm and said, "No, Uncle William, Lucas is my neighbor."

"And your neighbor comes over for coffee before 8 a.m.?"

Ignoring his insinuation, Charlie looked at me and asked, "Why is it that everyone assumes they have the right to comment on my personal life?"

I shook my head. I wasn't stepping in the middle of this. William, incorrectly taking my silence for agreement, said, "Because you need looking after."

I didn't like the way his words echoed my own from the day before. Charlie did need looking after, but I knew in my gut that William Davis and I meant two completely different things when it came to looking after Charlie.

Proving me right, he said, "This is just one more

problem from you, Charlie. When are you going to give up this foolish rebellion and move home? Aiden needs a hostess. Since he can't manage to get himself married again, that has to be you."

"I don't want to be Aiden's hostess," Charlie said. "I don't want to move home. And besides that, I'm still mad at Aiden."

"This is what I'm talking about. Aiden did the right thing in firing you from the company. He never should've hired you in the first place. I've been telling him since you were a teenager that a young woman like you has no place in business. I'm glad to see he's finally listening."

I'd swear I could hear the low sound of Charlie's teeth grinding together as she stared at William Davis. While she struggled to formulate a respectful response to this man who was obviously important to her but clearly out of touch, I couldn't help poking at him a little more.

Gesturing with my empty mug, I said, "Coffee?"

William narrowed his cool brown eyes at me, raising one eyebrow in a perfect expression of privileged disdain before saying, "Why don't you go back home and let me talk to Charlie in private? You're not needed here."

Charlotte's face flushed red. Before she could speak, I said with a casual shrug of one shoulder, "So . . . no coffee then? Charlie? More coffee?"

Not needing an answer—I knew damn well she needed more coffee—I plucked her mug from her hand and crossed the room to refill it.

"Uncle William," Charlie said evenly, "Lucas is my neighbor and my friend. There's nothing you can't say in front of him. And it's completely inappropriate for you to ask him to leave when we are in *my* house. Just because you're upset doesn't mean you can forget your manners."

She finished with her chin up, looking down her nose at William even though he was taller than her. I kept my eyes on the coffeemaker, hiding my grin. On William Davis, privileged disdain was irritating. On Charlie, it was adorable.

William let out a sigh. In a low voice, he said, "Charlie, surely, you know you can do better than this."

William's eyes slid to me. It wasn't hard to read that he knew I'd heard and didn't care. I didn't care either. If anything, I needed this kind of in my face reminder that Charlie and I were worlds apart.

I thought about leaving. I didn't need to put up with this bullshit. But I didn't want either of them to think this douche-bag could run me off. I added a splash of half-and-half to Charlie's coffee the way she liked it and handed her the mug.

She took it, shooting me an apologetic look. I gave her a small shake of my head. It wasn't Charlie's fault this guy was an ass.

"Uncle William, I don't want to be rude, but if you say anything like that again, I'm going to ask you to leave." She took a deep breath, as if bolstering herself. Then she said, "Jacob is still upset with you after the things you said to him about Abigail. Please don't put me in that position."

William gave her a hard stare, not appreciating being put in his place by a woman he still considered a child. But even he couldn't argue with her logic. I wondered what he'd said to Jacob Winters about Abigail.

I could guess. Abigail had had a sterling reputation until she'd married Big John's son. William Davis probably hadn't considered her good enough for Jacob. It made me wonder exactly who *was* good enough for the Winters children. Did he have a crown prince lined up for Charlie? I wouldn't be surprised.

William huffed out an exasperated breath. "You always were a handful, Charlie. You and Annalise both. Will you at least go see your brother? It's not right to hold a grudge."

"I saw him yesterday."

"And did you apologize?"

"No." Charlotte's eyes narrowed dangerously, the blue of her eyes a dancing flame. "No, I did not apologize to Aiden for firing me, without cause, from my job."

"He was only doing what was best for you, Charlie."

William's placating words set my teeth on edge. Based on the tight muscles of her jaw, he was doing the same to Charlie.

"Newsflash, Uncle William. This is a whole new century where women are allowed to decide what's best for themselves instead of letting the men in the family figure everything out for them."

William shook his head sadly. "All this feminism stuff just complicates things. I don't know why you girls can't see that."

Charlie made a sound that was half laugh and half sigh. "You know you're a dinosaur, right? You're letting the world leave you behind."

"I like my world just how it is, young lady." William was at least self-aware enough to give her a gentle smile. Still ignoring me, he said, "So, is this your new business? You're going to rehab houses and sell them? There's good invest-ment value in the Highlands. But you really should live in Winters House. This place looks like it's going to fall down around your ears. And it's in the Highlands. So urban."

He shook his head again. I bit back a laugh. Only a man like this, clearly born with a platinum spoon in his mouth, would call the Virginia Highlands area of Atlanta 'urban' in that snotty tone.

Most of the houses around us were well over a million dollars. Both Charlotte's and mine had originally been under the million-dollar mark, but when they were done, they too would be worth a lot more. The neighborhood was diverse and the location was ideal, but it was expensive. Very expensive.

"You think anything that's not an estate in Buckhead is urban," Charlie said and sipped her coffee. "You're such a snob, Uncle William."

I don't know how she managed to be both exasperated and affectionate. I wanted to shove the guy right out the back door.

"Do you want a tour?" she asked.

William let his eyes roam the house, stepping out into the hall so he could see the front rooms. His gaze lingered on the pile of drop cloths, the heater, the scrapers we'd been using in the living room, and the caution tape Charlie had tacked across the front door. He shook his head.

"You can show me around when it's finished, sweetheart."

"Okay," she agreed. "Are you seeing Aiden today?"

"For lunch. Yes."

"You going to give him a lecture about getting me in hand?" Charlie asked with a cheeky smile.

William shook his head with the same mixture of exasperation and affection I'd seen on Charlie's face a minute before. Stepping forward to kiss the top of her head, he said, "I was planning on it, yes."

"Why don't you tell Aiden to find himself a real girl-friend so he can get his own hostess?" she asked.

William turned for the back door as he said, "That's also on my list."

"Good, then you can bug him instead of me."

Standing in the open doorway, William faced Charlie. His eyes flicked to mine and back to her. Quietly, he said, "I know I annoy you children with my out-of-date expectations and my nagging. But your parents are gone, and I'm only trying to stand in for them as best I can."

He left, firmly shutting the door behind himself. Charlie stared after him, the gleam of tears in her ocean blue eyes and a bereft expression on her face. She wiped the tears away with the back of her hand.

"I'm sorry he was so rude," she said, not meeting my eyes. "He really is a dinosaur. He doesn't seem to get that it's not okay to be such a snob. Jacob is so mad at him. If William doesn't apologize soon, Jacob may never speak to him again. He's crazy in love with Abigail, and from what I heard, William said some things. Abigail overheard . . ."

She shook her head. "I wasn't there, but everyone said it was ugly. Anyway, he was our parents' best friend. My parents' and my aunt and uncle's. He's been there for us our whole lives. It was bad enough when Uncle James and Aunt Anna died, but when my parents . . ."

She trailed off again before finishing. "Aiden was just in college and it was so much, between the company and the press. Annalise and Holden and Tate and I were so young. We couldn't have gotten through it without William. But I'm sorry he was such a dick."

"Don't worry about it, Princess. He didn't bother me. Once he realizes I'm not going to be around long-term, he won't bother being rude."

Charlie's back went stiff and she looked away. She didn't like the reminder that we weren't really together.

If I were being honest, my gut clenched a little when I said it.

We both needed to remember this was temporary, especially after that little scene with William. I wasn't her kind of people. If William had been an asshole to Abigail, who had a sterling pedigree until she married John Jordan, he would go completely ape shit if he thought there was any possibility of a real relationship between Charlie and me, so it was a good thing there wasn't.

She was convenient sex and that was it.

That didn't mean I liked the hurt look on her face.

Before I could open my mouth and say something to take that look away, something that would erase my earlier words and make us forget reality, I made an excuse about work, reminded her to set the alarm behind me, and left.

Chapter Fourteen
Charlie

I spent the rest of the day stripping paint. It wasn't the most fun I've ever had, but the sense of satisfaction I got from seeing my progress was worth my aching arms.

As a side bonus, I could watch the crew on my front porch through the living room windows while I worked. I knew my life had taken a turn when a brand-new front porch was enough to make my day.

The workmen were faster than I was. They finished laying the new decking on the front porch by lunch and had moved to the back of the house. The deck off the kitchen was in much better shape than the front had been, and only a few rotten boards needed replacing.

By mid-afternoon, they were gone for the day. Tomorrow, the contractor had plumbers and electricians coming to finish up the second floor and the attic, but for the rest of the day, I was on my own.

It was early evening but still light out when I finished scraping the last speck of paint from the trim in the living room. I still needed to sand it all and repair the dings and scratches, but I was one huge step closer to a finished room. Satisfaction sang in my chest, better than any I'd felt before. No business deal had ever made me feel like I could conquer the world.

Not like this. For the first time, it sank in.

I wasn't going back.

Not to Winters Inc.

Not to another company.

I didn't have a plan yet, but whatever I was going to do, I wouldn't be behind a desk.

Feeling oddly lighthearted, I unplugged the heater, placing it carefully on its handle the way Lucas had the day before, and finally paid attention to my growling stomach.

I really needed to buy some food. I had cereal and milk and a little yogurt, none of which were appetizing after hours of hard work. I wanted an Italian sub with extra hots. Or maybe meatball.

There was a great sandwich shop a couple of blocks away. I grabbed my phone and keys, set the alarm, and headed out the door, ignoring the chill down my spine at the memory of the last time I'd gone for a walk to get dinner.

This was different. For one thing, it was still daylight. For another, I had the panic button in my pocket. I hadn't been more than a foot away from it all day.

I wasn't going to hide, but that didn't mean I had to be reckless.

I decided on the meatball sub. Extra cheese. Extra cheese was good on everything. Even salad was better with extra cheese.

Pushing open the door to the shop, I placed my order and waited, playing a game on my phone until it was ready. The smell of toasted bread and marinara sauce was killing my empty stomach.

As soon as I got my food, I was going to go home, eat my sub, start working on the trim in the front hall, and go to bed early. I was exhausted.

Staying up half the night so Lucas could give me multiple orgasms was absolutely worth being tired.

I flinched a little inside at the thought of Lucas. I was starting to get attached. That made him sound like a lost puppy. He was anything but a stray pet.

Lucas was a man with plans and ambitions that had nothing to do with me. I knew he liked sleeping with me.

I should be past euphemisms by now.

He liked fucking me. Lucas Jackson liked fucking me. That was it.

He lent me the tools to strip paint, helped me for an afternoon, came to my rescue when I was attacked, and told me a little bit about his family.

After the way he'd left that morning, I was painfully aware that our interactions had already gotten way more personal than he'd planned.

Lucas wasn't sticking around.

When he got tired of fucking me, and he inevitably would, he'd walk away. He'd let me down easy. Lucas wasn't a jerk. But we'd both been clear about what we wanted when this started. Sex. No one was supposed to get attached.

After it was over, I'd go back to ogling him while he mowed the lawn and he'd forget all about me.

I tried not to remember the visit with William that morning, but his careless snobbery echoed in my head. The thing was, I understood William. He was wrong and he was incredibly rude, but he wasn't the only person like that whom I knew.

The world we inhabited was filled with people who

thought they were better than everyone else. That was life. Every social stratum had people who thought they were better than the people around them.

In mine, money and breeding were the excuse. Half the time, when William was berating one of us over our behavior, he harped on the Winters name. Like anything we could do would eclipse four scandalous, violent deaths. The family name had been dragged through the mud long before we were old enough to do any damage.

I'd been young when my parents had died, but I remembered them. Aiden and Jacob had told me stories. My mom and dad hadn't been snobs. They'd loved us for who we were and wanted us to grow up into good people who found love and made happy families.

Not people with the right jobs and the right houses in the right neighborhoods. I knew that William thought he was speaking for our parents when he said things like he did that morning. He was wrong.

I refused to believe that my parents would have been that narrowminded. Lucas had enjoyed poking at William, but he hadn't seemed hurt by William's unkindness. The idea of someone like William hurting Lucas seemed absurd.

Lucas was strength and power. Still, he had feelings. I'd listened to him tell me about his brother, about leaving home because the town thought his family was trash. He knew loss, grief, and pain. He deserved better than to be the target of William's crap.

I rounded the corner to my block and my nerves prickled. It was still light out. Still early. There were cars on the street, people in their front yards and on their porches.

It wasn't like the other night. Nothing was going to happen.

That didn't mean my shoulders weren't tight. I picked

up my pace, looking over my shoulder once or twice when I couldn't help it.

My house looked exactly the way it was supposed to. Everything was locked up tight. The raw, unstained decking was beautiful on my front porch.

I skidded to a halt in front of my driveway and looked again. The house appeared untouched. My car was still in the driveway. The gate to the backyard was closed.

The mailbox door hung open.

I racked my brain for a good reason the mailbox would be open. I hadn't changed my address yet so I shouldn't be getting mail. In fact, the mail was being forwarded to Winters House because I hadn't anticipated moving in yet.

The mailbox had been closed when I left to get dinner and the mail had been delivered to my neighbors earlier that afternoon.

I slowed my steps as I approached the mailbox. It tilted a little on its wooden post, but that wasn't new. I was planning to replace it at a point. I just hadn't gotten around to it yet.

Inside was a square white envelope, the same style you might use for an invitation or thank you note. I reached for it, then snatched my hand back.

It was probably a note from a neighbor, welcoming me to the street.

Or someone soliciting business.

It was probably nothing.

But if it was something, I didn't want to touch it and get fingerprints all over it.

I ran across the yard into the house, turning off the alarm after I sprinted in the door. On the floor next to the mini-fridge, I found what I was looking for—a plastic grocery bag. I'd been saving them to recycle, but now I could use it to protect whatever was in my mailbox.

Thinking that if this was a note from a neighbor, I was going to feel very silly, I left my sandwich on top of the refrigerator and went back out to the mailbox.

Wrapping the bag over my hand, I reached in the mailbox and gripped the corner of the envelope, carefully pulling it out. My name was hand-printed on the front.

CHARLOTTE WINTERS.

The envelope wasn't sealed. Inside was a square note card with beveled edges. It was blank except for a message in block print: *I'm watching you. You'll get what you deserve.* Rusty streaks of red stained the snowy white card, crossing the black ink like claw marks.

Something was stuck in the bottom of the envelope, keeping me from pushing the card back inside. Tilting the envelope into the plastic bag, I shook it carefully.

Out slid a clump of dark auburn hair, bound at the root by a rusty red chunk of flesh.

My hair.

I remembered the burning pain when it had been torn out of my head two nights before. The spot at my temple was still raw.

The attacker had kept my hair. Another rusty streak of red marred the inside of the envelope.

My blood.

The implications of the note in my mailbox and my hair in the envelope hit me like a freight train, hard and fast, stealing my breath and sending my head spinning.

My vision blurred. My heart raced in my chest.

I had to move. I had to do something.

My hands still protected by the grocery bag, I shoved

the card back in the envelope and dropped the envelope in the bag.

Carefully, I closed the mailbox door, giving it an extra push to make sure it was shut. Nausea lurched and rolled in my stomach. My skin prickled with goosebumps. Cold sweat froze my spine.

Striding across the lawn, I was fairly sure I was going to throw up. I heard my name called out behind me. I didn't slow down. I raced up the steps and through the front door, slamming and locking it behind me.

Vaguely, as if at a great distance, I heard the thump of feet on wood and a banging on the door. I would deal with that later. I'd deal with everything later.

The grocery bag with the note fell from nerveless fingers to the floor in the hall. I went to my knees in front of the toilet, braced my arm on the cold seat, and vomited.

There wasn't much in my stomach. I hadn't eaten since my bowl of yogurt and granola at breakfast. That didn't stop my body from heaving. Over and over, the sour taste of bile filled my mouth. I spit into the toilet, flushed, and threw up again, shaking and gasping for breath.

I needed to get it together.

Needed to think about what to do next.

Thoughts flitted around in my brain, unfocused and drenched in fear. Every time I thought about the note and what it meant, my torso curled over the toilet and I heaved again.

"Jesus Christ, Princess, what the fuck?"

A big hand settled between my shoulder blades, warmth chasing off the chill of sweat coating my body.

"What happened, Charlie? What is it? Talk to me."

Lucas sounded frantic. I had to answer him. I had to get it together before he really freaked out.

I was fine. It was just a stupid note. Why was I more upset by that than someone attacking me?

I knew the answer already. Because the attack could've been random. People got mugged every day. The note proved it was anything but.

I braced my arm on the front of the toilet seat, rested my forehead on my wrist, and pointed with my other hand at the grocery bag in the hall.

Lucas rose, taking his heat with him. Plastic rustled. He swore under his breath. His phone beeped. A few seconds later, he spoke.

"Brennan. I'm at Charlie's." A pause. "No, but she got a note. A threat. No, she was smart. Wrapped it up and didn't touch it. Can you . . . yeah, we'll be here."

He was behind me again, rubbing his big warm hand up and down my spine. I relaxed, knowing he was there. Lucas was a wall between me and the rest of the world.

As long as he was at my back, nothing bad could happen to me.

"Brennan will be here in fifteen. Can you stand up?"

I nodded and tried to get to my feet. Lucas's arm came around me, lifting me. He reached past me and turned on the shower. "Let's get you warmed up, okay?"

Impersonally efficient, he stripped off my T-shirt and jeans, focused only on getting me in the shower.

I would've stumbled if he hadn't been there, steadying me, guiding me. When I was under the warm spray, he drew back, saying, "I'll get you some dry clothes."

I tipped my face back under the shower, letting the hot water rinse away the cold sweat of panic, the stink of fear. The water stung the raw skin on my cheek and temple, but the penetrating heat was worth a little pain.

I flipped open my tube of body wash and took a deep

sniff, letting the smell of fruit and flowers soothe me. Mechanically, I washed my hair and my body, then stepped out of the shower, dried off, and smoothed lotion over my skin.

Squeezing out an extra-large glop of toothpaste to brush my teeth, I scrubbed every nook and cranny of my mouth to get rid of the taste of vomit.

When I stepped out of the bathroom, towel wrapped securely around me, I heard voices in the kitchen. Lucas and Detective Brennan. Brennan was fast. I slipped into my room and closed the door behind me, wishing I could crawl into the futon and go to sleep.

I wanted this whole mess to go away. It didn't look like that was going to happen, and hiding in bed wouldn't help anything. Lucas had laid out a stack of clothes on top of my pillow, a T-shirt, sweatshirt, and a pair of yoga pants.

No underwear. Amusement muscled aside my nerves for a second and I rolled my eyes. Lucas didn't make mistakes. He wanted me commando. A tiny grin tugged up one side of my mouth as I pulled on the clothes he'd chosen. If I couldn't crawl into bed, at least I could be comfortable.

Lucas stood in the center of the kitchen, arms crossed over his chest, jaw set, eyes grim. Detective Brennan was holding the plastic grocery bag, examining its contents without touching them, the same way both Lucas and I had.

Hearing my feet on the floor, Detective Brennan looked up. His eyes were as grim as Lucas's.

"How are you holding up?" he asked kindly.

"I'll be okay," I lied.

I was not at all sure I'd be okay, and I was extremely unhappy about that goddamned note. But I didn't want to be a whiner. None of this was Detective Brennan's fault. He seemed willing to let me get away with the lie.

Lucas stepped in front of me with a clump of ointment on his finger and a fresh bandage for my temple. I stood there, acquiescent, as he doctored me. For the moment, I was all out of independence. I needed help, and if Lucas wanted to give it, I wasn't going to make it harder for him.

His strong fingers smoothed the bandage against my skin. He wiped the extra ointment on his cargo pants and wrapped an arm around me, pulling me into his side. It felt like being wrapped in a shield. Safe. Protected.

"Can you think of anyone else, anyone you haven't already mentioned, who might be targeting you?" Brennan asked.

He let the envelope fall into the bottom of the plastic bag and loosely tied it shut. I shook my head. I'd told him everything I knew already. If I had any idea who might be doing this, I wouldn't keep it a secret.

"Hayward has an alibi," Lucas said abruptly. I glanced between Lucas and Brennan. Neither of them looked happy.

"For the other night?" I asked.

Lucas shook his head. "For everything. He's got eyes on him around the clock."

"It's always possible he's hired someone," Brennan said. "The FBI is all over him, so if Bruce Hayward is behind this, he's got someone else doing his dirty work."

"We pulled up the last few hours on the cameras, but all they show is someone in a hooded sweatshirt and jeans stopping at your mailbox about an hour ago," Lucas said. "Whoever it was, they look to be about the same height and weight of your attacker Wednesday night, but we can't be sure."

"So what does that mean?" I asked.

"It means that we don't have a solid suspect," Brennan

said. "There's also the problem of the pictures. Whoever was sending those pictures to your family is still out there. If they've escalated their harassment, this could be the same person. Sending your brother and your cousin photographs, but you a personal note . . . that may be an escalation, or it could just be that they're acting out differently because you're younger and female. Without knowing who the perp is, it's impossible to say."

"Okay, then what happens now?" I asked.

"I'm going to take this back to the lab, see if we can get anything off it," Brennan said, lifting the plastic bag with the envelope inside. "Maybe we'll get a break. In the meantime, the best thing you can do is avoid making yourself a target. I don't want you alone anywhere, if you can help it. Let's not make it easy on this guy to get to you, okay?"

"But I have an alarm," I protested.

I agreed with Detective Brennan. I didn't want to make it easy for anyone to get to me. But isn't that why I had the security system put in? To keep me safe? I wasn't going to be stupid, but I didn't want to be run out of my own home.

"You do," Brennan agreed. "And it's a good system. Better than good. I guess it helps to be on the Sinclairs' Christmas list."

He grinned and winked at me, letting me know he wasn't making a crack at my family or my connections. I gave him a weak smile in return.

"Sometimes it is," I agreed. "Most of the time, I could do without the extra set of big brothers, but they come in handy. Especially when I'm being stalked by some psycho."

A muscle clenched in Lucas's jaw and he narrowed his eyes at me. "Don't joke about this," he said. Turning his intent green eyes on Brennan, he went on, "I'm staying with her at night. We'll figure out the rest, but I'll make sure she's not on her own during the day either."

Brennan raised an eyebrow. "You in town for a while?" he asked.

"For the moment," Lucas answered vaguely. Brennan nodded at him.

"If that changes, let me know. I'll arrange for some drive-bys, but it's not a substitute for being careful," he said to me.

"I'll be careful," I said.

Lucas walked Brennan to the door. I stood in the middle of the kitchen, hugging myself, my hands threaded through the opposite sleeves of my sweatshirt, trying to warm up.

Even after the hot shower, I was still chilled deep inside. My meatball sub, wrapped in brown butcher paper, sat on top of my mini-fridge. I should have been starving.

My stomach still rolling with nausea, I didn't want to eat.

Lucas came back into the kitchen, stopped in front of me, and pulled me into his arms. I collapsed against him, absorbing his warmth and strength.

He was so tall, my head only came to his collarbone, and though I wasn't a small woman, his big frame engulfed me. Just then, it was exactly what I needed. I burrowed into him, shuddering as his hand rubbed up and down my back, soothing me.

Reminding me I was safe.

"We're going to find this asshole, Charlie. I promise," he said in a low murmur. I shuddered again, feeling heat on my cheeks. I realized I was crying.

I never cried. I had a little trick I'd used since I was a kid and I didn't want the media to catch my tears. I'd bite my lip, hard, on the inside of my mouth where the flesh was tender and sensitive. It hurt like a bitch, but the pain was usually enough to push back the tears.

I drew in a breath and set my teeth into my lip.

Before I could bite down, Lucas placed a soft kiss on the top of my head. I sucked in a breath, startled by his tenderness. Lucas was protective, but he'd never been sweet.

With one hand, he cradled my head against his chest, stroking the callused flat of his thumb over my cheek, wiping away my tears. Normally, I was appalled at the thought of anyone seeing me cry. Anyone—my brothers, my cousins . . . so why, with Lucas, was it so hard for me to stop?

Maybe if he'd chided me, told me to get it together, it would've been easier to force my emotions under control. But I was terrified, off-balance, and the soft stroke of his thumb on my skin seemed to draw the tears out as much as it brushed them away.

I don't know how long I stood there crying all over Lucas. Longer than I wanted to. Finally, I wept myself dry and tried to pull back. He didn't let me. His arms wound tight, he said against my hair, "It's still early, but you're exhausted."

I was. I really was. With my cheek pressed to Lucas's chest and the reassuring thump of his heart filling my ear, tension drained out of my spine and my stomach growled. In the quiet of my kitchen, it was loud.

"Do you think you can eat that sub you brought home?" Lucas asked, his voice gentle, his fingers threading through my hair.

"Yeah, I should at least try. If I don't, I'll wake up in the middle of the night starving." Middle of the night kitchen raids never went well, even in an understocked kitchen like mine.

"Where do you want to eat?"

"I'll just sit on the floor in here," I said. Lucas released me to go grab my sandwich and I sat, leaning against the wall. Tomorrow, I was getting a table and chairs. Nothing fancy, just a folding card table and some folding chairs. They'd come in handy later when I needed extra seating, and I was getting tired of eating breakfast standing up.

Lucas handed me my sub and a paper towel before taking a position across the room, leaning against the wall, his arms folded across his chest. I wasn't sure I had an appetite until I took the first bite of the meatball sub. It was cold, but it was still delicious.

The second the tang of marinara sauce hit my tongue, I realized I was ravenous. As I chewed and tried not to look like a pig, I thought about what had happened. Everything. Aiden firing me and my moving in here. Getting jumped in my yard, the threatening note . . .

I needed to figure out what to do.

I knew what I *should* do. And I knew what I wanted to do. Halfway finished with my sub already, I swallowed and looked up at Lucas. There was worry in his green eyes.

I didn't know if I liked that or not. I didn't need another overbearing male worrying about me, but it was nice to know he cared. Unless he was just worried I was going to get killed and then he wouldn't be able to have sex with me anymore. That was a possibility. At the moment, it wasn't important.

"I don't want to move back in with Aiden," I said. "I want to stay here. In my house."

"I get that," Lucas said evenly.

"But you think I should move back into Winters House."

"You'd be safer."

I looked down at my sub and took another bite. I

couldn't argue with his logic. Winters House was on ten acres, behind gates, and built like a fortress. It wasn't impenetrable, but it had layers of security. Intruders were far easier to spot than they were here.

Lucas interrupted my thoughts.

"Unless you stay at Winters House twenty-four seven, you'll still be exposed. You've got a solid security system here, and I'm next-door."

"I don't want to move back into Winters House," I said, resting my head against the wall and closing my eyes. My voice wavered with tears and exhaustion. "I want to stay here."

"Then you'll stay here. You need to be careful. We'll talk about taking precautions in the morning. For now, you need to eat, and then I'm taking you to bed."

Tears pricked my eyes again. Dammit. What was with all this crying? Lucas's gentle consideration when I suspected he'd rather just tell me what to do softened something inside me.

I didn't know what to say, so I finished my meatball sub and stood so I could throw out the wrapper.

"You look like you're about to pass out standing up," Lucas said. He wasn't wrong. I could feel myself wobbling a little. Every muscle in my body was drained.

My brain was done. Just done.

I didn't want to think about anything. I wanted to sleep.

Lucas wound his arm around me and urged me down the hall, stripping off my clothes and nudging me onto the futon. He disappeared into the bathroom for a few minutes before he came back and started to undress.

I don't know what I was expecting. My mind was too sluggish to consider sex. Watching Lucas strip through half-closed eyes, it occurred to me that it might not be time to pass out quite yet.

Lucas wasn't my boyfriend. And I wasn't a client.

He wasn't spending the night on a futon too small for him because it was fun. Our whole thing was about sex. That was why he was here.

It was okay. I'd get into it as soon as he started touching me. With Lucas, it didn't take much. He slid beneath the blanket, lying on his back. I rolled into him, hiking one knee over his legs and pressing my palm to his chest, intending to let my hand drift south.

My fingers skimmed his warm chest, dipping into the grooves of his muscles, tracing the line of his abs. He caught my hand when it hit his hipbone, wrapping his fingers around mine and pulling them back up to press my palm over his heart.

"Go to sleep, Princess."

"But—"

Lucas passed his hand over my hair, starting at my temple and sliding around the back of my skull and down my neck. "Go to sleep. If you're too wired to fall asleep, I'll fuck you. Promise."

I grinned into his chest and let my eyes close. I doubt it took more than another minute or two before I passed out, lulled by the heat of his hand stroking my hair and the pulse of his heartbeat echoing in my ear.

CHAPTER FIFTEEN
LUCAS

I was sucked into work, eyes focused on my laptop as I burrowed my way into line after line of code for a client. Beside me, my phone beeped an alarm. The security system. Not Charlie's, mine.

Proximity alert on the driveway.

I tapped the app on my phone and watched Aiden Winters unfold himself from what I knew was a very expensive and almost impossible to get Aston Martin. Damn, that was a gorgeous car. One of the perks of being a billionaire.

Didn't bother me. I wasn't a billionaire, but I had enough money socked away to buy my own Aston Martin if I really wanted one. Someday, maybe. For now, my capital and my attention were on building my business and playing around with rehabbing houses. An expensive luxury car didn't fit in.

With a sigh of annoyance, I logged out of my laptop and closed it. This particular client wasn't in a rush, but the job was taking longer than I'd estimated since Charlie's life had intersected with my own.

I didn't have to guess why Aiden Winters was here.

After William Davis's visit, I'd been expecting Aiden to stop by. If he thought he was going to roll in here and scare me off Charlie, he was very much mistaken.

Charlie was mine for as long as she wanted to be, as long as this thing between us stayed good, and nothing her brother had to say would change that. I knew guys like Aiden Winters. Rich, entitled, used to thinking the world existed to serve them.

When you work in my business, you run into more than your share of men like him. I let him ring the doorbell and took my time answering it. When I swung the door open, I was taken aback by how much he reminded me of Charlie.

In pictures, they didn't look that much alike. Her blue eyes were so striking, they overshadowed the features she shared with Aiden. It was disconcerting to see her lower lip and those defined cheekbones in a male face.

Aiden met my eyes with a direct stare and said, "Lucas Jackson?"

I nodded, affirming his guess.

"May I come in? We have things to talk about."

I stepped back, holding the door open. "Charlie is at Winters House," I said. I'd dropped her off myself not more than an hour before.

"I know," Aiden said with a quirk of his lips that was almost a smile. "She's playing with Maggie's dog. I told her I would do it, but she said I wouldn't spend enough time letting him drool all over me. She was probably right. You drove her?"

"I did," I said. It might be overkill, but I was serious about not leaving her on her own. She was behind a gate at Winters House, protected by multiple layers of security. I still didn't like her being on the other side of town without me.

Echoing my thoughts, Aiden said, "I'm surprised you let her out of your sight."

So was I.

Which was a problem. It was supposed to be easy to let go of Charlie. That was the whole point of our arrangement.

No relationship. No attachments.

I wasn't sticking very well to my own ground rules. Until I knew what Aiden was getting at, I wasn't going to respond. I gave a half-shrug and waited.

"I talked to Evers this morning. Brennan told him about the note. I can't help but notice that no one told *me* about the note."

"Charlie specifically asked Brennan not to tell you," I said. "He's doing his job, which is to build a case against whoever is after her while they look for the guy. His job is not to keep Charlie's family posted on his progress."

Aiden narrowed his eyes at me. I stared back with a level gaze. When he realized I wasn't going to give him anything else, he said,

"I'm aware of what Detective Brennan's job is. Evers assures me that the system he installed on her house is as airtight as he can make it while it's being renovated. I still don't like it."

"Are you going to try to force her to move home?" I asked. I crossed my arms over my chest, bracing for his answer.

"Do you think it would work?" Aiden asked, raising an eyebrow at my stance. He went on, "Charlie's already angry with me. Trying to strong-arm her into moving home when she obviously doesn't want to would be an exercise in futility. I don't like to waste time."

"Why did you fire her?" I asked. The change of subject was a one-eighty, but I needed to know.

"Because it was the most efficient way I could think of to start making up for my mistake."

"And what was the mistake? Hiring her in the first place?" I asked. Every report I dug up about Charlotte Winters said she was exceptionally good at her job. Firing her didn't make sense.

"No. Not exactly. But that was part of it. And this really isn't any of your fucking business."

"Humor me," I said.

"No. I'm not in the habit of talking to strangers about my family."

"Smart, considering your family. But I'm involved with your sister. I'm not a stranger. And I'm curious. You two are close. She poured her life into that job. Before I trust you, before I tell you things that she may not want me to share, I have to know why you would do that to her."

Aiden absorbed my words in silence, words I hadn't been aware I was going to say. Aiden might be here to warn me off his sister, but since he'd led with Evers and Brennan, I was thinking he was also here to find out how Charlie was really doing.

I wasn't going to let him in until I understood his relationship to Charlie better. He took a breath and seemed to come to a decision.

"It's a little early for beer," he said. "Do you have any coffee?"

"Follow me," I said, leading Aiden through the front rooms of my house into the kitchen at the back. My house was smaller than Charlie's overall, but the lower level was about the same size and laid out in a similar way—living room and dining room off the front hall, kitchen in the back.

Where she had the office and bathroom, I had a family room with a flat screen open to the kitchen. And unlike Charlie's mess of construction, my house was mostly finished.

The front rooms didn't have furniture yet. I hadn't had time to deal with them. But the kitchen was done and it was just about perfect. Dark cabinets, a custom poured concrete counter and matching island, high-end appliances, a wine fridge, two farmhouse sinks, and a wet bar in the butler's pantry beside the family room.

It was good-looking enough to make a decorator happy and functional enough for a guy, whether he liked to cook or just liked having cold beer close to his TV. It suited me, and I knew if I ended up flipping it, buyers would love it.

I had the same style single-cup coffeemaker Charlie did, and I had Aiden's coffee brewed a few minutes after we hit the kitchen.

He took it and said, "You redid this place?"

"You don't already know?" I challenged. I was curious to see if Aiden Winters could cut through the bullshit. It turned out, he could.

"I was going for polite, but if you'd rather do it this way, I'm good with that too."

"I don't like to waste time either," I said.

"Fine. I know you redid this place practically from the studs. Nice job, by the way."

I acknowledged his complement with a nod but didn't interrupt.

"You paid for the house, and all the work, in cash. You have zero debt. According to your tax return, you made well over a million dollars last year. It would've been a lot more if you hadn't gotten sidetracked avenging your brother, for which you took no money at all.

"You're former Army, and even Cooper couldn't find out what you were doing for them after you transitioned out of the Rangers, but whatever it was, they didn't want to let you go. You're trained in security and protection, but as you've built your business, you've left that behind in favor of hacking jobs that are mostly white hat. What I don't know is why a guy like you is rehabbing a house in the Highlands."

"I thought you were going to ask what a guy like me is doing with your sister," I said.

I wasn't thrown by his recitation of my history. Aiden Winters was tight with the Sinclairs, tightest with Cooper. I knew Cooper Sinclair, knew all of them. Cooper could find out anything. He was almost as good with the keyboard as I was.

I was surprised that Aiden appeared to be dodging the issue of my fucking Charlie. If she were my sister, I would've started with that. I probably would've started with a punch to the jaw.

"I don't have to ask what you're doing with Charlie," Aiden said, shaking his head. "Charlie is a beautiful woman. She's smart, and funny, and any man would be lucky to have her attention. When I heard about this, I didn't wonder what you were doing with Charlie. I wondered what it was about you that made Charlie stop and look.

"She has men after her all the time. If she were ugly and dull, she'd still have men after her all the time because she's a Winters, which makes her a target. But she's not ugly and dull. She's Charlie. She can fend off attention from men in her sleep, and most of them, she ignores. So what's she doing with you?"

Annoyed at his tone and the question, I shrugged. "Maybe she's just slumming," I said.

Aiden laughed, amusement bringing his austere features to life.

"Don't ever make the mistake of underestimating Charlie," he said. "She's not slumming."

"How do you know?" I challenged. "You're not going to tell me I'm her type."

"I don't know if Charlie has a type. God knows, the men she's dated haven't worked out. I think she's still trying to figure that part out. But I know she's not slumming because no one she'd bother to spend this much time with would be a step down. Do you get me?"

I wasn't sure I did. Not that I considered myself beneath Charlie. All of that was bullshit. But I knew most people looking at us would see it that way. William Davis certainly had. Charlie didn't, but I'd assumed her brother would.

Apparently, I'd been wrong.

"If you respect her judgment that much," I asked, "then why did you fire her from a job she loved?"

"Because she was miserable. She was fucking miserable. And she didn't love that job. I know, because I *do* love it. I work long hours, but I do it because I love it. I love the company. I love that I'm able to continue my family's legacy, to grow it.

"Charlie never felt that way. It was killing her. She was always stressed, headaches, not sleeping. I stopped hearing her laugh, and then I stopped seeing her smile. I love my sister, and the only reason she started working at Winters Incorporated in the first place was because she thought it would make me happy. Everyone else took off to do their own thing, and she wanted to support me so she decided she was going to take Gage's place and help me run the company."

"And you let her?" I asked. His answer wasn't what I'd expected. I thought he'd blow me off again or lie.

"At the time, I didn't really think it through. At first, she just wanted to intern, and she was a teenager. Then, she was there more and more and I was distracted with changes in the company and my marriage—"

He cut off and shook his head, his eyes tired. He pressed his lips together, digging grooves into the skin of his cheeks and around his mouth. Aiden might love his job, but he looked like he could use a day off.

"I should have done a better job raising her after our parents died. I left her with Elizabeth too much, and Elizabeth wasn't the maternal type. I didn't do right by Charlie. I let her think the company was where she belonged. I liked having her around, and she was damn good at her job, so I let things slide.

"When I finally saw how unhappy she was, I knew I had to do something about it. Believe me, I tried talking to her. I told her she had to slow down, that she needed a life outside of work. But I'm a shit example because I'm even more of a workaholic than she was. She ignored me and kept working herself harder until she was utterly miserable. So I fired her. Yes, I get that she's pissed, and yes, it was a dick move. I know that. I can own it."

Aiden's glare was defiant, but he'd answered my question. He might have gone about it the wrong way, but Aiden Winters adored his sister. More than that, he respected her. Good enough for me.

"She got her revenge with your Macallan," I said, not hiding my grin when his glare turned into a scowl. "That was the best whiskey I've ever had. If you want to buy another bottle and then piss her off again, let me know so I can make sure I'm around."

"God damn, Charlie knows how to twist the knife. That was a fifteen thousand-dollar bottle of whiskey." Aiden saluted me with his half-full coffee cup. "Pay attention, Jackson, so you know what you've got coming when you eventually piss her off. You'll have to stay on your toes with Charlie."

Shit.

I thought he was coming over here to warn me off, and instead he was giving me his blessing. A problem because Charlie and I weren't dating. We weren't together. She wasn't my girlfriend.

Shit.

"I don't think you understand," I tried. "Charlie and I aren't . . . we're not . . . she doesn't—" I shut my mouth. There's no good way to tell a man that you're just fucking his sister.

"I really don't need to know the details," Aiden said with a grimace. "Charlie is a grown woman. She can figure this shit out on her own. If she needs advice, she's got Maggie. If you fuck her over and she wants your ass kicked, that's a different story."

He eyed me, tracking me from my toes to the top of my head before he grinned into his coffee cup.

"You've got a good four inches on me, so I might have to call for backup."

"I'll keep that in mind," I said, amused.

Aiden looked like he was in good shape, and he was no lightweight, but I'd been trained by the best. He'd need a lot of backup if he thought he was going to take me down.

I wasn't worried about it. By the time things ended with Charlie, she'd probably be happy to see me go.

"Cooper says you don't take jobs like this very often anymore, but I want to hire you."

"Jobs like what?" I asked, pretty sure I knew what was coming.

"Security. Bodyguard. I want to hire you to guard Charlie."

I didn't bother to cover my laugh. "No fucking way," I said once I had myself under control. "Don't get me wrong. I'm not scared of your sister, but I'm not going out of my way to give her an excuse to put my balls in a vise. Jesus."

"I know you can keep your mouth shut. And I know you have other work on your plate, but I want you to watch over Charlie full-time and I'm willing to make it worth your while."

"Why me? Why not get someone from the Sinclair team? They have a whole division trained for exactly this kind of thing."

"You're already with her most of the time, anyway. And if I try to put a bodyguard on her, she'll go ballistic. Anyway, do you really want one of the Sinclair guys on her twenty-four seven? Sleeping in her house? Driving her around?"

Fuck, he had a point. I most definitely did not want one of the Sinclair team attached to Charlie at the hip twenty-four seven. That would put a serious crimp in my plans.

Goddammit.

An unwelcome thought occurred to me. Charlie had invited me into her bed, so I knew she liked my type. Big, rough, dangerous. Sinclair had a diverse team, but I could guess that the guy he'd put on Charlie would be muscle. Meaning, a lot like me.

Charlie was mine. This wasn't long-term, but for now, she was mine, and I wasn't sharing her with some fucking meathead, with a gun, that Sinclair thought was good enough to keep her safe.

Fuck that.

Making a decision, I said, "I have a job running that I can finish today if I put in a few more hours. Everything else is flexible for the next two weeks. I'll be on her around-the-clock as soon as I get this job wrapped up."

"That works," Aiden said. "Just send me an invoice when it's done, and I'll take care of it."

I resisted the urge to chuck my coffee cup at his head. "I'm not sending you a fucking invoice. You're not paying me to watch Charlie. I'm watching Charlie to keep her safe from the psycho after her."

"I'd rather you didn't tell Charlie about this conversation," Aiden said.

This guy just kept getting funnier and funnier. I shook my head.

"No fucking way. I'm not setting myself up for that. And tell your friend William Davis to get off her case."

Aiden took the last sip of his coffee and crossed the room to put the mug in my sink. "I already did," he said. "I told him to back off of Charlie—and you—if he comes by again. I'm sorry about that. We all love William, but he's a relic. He wants the girls married and having babies while they do what their menfolk tell them. He can't quite absorb that the world has moved on. He's so obsessed with telling us what he thinks our parents would say that I think he forgets he used to argue with them all the time about this stuff. He means well."

"He might mean well, but he's a jackass," I said. I was beginning to understand William Davis's role in all of their lives, but that didn't mean I was gonna let him upset Charlie. Aiden nodded.

"If he comes by again, let me know. I'll see what I can do, though he doesn't listen to me any more than he used to listen to my dad. Just nods his head and then goes on giving me the same speech he always does."

"Yeah?" I asked, suddenly curious. "What does he give *you* shit about? I thought you were the king of the family."

"I am," Aiden agreed with a glint of laughter in his eyes. "But apparently, I never should've divorced my first wife—who was a raging bitch, as Charlie will be happy to tell you—and it's high time I found a new wife and started breeding the next generation of the Winters family. He recommended I find someone who will do what she's told and represent the family appropriately. He threatened to bring me a list of candidates."

"Jesus, that's sucks," I said, openly laughing at him.

"Believe me, I know. It's only gotten worse since Vance and Maggie got engaged. Maggie is old Atlanta and William is over the moon that Vance—whom he's given lecture upon lecture about the art, the tattoos, and the long hair—managed to snag Magnolia Henry. He thinks she's redeeming him. Yet I'm still single. And after all his resistance to Abigail, he's throwing her in my face, too."

Imitating William's patrician voice, Aiden said, "I fail to understand how Jacob and Vance have managed to find appropriate women and you are still single. You're letting down the Winters family name, Aiden."

"I'm seeing that Charlie might have it easy," I admitted. Aiden's expression turned serious in a flash.

"Regardless, I don't want him bothering her. If he does, I'll have another word with him. She's got enough going on right now. She doesn't need extra stress from William over things that don't matter anyway."

I followed him to the door. "We'll keep you posted if anything changes."

"I'd sleep better if I knew I was in the loop," Aiden said.

I nodded. I didn't have a baby sister, but I'd had a younger brother and I got what he was saying.

"I'll talk to Charlie about it," I said. "I don't like that note. And I don't want her scared. If anything else happens, we'll let you know."

I watched him jog down the steps and get in his Aston Martin. That visit hadn't gone the way I'd expected. Understatement. I hadn't expected to feel a kinship with Aiden Winters, of all people. It was there all the same. I knew where his head was. I'd been the older brother trying to keep his family together.

I didn't have generations of tradition weighing me down, but I'd felt the same love, love weighted with responsibility. The same need to protect. I'd mostly failed my own family, while Aiden was still trying to save his.

It didn't hurt that he wasn't an asshole. It was hard to dislike a man who loved his baby sister the way Aiden loved Charlie.

I wasn't looking forward to telling Charlie about his visit. She wouldn't like that Aiden had come by behind her back, and she definitely wouldn't like having a bodyguard. She was going to have to deal with it. I locked the door and went back to my laptop. If I was going to clear my schedule for Charlie, I had to get this job done.

While my laptop woke up, I sent her a quick text to check in. I'd feel better if I had confirmation that she was still safely behind the gates and the security. I'd given Aiden a hard time, but we were on the same page.

I didn't like her out there on her own, and I wouldn't, until we caught whoever was after her and put him behind bars.

CHAPTER SIXTEEN

CHARLIE

L ucas was driving my car when he pulled into the circular drive at Winters House. My sedan wasn't small, but Lucas's tall frame filled the driver's seat so thoroughly I was certain he had to be uncomfortable.

I thought about offering to drive back, then changed my mind. I didn't have to ask to know that Lucas was one of those men who didn't like anyone else to drive the vehicle he was in.

I hadn't spent my life surrounded by overbearing men without learning to pick my battles. I didn't wait for him to knock before opening the front door.

"Hey," I said. "Thanks for coming to get me. Sorry I took so long."

Lucas bent his head, his lips gliding across mine in a kiss that held more affection than passion. "No problem," he said. "I had a job I was trying to wrap up, anyway."

"Did you get it done?" I asked, linking my arm through his as he led me down the steps. Looking back over my shoulder at the door I'd left half open, I said, "Oh, wait. I have some stuff for the house in the front hall. I should grab it."

"You can get in the car. I'll get your stuff."

Lucas opened the passenger door and stood over me as I sat and fastened my seatbelt. It's not that I didn't appreciate his protectiveness, but he seemed edgier than usual, his eyes scanning the courtyard and the closed gate, alert for any threat.

Assured that I was safely strapped into the car, he went back in the house for my loot. I'd raided the attics for some extra things no one needed.

Not much. Furniture would only get in the way of the renovations. Just a card table and three folding chairs, plus a few camp chairs—the kind that folded out into a lounger with a footrest.

Not having anywhere to sit except the futon was getting on my nerves. Lucas loaded the trunk and joined me in the car, starting the engine and pulling out of the courtyard.

"Did you get your job finished?" I asked, feeling oddly domestic. Lucas looked over at me and grinned, his green eyes lighting up even as shadows lurked in his face.

"I did," he said. "Closed it out with the client right before you called."

"Good timing," I commented.

"Yeah," he said. He fell silent, drawing in a half-breath like he was going to speak, then letting it out in a whoosh.

"What?" I asked. Something was bothering him.

"Your brother came to see me," he said finally, shooting me a quick, worried glance before focusing again on the winding road through Buckhead.

"Which one?" I asked, torn between dread and exasperation.

"Aiden."

"Was he awful?" I asked, bracing for the worst.

Lucas surprised me. "No, he was cool. He tried to hire me to be your bodyguard."

"Okaaay." I drew out the word, inviting an explanation. None was forthcoming. Finally, I asked, "What did you tell him?"

"Are you pissed?" Lucas asked.

"I don't know yet. How much did he offer to pay you?"

"We never got that far," Lucas said. "I told him I already planned to keep you safe. You're not a job, Charlie."

"Okay," I said again. "Then I guess I'm not pissed."

"Not pissed at me or not pissed at Aiden?"

"Definitely not at you," I said. "I appreciate your telling me and not letting me find out on my own. Did Aiden ask you to keep it a secret?"

Lucas's silence was its own answer.

"Harrumph." The disgruntled sound rumbled in the back of my throat, drawing a laugh from Lucas.

"So, you're still pissed at Aiden?" he asked, still laughing.

"Mmm. Maybe. I don't know."

I was and I wasn't.

It was hard to be angry with someone who loved me so much. I remembered the cool, calculating look in his eyes when he said, "You're fired."

No, I was still pissed.

"Yes and no," I explained. "I'm not mad at him for going to see you. I'm still furious with him for firing me."

"I would be too," Lucas said.

"You're not going to try to convince me to forgive him?" I asked.

"No. He loves you and you love him. That doesn't mean you don't have a right to be pissed. I wanted to beat the shit out of Gunner half the time. We didn't agree on anything. Doesn't mean I didn't love him."

"That pretty much describes my relationship with all of my male relatives."

"I figured," Lucas said, laughter still in his voice.

"Does he know we're . . . involved?" I asked carefully.

"He does. Does that bother you?"

Without thinking first, I reached out and lay my hand over Lucas's where it rested on the center console. His fingers curled around mine with a light squeeze.

"No, of course not," I said. "Does he know we're not . . . that it isn't . . ."

I stopped talking, feeling childish for being unable to articulate our relationship. Calling us *fuck buddies* out loud sounded so much cheaper than it did when I said it in my head. Lucas squeezed my fingers between his and let out a low chuckle.

"You mean, did I tell him I wasn't your new boyfriend, and that we're just fucking for fun?"

My cheeks burned. "Yeah. That."

"No. We didn't get into specifics."

I let out the breath I'd been holding and relaxed, absently stroking my thumb over Lucas's fingers.

Were we holding hands?

I looked down at the center console and Lucas's much bigger hand wrapped around mine, his fingers curved over mine protectively.

This was weird.

So far, we'd had a lot of sex, a few arguments, two major crises, and he'd helped me strip some paint. The closest we'd come to doing normal couple stuff was the night we went out and got dinner together.

Holding hands was a tiny, unimportant thing. It should be. Shouldn't sex be the thing that made the difference?

It wasn't with us. Sex had been easy. If I were lucky, it would continue to be easy, because God knew, sex with Lucas Jackson was fucking phenomenal.

But this?

Holding hands was something entirely new. He wasn't comforting me after I was attacked or got a threatening note. This wasn't a crisis. This was just Lucas picking me up at my brother's house and driving me home while we talked about our days.

Normal stuff. Couple stuff.

I should put the brakes on right now. I should pull my hand back into my lap. We weren't a couple. Lucas wasn't my boyfriend.

The fact that I was kind of sort of starting to hope that he might be . . . that wasn't optimism. That was me heading straight for a broken heart.

As if that weren't bad enough, the next thing Lucas said told me that if I thought I was headed for a broken heart now, it was about to get so much worse.

"Aiden and I didn't talk about you and me," he said, glancing at me as if to gauge my mood. "But we did talk about your security. After that note, you've got two options. Everyone agrees you need someone with you twenty-four seven until this is resolved. Your choices are someone from the Sinclair team or me."

"What if I choose not to have anyone watching me at all?" I asked, already knowing what he would say.

"Don't go there, Princess," Lucas said calmly. "Be smart. My guess is that Hayward hired someone to go after you. The FBI is watching him too closely for him to be doing this himself.

He's alibied for everything. Brennan's theory is that whoever was leaving those pictures has escalated. He could be right, but my gut tells me this isn't about your family. This is about you."

"And you're sure I need to be watched around-the-clock?" I asked.

I wanted to be safe. I really, really didn't want to get hurt. Still, constant supervision sounded extreme. And annoying.

Lucas shot me another quick sideways glance.

"Yes. Here's the thing about stalkers. They always escalate eventually. But it's not a stable escalation. We don't have a flowchart to say that after a certain thing happens—a note, a phone call, sending you flowers, whatever—after that thing happens, *now* it's dangerous. This guy started with physically attacking you and then sent you a threatening note. Most of the time, it's the other way around."

"Do you have a theory on why he's coming at me backward?" I asked, curious.

I'd spent too much time being scared or ignoring the problem to think about the psychology of my stalker. Mostly, I just wanted it to stop.

"I have some ideas. I want to get a better picture of why Hayward is focused on you rather than your brother or someone else at the company. But as far as his approach being upside down, I think he saw all the security go in and realized it wouldn't be as easy to get to you as he planned so he dialed back his approach. That doesn't mean he's not waiting for an opportunity. The whole idea of constant protection is to keep him from finding that opportunity."

"Okay," I said." I'd rather have you than one of the Sinclair guys. But don't you have work? I don't want to get in the way."

I didn't. Watching over me instead of working was a

massive intrusion into his life. I was going to wear out my welcome with Lucas Jackson, and when this was over, he'd be so eager to get away from me I'd never see him again.

The thought was depressing.

"It's not exactly a sacrifice, Princess," he said with a quirk to his lips.

"I can pay you for your time while you're guarding me," I said, wincing when his fingers closed tightly over mine, then let go as he yanked his hand back and dropped it into his lap, leaving my fingers cold.

Dammit.

"What is it with you Winters'?" he demanded. "Do you always throw money at your problems until they go away?"

"Yeah, because that works so well on most of our problems."

If I sounded bitter, it's because I was. Money doesn't erase problems. For every problem you get rid of when you throw money at it, another springs up in its place.

I don't mean to sound ungrateful. I appreciated all the benefits of being a Winters. It was nice not to have to worry about bills or tuition. But money wouldn't bring my parents back. It wouldn't heal our damaged souls or mend our broken hearts.

Money didn't save Vance. And money couldn't help Annalise or Gage, who'd both run from home, fleeing their own demons. In Annalise's case, literally.

"I wasn't trying to be rude," I said through clenched teeth. "But I recognize it's a lot to ask. What do you usually charge for around-the-clock protection? I'm guessing it's a lot. I don't want to take advantage of your being a nice guy by expecting you to watch out for me for free, that's all."

Lucas busted out laughing. His hand came back to the

center console and closed over mine, his fingers twining with my own.

"Princess, you've got business on the brain. Look, I'm not taking money for this. This thing with us works for me. Just because it's not going anywhere long-term doesn't mean I don't care about you, okay? I won't let anything happen to you. I already told you, you're not a job."

"But—" I started to protest.

"Charlie, just because I drive a truck and don't belong to the country club doesn't mean I don't have money, okay? I'm just not into buying stuff. Some people grow up poor, and the first time they have money, they blow it all. I know that feeling, that rush when you can have the things you always wanted. It's almost impossible not to go crazy."

"But you didn't?" I asked.

"No, I did. I blew through my first few paychecks from the Army so fast they might as well have gone up in a puff of smoke."

"What did you buy?" I was curious. More curious when Lucas gave me the side eye, pressed his lips together, and shook his head.

"Nothing appropriate for your ears, Princess."

"Hey, I've had my mouth on your cock," I said. "I think we're past appropriate."

Ignoring me, he went on, "Anyway, after that, I realized that if I wanted to get ahead I needed to be smarter. I started saving, and once I got out of the Army and was making real money, I was already in the habit of socking it all away. I don't live large because I don't need to. If I wanted to, I could retire today and never have to work again."

"Really? You're pretty young."

"I have specialized skills. They're worth a lot of money. I

like my work, so I'm going to keep doing it. And when I do retire, I'd like to do it with enough money to live very well. I've got a few years left in me before I'm ready for that. But I don't need your money, Princess. Are we clear?"

"We're clear. I'm sorry if I hurt your feelings."

"Hurt my feelings?" He made a noise somewhere between a laugh and a grunt. "I'm a badass, Princess. I don't have feelings."

"Harrumph." That statement didn't deserve a true response.

Since the subject was closed, I went back to something he'd said that bothered me. "You think Hayward is stalking me?"

"What would you call it?" Lucas asked.

"I don't know. But my cousin Annalise had a stalker and it wasn't anything like this."

"You okay with pizza for dinner?" Lucas asked out of nowhere. I checked the dashboard clock and realized it was almost dinnertime.

"Sure." Was I ever not okay with pizza? No, I could eat pizza every day.

Lucas turned into the parking lot of a pizza place not far from our street and parked.

"Let's talk about this in the car, where no one can overhear," he said. "Tell me about your cousin's stalker."

"It started when we were in high school," I said, thinking back. None of us liked to dwell on the stalker episode, Annalise least of all. "It was so subtle at first that we all thought she just had a secret admirer. She's seven years older than me, so I missed a lot of the details. But it was mostly sweet notes left where she would find them, then little presents, then longer notes that started to get creepy. They stopped for a few years after my parents died."

"How old was she when your parents died?"

"Eighteen. She'd just started her freshman year in college, and she moved back home for the rest of the year. She was at Emory—"

"Did all of you go to Emory?" Lucas asked.

"Aiden was at Harvard," I offered. "Then when our parents died, he came home and finished school at Emory. It's an excellent school and it's a family tradition."

"Did they mind that Aiden wanted to go to Harvard?"

"No." I shook my head remembering the party they'd thrown when his acceptance letter had come in. "No. They never pushed us like that. They were so proud of him. We actually all thought that Annalise would go to RISD or another art school like Vance did. But she was close to my parents and she didn't really like being away from home. Ironic, since she hasn't been home in ages."

"So what happened?" Lucas rubbed his thumb along mine, the touch of his skin comforting.

"Like I said, the notes and presents stopped after my parents died. But only for a year. Annalise moved back into the dorm and it started again. But this time, she felt like someone was following her. I don't know exactly what happened to scare her so badly. Things were confused back then. There was a lot going on, and if you think Aiden is protective now, you should have seen him those first years after Mom and Dad were gone. No one would tell me anything."

"But something happened."

"All I know is that not long after she graduated, Annalise came home one night terrified. She wouldn't leave the house for days, and then she left and she didn't come back. Now, she travels all the time. She's never home. She takes the most beautiful photographs and makes a good living selling them, but she'd do better if she had a show or got hooked up with a gallery. I think she's afraid to stay in one place that long."

"And they never caught the guy?" Lucas asked.

"Never came close. He was very, very smart. We knew it had to be someone local, and that seems to have held up because it stopped after she left Atlanta. That's why my thing didn't seem like stalking. What happened to Annalise was gradual. It grew so slowly, I don't think any of them realized how bad it was until it was too late."

"It does sound like a textbook case," Lucas agreed. "Your cousin's situation is the most common variety, but not the only one. And before we go in and get a pizza—"

"And garlic knots," I interrupted.

"And garlic knots," Lucas agreed, squeezing my fingers, "I want a quick rundown of what happened with Bruce Hayward. Did you have any indication he might have an interest in you before the FBI went after him?"

"I don't think he has an interest in me. At least not the way you mean. I was working with him on a project. He was providing materials and some staff for a joint development. As things moved forward, I became aware that he was violating the law in a number of different ways."

"What ways? Specifically."

"Counterfeit materials, illegal workers . . . it was a long list. I talked to Aiden about it and we agreed that we needed to contact the FBI. We knew it wouldn't be a popular decision and might be bad for the company, but we weren't going to sit there and condone his behavior by not doing anything."

"So why is this focused on you and not Aiden?"

"Because I'm the one who worked with the FBI. Aiden

and I decided together, but I had the evidence, and I was in the best position to gather more."

"They fucking sent you in undercover?" Lucas demanded, his fingers closing over mine tight enough to hurt. I rubbed my thumb across his, soothing his anger.

"That makes it sound so cloak and dagger," I said. "It wasn't really like that. I just kept doing the job I was already doing, only I gave copies of things to the FBI and I took pictures when no one was looking. That part wasn't even a big deal. I just said I was documenting the progress for my report to Aiden. Hayward is so arrogant it never occurred to him that a mere woman might bring him down. Plus, he's one of those people who doesn't think the law applies to him. Regulations are for everyone else, not Hayward. He never saw it coming."

"So, there *is* a reason he's focused on you," Lucas said. "Did he ever ask you out?"

"Once," I admitted. "Aside from the fact that he's old enough to be my father, ugh. Bruce Hayward is sleazy. The stories I've heard from the women in his company, the few he hires, are not good. Groping, innuendo, and lots of threats if anyone mentions a sexual harassment suit. I turned him down as politely as I could and he never asked again."

"Aiden let you work with this guy?" Lucas asked, his eyes narrowed.

I narrowed mine right back.

"Do you want to ask me that again?" I asked, my voice dangerously calm. "And this time, think before you talk?"

What did he mean, *let me* work with that guy?

Lucas let out a grunt and scowled at me. "He should have been looking out for you."

I pulled my hand from his and crossed my arms over my chest.

"First of all," I said in a cool tone, "my brother has always looked out for me. More than I'd like him to, his firing me case in point. Second of all, there are assholes in every walk of life. I'm going to run into them unless I hide in my house. Aiden didn't like me working with a pig like Bruce Hayward, but it was *my* project, in *my* department, and it was too big to pass off to someone else. Don't you run into assholes? Do you turn down every asshole client you meet? Or do you weigh your options and sometimes take the job anyway?"

I knew I'd made my point when he grunted again and reached out to reclaim my hand. He squeezed my fingers gently before kissing them.

Apology accepted.

"So," Lucas said, all business again, "he's angry with you for turning him in to the FBI, more so because you're a woman who brought him low, *and* one who refused his advances. Does that sum it up?"

"Pretty much," I said. "Are you sure this is Hayward?"

"Not positive, no. We're keeping our options open. Hayward is the most obvious suspect." With a final squeeze of my fingers, he released my hand and turned off the car. "You ready to eat?"

I was. Like a good girl, I waited for Lucas to round the car and open my door for me. It wasn't so much about being a gentleman, more that he didn't want me exposed in the parking lot unless he was right next to me.

Either way, I won't deny enjoying the heat of his palm against my lower back as he led me into the pizza place. The scent of garlic, cheese, and spicy sauce assaulted my senses. My mouth flooded with saliva.

Pizza was on my top five list of favorite foods. Fortunately, Lucas and I shared the same tastes. Pepperoni, Italian sausage, mushrooms, and black olives. Yum.

He led me to a booth and slid in on the same side, effectively shielding me from the rest of the room. I got annoyed when my older brothers and cousins were too protective, but with Lucas, I liked it. Most of the time.

I was glad he'd turned down the money. I didn't want to be a job. I wanted Lucas to be here for me.

For now, he was. But I was in trouble, falling for him fast.

Way too fast, and way too far, sliding under, seduced as much by his company, by him just being Lucas, as I was by his body and his passion.

I couldn't keep him forever. I knew that. And I knew he'd end up breaking my heart.

I didn't care. Tucked into the wooden booth, his strength and his heat pressed against me, I let myself pretend that we were on a normal date. That Lucas was mine. If my heart was going to break, so be it. It wouldn't be the first time.

Being with Lucas was worth the pain.

Chapter Seventeen
Charlie

Lucas stuck by my side for the next three weeks. If you'd asked me, I would have guessed that at a point, it would get annoying. Maybe it did for Lucas.

For me, it was like a dream. We worked out a decent system that let him keep an eye on me without hovering. As soon as we finished the woodwork in the living room and prepped it for staining, we set up the card table and chairs in there, giving Lucas a place to work.

Days passed in easy harmony. We'd eat breakfast, Lucas grumbling about my yogurt and granola, and I'd go to work on stripping paint. Sometimes, Lucas would help me, and sometimes, he'd be on his laptop.

I didn't bother to ask what he was doing, knowing his work was confidential. He'd said enough to give me the impression he was some kind of good guy hacker. *Good guy* meaning he wasn't going to get arrested for most of what he was doing. That was all I knew.

He had an amazing ability to focus. Despite the noise,

he never got distracted. And it was seriously noisy in Casa de Charlie.

I'd switched up the renovation schedule, trading my master bath for the kitchen. I don't know what I'd been thinking when I started the project. I could do without a luxurious bathroom. Not so much without a kitchen.

The first floor of my house was chaos, but it never seemed to bother Lucas. I figured if it got bad enough, he could suggest moving over to his place, but he never did.

In all this time, I'd never seen the inside of his house, even though it was just next door.

Weird, I know.

Not seeing a guy's house was usually a good indication he was married or was cheating on someone, but I knew that wasn't the case. I also knew his house was in much better shape than my own, and I would've bet his bed was far more comfortable than my futon.

Day by day, we rubbed along like an old married couple, bickering about little things, enjoying comfortable silences, then fucking like crazy all night.

Okay, maybe not like an old married couple. Maybe more like newlyweds.

I thought I understood about his house. As long as he never brought me next door, he could compartmentalize. I was there to protect and to fuck. If I got comfortable in his house, we'd start a quick slide into relationship territory.

I got it, but it still bugged me.

His house beckoned from across the narrow strip of lawn between our driveways, mysterious, the source of all things Lucas. Everything he kept from me. Everything he wouldn't share.

I didn't say anything about it. What was there to say? It

made sense to stay at my house, practically speaking. It was convenient if less comfortable.

Lucas never complained. Neither did I.

I would take him however I could get him, for however long he was willing to stay.

Yep, that's what I was reduced to. I'd agreed to this whole *fuck buddies/friends with benefits* thing thinking it would be no big deal. It never occurred to me that Lucas would insinuate himself into every aspect of my life. Without meaning to, he'd become essential to my happiness.

I was totally screwed. Well, yes, I *was* totally screwed. I liked that part of it. Sex with Lucas only got better the more we did it. I knew things now. That spot on the inside of his thighs that was so sensitive I just had to blow on it and his cock would surge in my hand.

Lucas was the same with me. At this point, all it took was a certain look, slanted from beneath his dark lashes, and I was instantly wet, instantly ready to be his.

Yep, totally screwed. For him, it was about our bodies and hanging out and keeping me safe. I had no illusions that I'd made a place for myself in his heart, the way he'd taken residence in mine.

Lucas had been watching over me, nonstop, for three weeks, and other than progress on my house and a lot of sex, nothing had happened. We still didn't know if my stalker was Bruce Hayward or someone working for him, but either way, they were leaving me alone.

Both Aiden and Lucas thought that Lucas's constant presence had scared them off. If that were true, it left us in a bind. As long as Lucas was never more than a few feet away, the stalker wouldn't make another move, and we'd never have the chance to catch him.

Since I wasn't eager to give Lucas the perfect excuse to leave me and I wasn't interested in being bait for another violent attack, I let things stay as they were. I didn't want to do anything to rock the boat—a problem, since I had a question to ask Lucas. One that had been bothering me for weeks. There was a benefit tomorrow night and I had to go.

And if I was going, so was Lucas. I'd put off mentioning it for weeks, at first because going to a benefit with me was a boyfriend thing, not a fuck buddy thing. I wasn't going to ask just to hear him turn me down. Once Lucas became my bodyguard, he'd have to come with me if he was going to keep me safe.

Still, I hadn't said anything. Now, I was out of time.

I wasn't ready to find out how much of our relationship was a job and how much was about us. It didn't help that he'd been irritated with me all day.

Apparently, Lucas was not on board with my plan to trade my sedan for a used pick-up truck. I don't know what his deal was. He drove a pick-up, though his was new and much nicer than the trucks I planned to look at.

My car came to a stop, startling me out of my reverie. Lucas turned to look at me, a scowl marring his handsome face, and said, "Are you absolutely sure you want to do this?"

"I told you I was," I said irritably. "I don't know why you're making such a big deal of it."

"You should get something nicer."

"I don't want to spend that much money," I said for what felt like the fiftieth time that day. "I don't need a car payment right now and I don't want to drain my savings."

"At least get something new," he said. "Your brother would give you the money if you asked."

"You know, for someone who got all offended when he

was offered money to be my bodyguard, you're pretty cavalier about expecting me to take a handout."

"It's not the same. It's your family."

"It's exactly the same," I said, exasperated.

I didn't know what the big deal was. I was trading in my sedan for a used truck. People traded in their cars every day. When I told Lucas I was getting a new car, he must have envisioned me picking up a new version of the car I was trading in.

When it was new, the sedan Aiden had given me when I turned sixteen was pretty sweet. Expensive. Eight years later, it wasn't worth that much. I sure as hell wasn't trading it for a massive car payment on a vehicle I'd be afraid to drive to the home improvement store.

I didn't need a luxury sedan. I needed a truck.

Lucas called me *Princess* all the time.

Mostly, I took it as an endearment.

Sometimes, it felt like an accusation.

I was more than my family, more than my upbringing. He'd spent his entire life working to separate himself from who he'd been growing up and he'd succeeded brilliantly.

Why couldn't I do the same?

Because I was a Winters, living in Atlanta. Maybe if I'd moved away, it would've been easier to just be me. The next time I saw Annalise, I'd have to ask her.

Apparently finished grumbling at me, Lucas got out of my sedan and came around to open my door. A salesman greeted us the second my feet hit the lot.

I set him to work appraising my car for trade while Lucas dragged me around to inspect every used truck they had, treating me to a rundown of everything that was wrong with them.

Finally, I settled on one I liked that I thought was in my

price range. It wasn't pretty and it didn't have any of the bells and whistles a new vehicle would, but it didn't have too many miles and was in good condition.

It was also a good size, not a toy truck, but not as big as Lucas's. I needed a truck, but I wasn't entirely confident about transitioning from my normal-size sedan to such a big vehicle. This truck was perfect.

Lucas crossed his arms over his chest, planted his feet, and shook his head.

"Not this one."

I threw my hands in the air and said, "What? What's wrong with this one? I like this one. It's in good shape."

"It's only got thirty or forty thousand miles before the transmission falls out. These trucks are only good to a hundred thousand miles."

"That's fine," I insisted. "It'll be years before I hit a hundred thousand. I don't drive that much. Maybe by then, I'll be able to afford something new. I don't even know if I'm going to like driving a truck. I don't want to spend a lot of money."

"Fine. Then I'll buy you a truck."

I stared at him, dumbstruck.

What did he mean, he would buy me a truck?

He hadn't even let me see the inside of his house, and he was going to buy me a truck?

And he'd accused my family of throwing money at our problems. Lucas seemed to realize he'd gone too far. He looked away and shoved his hands in his pockets, studying the truck's tires.

"You're not buying me a truck," I said. "I'm getting this one. And I don't want to fight about it anymore. This is stupid. It's just a truck."

"Fine," he said.

"Fine." We both knew it wasn't just a truck. It was Lucas thinking that I really was a princess, too good to drive a truck—especially a used one—despite all he knew of me.

It shouldn't bother me. It wasn't like we were long-term anyway. What did it matter if he thought I was a spoiled little rich girl? Why did I even care?

I bit the inside of my lip to force back the prickle of tears in my eyes and flashed a smile at the salesman when he came back. I opened my mouth to greet him when Lucas stepped in front of me.

With a quick look over his shoulder, he said in an undertone, "Let me, okay? Please?"

I nodded and stepped back. I didn't want to fight with Lucas anymore. While I was perfectly capable of negotiating the sale, I was sure Lucas could handle it. He definitely knew more about trucks than I did.

I sat back and let him take care of everything, hiding a grin of triumph as he negotiated my trade-in up and the sale price down. I ended up writing a check for my new truck, but it was a smaller one than I'd expected.

Score.

I decided I wasn't that annoyed with Lucas anymore.

Lucas didn't argue much when I insisted on taking the wheel on the way home, though I drove a lot slower than usual. I liked my new truck, but it was definitely bigger than my sedan, blocky and harder to turn.

To be completely honest, I was a little bit nervous driving it. Not so much through the main roads, but once we got into the Highlands, the roads were narrower and I found myself slowing down.

I was so careful to avoid sideswiping the cars as I passed them that I missed it until I was parked in my driveway.

Then, when I finally looked up, I was so shocked my brain couldn't register anything.

Spray-painted graffiti was all over the front of my house. Mostly squiggly lines, but here and there, I could make out the words *bitch* and *cunt*. In places, bright swathes of red paint stained the siding and covered the windows, as if someone had opened a can of paint and tossed the contents at the side of the house. I stared at the pointless destruction, heart pounding in my chest.

The clink of metal sounded beside me and I jumped. Lucas swung open my door and said roughly, "Get out. I already called Brennan. He's on his way. I've got Sinclair pulling up the video feeds. Must've happened while the crew was at lunch."

Lucas pulled me from the driver seat, barely giving me time to grab my purse before he wrapped an arm around me, angling me into his chest so that I couldn't see the front of my house, and hustled me across my driveway, over the strip of lawn separating our houses, and up onto his front porch.

He had his door unlocked and was ushering me inside before I got my bearings.

I'd finally reached the inner sanctum and I was too shocked to care. I closed my eyes, seeing the front of my house in my mind. The siding had been prepped for paint, the windows brand new.

I didn't get it. Obviously, it was meant to make me angry or scared. Probably both. But why bother? I'd already turned in all of my evidence to the FBI. Threats wouldn't stop me. There was nothing to stop. My part in Hayward's prosecution was done. Why waste time harassing me?

Lucas sat me in a chair and crouched in front of me. He slid a knuckle beneath my chin, raising my face to his.

"Hang in there, Princess. We're going to figure this out. Brennan and Evers are on their way. We'll take a look at the cameras and see what happened. When they get here, I'm going next door to get your stuff."

"Why?" I asked, too heartsick to keep up.

"You're moving in with me."

Detective Brennan and Evers arrived within a few minutes, Aiden close behind. I sat in Lucas's big leather chair, staring blindly at the black screen of his giant television, unable to take anything in.

After three weeks of relative peace, the graffiti was a shock. In the big picture, it wasn't that big a deal. No one got hurt. The damage could be repaired, though it was going to cost a lot.

Lucas, Evers, Brennan, and Aiden shouted over my head, gesturing angrily and swearing when they pulled up the video feeds on Lucas's laptop. Brennan muttered under his breath, "Got him. It's a teenager."

"I guarantee when you pick him up, he'll say he was paid for the job," Evers said.

Lucas grunted in agreement. "Another dead end. Goddammit."

Aiden sent a careful look my way and said, "Sweetheart, why don't you think about coming home for a while?" He glanced at Lucas, then back at me.

Lucas sent him a dark scowl, his green eyes hot and angry.

"She's staying with me," he said. "I may not have a wall around my house, but I can goddamn guarantee you no one will get to her here. If I thought she'd be safer with you, I'd fucking deliver her myself."

Aiden and Evers exchanged a look. Evers sent him the

tiniest of nods and Aiden relaxed slightly. "Would you rather stay with Lucas?" he asked me gently.

I nodded. I didn't know what was going on with Lucas, but he made me feel safe. And more than that, I had this growing fear that if I walked away, so would he.

I knew I'd lose him eventually. He'd made it clear he didn't want me forever. I'd have to live with that.

But for now, I'd take what I could get.

CHAPTER EIGHTEEN
LUCAS

I couldn't seem to shake the knot in my chest.

Was it anger? Fear?

Fuck that. I don't get scared.

There was no denying we'd all been lulled into a false sense of security over the last few weeks. Charlie's stalker had backed off and we were all relieved. Me, most of all.

This thing with Charlie would run its course, likely sooner than later. As long as the stalker was out there, I had an excuse to stick close.

We'd moved way beyond *friends with benefits*. I didn't know what we were, but whatever it was, I liked it.

I liked being with Charlie.

Not just in bed, though that was fucking spectacular. Before Charlie, I'd never been a guy to go back for seconds. Honestly, I'd expected the whole thing with her would be over before it started.

In a million years, I never would've imagined she'd be this good. It wasn't that she was skilled. I'd been with women who had way more experience.

For the first time, sex wasn't about experience. It wasn't

about tricks and skills. It was all about Charlie. Not the way her pussy gripped my cock or how well she used her hot mouth. All of that would've been enough.

No, it was *her*. The way she smelled underneath her lotions and sprays, her natural musky sweetness. The silk of her hair. The way she never took my shit or let me boss her around.

It was everything. I was totally fucked. I knew it. Everyone who saw us knew it. As soon as we caught the stalker and she was safe, I'd be out of excuses.

I was turning down work every day. I picked up a few small jobs I could do from my laptop, but I turned down everything that would take me out of town.

Leaving Charlie unprotected was out of the question.

Never mind that Sinclair would have a guy on her the second I stepped away. No one could keep her safe the way I could.

No one.

Sinclair Security only hired the best. I didn't doubt that whoever they assigned to Charlie would be technically proficient. Considering that they thought of her as family, whoever it was wouldn't just be proficient, they'd be exceptional. But no one knew her like I did.

To them, she'd be just another client. They wouldn't get that she was precious. And it wasn't just about keeping her safe, it was about making sure she wasn't afraid. That she never had to be afraid again.

Fuck.

The look on her face when I ripped open the door to her shit heap of a truck left me sick with rage. Her ocean blue eyes had been wide with shock, her skin blue-white it was so pale.

She'd been so fucking proud of her front porch, the new

224

planking, the patches on the siding. It looked like a mess, but anyone who'd renovated a house could see the progress. Now, some asshole had destroyed it and stolen her peace.

When we finally managed to pin this on Hayward, I was going to fucking kill him.

Aiden had called a family meeting for dinner even though Holden and Tate were out of town at a gaming conference. After announcing the dinner, he left, taking Charlie with him. Letting Evers lead her out to the car, he stopped at the door to say to me, "You'll move her stuff over? And be at dinner tonight?"

I nodded. Aiden lifted his chin in goodbye and left. I kept waiting for him, for any of them, to object to Charlie sleeping with me.

The Winters clan was surprisingly laid-back. I didn't get it, because they were bossy as hell with every other aspect of Charlie's life. Aiden had fucking fired her from a job she excelled at because he didn't think she was happy, but they didn't mind her shacking up with me.

If I had a little sister, I sure as hell wouldn't want her shacked up with a guy like me.

Shaking it off, I locked my house and headed next door to get Charlie's things. I went in through the back door, winding my way through the crew working on her kitchen. It would be a while, but the room was starting to take shape.

Her design was the complete opposite of mine, but I liked it. Where my kitchen was dark, with bold colors and dense concrete countertops, hers was all light.

Custom white cabinets with glass doors on the top, all the appliances covered in the same white woodwork. Beautiful white marble on the counters and island, deep farmhouse sinks like mine and a huge gas range, also like mine.

It was smart, considering that the big window in the

kitchen looked out onto the covered porch. The view was pretty, but without direct sunlight, the room could've been too dim.

Charlie had chosen a funky black iron and crystal chandelier to hang over the island. It was an offbeat choice, but I could see, looking at the rest of the room, that it would be perfect. A spark of Charlie in an otherwise too-perfect kitchen.

She was good at this. If she decided to flip the house, she'd probably make a decent profit even considering how much she was using contractors.

She was planning on keeping this place, but I caught her checking out listings in the neighborhood on her tablet. I'd wondered if she was being so stingy about the truck because she wanted to keep her cash handy to invest in another house.

I hated that truck. I knew I'd been a dick at the dealership. And I respected that she wasn't wasting money. I did.

But Charlie was too good for a piece of shit truck. She deserved something better. If she'd let me, I would've bought her a new one.

Stupid, I know.

I was never reckless with my savings, but the second I'd offered, I knew I meant it. I wanted her to have something from me. Something I'd given her, something that she needed.

I didn't try to justify the impulse. I was afraid if I thought about it too much, I wouldn't like what it said about my feelings for Charlie. I should have been relieved she turned me down. I wasn't.

If she wouldn't let me buy her a truck, at least she was letting me keep her safe. I packed up her things with quick efficiency. She'd only brought a duffel bag from Winters

House, but in the weeks since, her belongings had expanded.

It took two trips, but I managed to get her moved in, making space on the other side of my dresser for her stuff. I was not going to think about the jolt in my chest at seeing her clothes neatly folded in her own drawer in my bedroom.

I was not going to think about the way they looked right, her T-shirts, her lace underwear and practical athletic bras. I wasn't going to take a deep breath, absorbing the flowery fruity scent of her lotion.

It didn't belong here.

She didn't belong here.

The sooner I got that straight in my head, the better.

It was time to draw some boundaries. For my own sake, if not for hers. Sleeping with her, moving her in with me, that was all tied up in protecting her and our previous arrangement as neighbors with benefits.

Going to dinner at Winters House? That was another thing altogether. It was as close to dinner with her parents as I'd ever get, and it sent everyone the wrong message.

Before I could think too much, I picked up my phone and dialed Charlie, intending to cancel. She could get a ride home with one of her brothers or Vance and Magnolia.

Charlie didn't answer.

"Problem?" Aiden asked brusquely.

Mentally shifting gears, I said, "No problem. Stuff has come up. I'm not going to make dinner. Can you give Charlie a ride home?"

There was a long pause.

Then Aiden said, "Bullshit. I wouldn't have taken you for a pussy."

Did he just call me a pussy?

Gritting my teeth, I said, "Fuck off, Winters. I said something came up."

"Yeah, and I said it's bullshit. You don't have to be scared. We don't bite."

"Now I'm agreeing with Charlie. You're an asshole," I said. I wanted to hang up on him. I wanted to go over there, snatch up Charlie, and drag her back to my house so we could avoid the whole Winters family scene.

Dammit.

"Fine." I ground out.

"Dinner is at seven. Be here by six." Aiden hung up.

Asshole.

I got in a few hours of work before I closed my laptop and headed to Winters House. Charlie had given me the gate code, so I didn't have to go through the pain in the ass of calling the house to get on the property.

I liked living in the Highlands, liked the energy and the people. But there was something awe-inspiring about rolling down the long drive, shaded by old-growth trees, to discover Winters House nestled in the hills.

On ten acres in the heart of Buckhead, Winters House was a fairytale, the kind of house I'd thought royalty lived in when I was a poor kid growing up in a trailer.

Built in a square around a central courtyard in a Mediterranean-style, the red tile roof and creamy walls were warm and welcoming despite the dark iron gates blocking access to the inner courtyard. They opened smoothly as I approached.

I'd been in houses like this before, mostly on the job or meeting clients. Rarely as a guest.

My years in the Army, and those I'd spent on my own after I went private, had given me the confidence to deal with people on every level of society.

Money didn't intimidate me. Neither did power. If I was here on a job, it would be business as usual. No big deal. I wouldn't have this niggling certainty in my gut that I didn't belong anywhere near Winters House. Or Charlie.

Day by day, being with Charlie was so easy, so natural, I forgot who she really was. I'd started calling her Princess to poke at her, but lately to me, Princess just meant Charlie.

My Charlie.

But Charlie had grown up here, like a real princess behind castle walls. She was so far out of my league it was like looking at the sun. I'd been right to try and cancel.

I already knew I was in too deep with her, but I wasn't ready to let her go.

Not yet.

Deep down, in the hidden parts of my heart I rarely examined, I had the fear that seeing me in Winters House, surrounded by her family, she'd realize I didn't belong and that would be the end.

I was here now. It was too late to run away.

CHAPTER NINETEEN

LUCAS

I parked in front of the garage beside a Range Rover and let myself into the house. I couldn't picture myself ever living in a place this size. It was fucking enormous. I'd stayed in hotels that were smaller.

Everything about the house spoke of old-world quality. I'd spent enough time rehabbing my own place to appreciate the smooth grain of the quarter-sawn oak and the way the ivory walls contrasted with the dark wood trim without being cold.

Winters House smelled of beeswax and faintly of flowers. My mother's trailer had reeked of stale cigarettes, undercut by the bleach that clung to her skin after long days of scrubbing toilets.

Memory and reality clashed, shoving me off-balance.

I followed the sound of voices through the front hall to what looked like the formal living room. The heavy crown molding, silk drapes, and expensive furniture called for cocktail dresses and suits, but the Winters clan was having none of that.

Even Aiden wore jeans with his button-down shirt. I

didn't think I'd ever seen him without a tie. Despite his casual dress, stress had drawn grooves on either side of his mouth and the dark circles beneath his eyes were worse.

When he saw me, he grinned in triumph. I stopped myself before I could growl in response.

I spotted Charlie a second later, curled up on one of the couches, trying gamely to hang onto her cousin Vance's daughter, Rosalie. The baby was five months old and didn't seem to want to cuddle.

Beside her sat Maggie, a shapely redhead I'd met a few times when she came by to see Charlie. Engaged to Vance, Maggie already seemed to think of Rosie as her own. Charlie looked up to see me and her eyes brightened.

"Hey. You're here. Do you want anything to drink?"

She passed Rosalie back to Maggie and picked up her beer off a side table.

"I'll take a beer," I said.

"Sure you don't want a whiskey?" Aiden asked, a gleam in his eye.

"After your Macallan, everything else is a step down," I said, grinning at him. I heard a hoot of laughter from across the room and saw Vance elbow Jacob, her brother.

"You owe me," Aiden said.

I shrugged and shook my head. "I don't think so. That would be Charlie. I was just in the right place at the right time."

"I'm jealous," Jacob said. "I asked him twenty times to let me try it. Nothing, the selfish bastard. How was it? "

"It was so smooth," Charlie interrupted, smirking at her brothers and Vance. "So good, I don't think words can do it justice."

"You know if any of us had stolen a fifteen thousand-dollar bottle of whiskey from Aiden, he would've beaten the shit out of us," Vance said blandly.

Charlie shrugged. "I've spent my entire life putting up with you overbearing Winters men ruining all my fun. There have to be some perks. Anyway, Aiden deserved it."

"Agreed," Vance said. At Aiden's noise of affront, he looked at his older cousin and said, "Sorry, man. But you did. Firing Charlie was an asshole move. You know it. I know it. Everybody knows it."

"He's right," Jacob said, ignoring Aiden's scowl.

"You guys always gang up on Aiden," a low, sweet voice broke in. Abigail Jordan. I had a feeling it wouldn't be long until she was Abigail Winters if the way Jacob looked at her was any indication. I hadn't seen her since the night I killed Big John, and then only the back of her robe as she ran for Jacob's safe room.

Tonight, she was dressed more formally than anyone else in the room in a light blue linen dress with matching shoes, her hair up in a complicated looking twist. Except for the last time we crossed paths, I'd never seen her casually dressed.

She looked directly at me, her eyes filled with an emotion I couldn't name. I wondered if she was afraid of me. I'd shot and killed a man only a few feet from her. That would be enough to scare anyone.

Turning to Charlie with sympathy in her eyes, she said, "I'm sorry, honey. I agree he didn't handle that very well. And I know sometimes, these guys go overboard when they think they know best. But he acted out of love."

"It's nice to know someone around here appreciates me," Aiden said, his smile at Abigail affectionate and gentle.

Jacob shook his head at his brother.

"Stop flirting with my woman," he said.

Abigail sent him an exasperated look. "Just because someone's nice to me, doesn't mean they're flirting," she said.

"You guys are such cavemen," Maggie complained. She held Rosalie up in front of her and nuzzled her nose into the baby's stomach. Rosie erupted into a fountain of baby giggles, the sound pure joy. "I shudder to think what Vance will be like when Rosie discovers boys."

"Rosie is never going to discover boys," Vance said. "Rosie is going to join a nunnery when she's twelve. If she behaves herself, I may pick her husband for her when she's thirty-five. Preferably a eunuch."

Jacob and Aiden both made sounds of agreement. Maggie just shook her head and ignored them.

A bell rang somewhere in the house, and everyone stood. Must be dinner time. Charlie handed me a beer she'd gotten from the wet bar by the door and looped her arm through mine as we walked to the dining room.

Abigail stopped us in the hall with a hand on my arm. Looking up at me with brimming eyes, she said, "Lucas Jackson. I'm so sorry I haven't been to see you since Charlie moved in next door. Jacob wouldn't tell me where you lived before."

"Why did you want to see me?" I asked, confused, and sent a quick glance at Jacob, who was eyeing us with an amused expression.

"I wanted to thank you for everything you did for me. I know trying to help me made the whole situation with Big John worse. You didn't have to do that."

"Yes, I did," I said. Abigail had been in a bad spot with her former father-in-law. I couldn't have left her to face it alone. She'd risked her future to help her sick mother. She didn't deserve what Big John was going to do to her.

"No," she said, her eyes meeting mine with a level gaze.

"You didn't. Except for Jacob, no one else helped me. I was in your way and you changed your plans to keep me safe. It means a lot and I wanted you to know. I wish I'd been able to thank you at the time, but—"

But I'd just shot a man and hadn't stuck around to chat. And Jacob hadn't been eager to let his woman anywhere near me.

"It's okay. You're welcome. I'm just glad to see you're doing so well. Is your mom hanging in there?"

She nodded. "Some days are better than others. I don't think she has a lot of time left. It's good to be able to visit her so much."

"I'm sorry," I said. Her grief when she spoke of her mother was palpable, weighing down her voice.

"Thank you, so am I. I hope you didn't get in too much trouble for, um, Big John. Jacob said you didn't."

"No, I didn't. Everything was fine."

"Good," she said with a smile.

Jacob swept by, sliding his arm around her waist. He swung her away from me with an exaggerated scowl in my direction and said to Abigail, "I told you to stop flirting. Especially with men who once threatened to kidnap you."

Abigail let out a lighthearted giggle, a sound I'd never heard from her before. She patted the side of his face before kissing his cheek. "Maggie is right. You *are* a caveman."

Jacob made a grunting sound and nuzzled her ear as he led her into the dining room, oblivious to Charlie and me behind them.

The formal dining room in Winters House was more suited to a state dinner than a family meal. A long, polished table stretched the length of the room, surrounded by heavy, ornately carved wooden chairs with dark velvet seats.

At one end was an enormous stone fireplace, left cold

this time of year. The beamed ceiling rose for two full stories, and along two sides of the upper level, a railed gallery gave access to a built-in library, the shelves filled with books.

I couldn't see a way to access the library from the dining room. There had to be a hidden door to the second level. Winters House was impressive, but that dining room was the coolest thing I'd ever seen.

From the size of the table to the secret library tucked into the walls above our heads, it was all I could do not to stare. I was usually cooler than this.

Turning my attention back to Charlie, I let her lead me to a surprisingly comfortable seat. Few chairs were a good fit for a guy my size. With its tall back and well-cushioned, wide seat, this one was perfect.

I couldn't imagine myself living in a house that could pass for a hotel, but there was something to be said for having a personal chef. Especially since the Winters family tastes ran more toward home cooking than haute cuisine.

On the menu tonight were stuffed pork chops, some sort of potato dish layered with cheese, and green beans almandine. I wasn't a huge fan of green beans.

Based on the way Vance was shoving them around his plate, half burying them under the potatoes, neither was he. I saw Maggie elbow him and his sheepish smile in response. I had a feeling he'd be eating at least some of those green beans.

The conversation flowed around the table, hopping from topic to topic. It wasn't hard to keep up. None of them treated me like I didn't belong. There was no posturing about my relationship with Charlie, no attempt to get me alone and 'explain things'. Nothing was said on the topic at all. The lack of challenge left me unsettled.

Was it possible they'd already granted their approval?

Or did they know our fling had an expiration date, so they weren't wasting their energy?

They didn't give me a clue, and I found it frustrating. I was good at reading a room, but I couldn't make sense of the Winters family. They defied my every expectation.

Wealthy but not elitist.

Controlling and bossy but supportive and loving.

This had nothing to do with my experience of family.

Focused on my food, I finished dinner and dug into the strawberry shortcake the housekeeper served for dessert. Lulled by the sound of Charlie's laughter beside me and my comfortable surroundings, I lost the train of the conversation.

It wasn't until I heard my name repeated that I looked up to find the whole table staring at me. Charlie's eyes were on me as well, but unlike the others, hers were worried and her cheeks were pink.

Normally, I loved it when she blushed. She could be so direct and ballsy that it was cute when she got embarrassed.

This time, it just made me nervous.

"What?" I asked.

"I asked if you thought it was safe for Charlie to come to the benefit tomorrow?" Aiden asked, his eyes on mine, his gaze penetrating.

I had the fleeting thought that he could see everything that passed through my mind. Taking the easy way out, I looked away.

Beside me, Charlie said in a low voice, "I forgot to mention it. There's a thing tomorrow, black tie. I'm supposed to go, but . . ."

She looked miserable and embarrassed. I was missing something. Maybe she didn't want me to go with her.

Maybe she didn't want to drag her tattooed badass fuck-buddy to a charity benefit. If the Winters family was attending, I could bet it would be filled with the highest echelon of Atlanta society.

"It's probably safe enough," I said, glancing up at Aiden. Beside me, Charlie whispered, "Do you mind?"

I still couldn't read her and I wasn't going to ask what was wrong. Maybe it would've been smarter if I did ask. I never saw the point of uncertainty when a question could erase it.

But I wasn't sure I wanted this uncertainty erased. Was I ready to hear her tell me I wasn't the type you brought to a black-tie benefit?

Aiden was right. I was a pussy.

Hoping I was saying the right thing, I looked down at Charlie. "I don't mind. If you're sure you want to go, you're not going without me. I doubt Hayward would dare to make a move with an audience like that. He wants revenge, but he doesn't want the attention."

Looking up at Aiden, I asked, "Will Sinclair provide extra security?"

"Already done," Aiden answered.

"Then we'll be there," I said. Charlie let out a breath of relief.

At least, I thought she was relieved. *Fuck.*

From across the table, Abigail sent me a delighted smile and said, "Thank you so much. I know it's not a great time to be out and about with everything going on with Charlie, but Cheryl was so helpful with our event last month. It was my first for The Winters Foundation, and I couldn't have done it without her. I wanted to return the favor."

Charlie closed her hand over mine and said, "We're looking forward to it. It should be fun."

From the look on her face, you'd think she'd agreed to attend her own execution. Dropping my lips to her ear, I whispered, "I can arrange for more discreet security if you'd rather go on your own."

I hated making the offer, but I had to do it. If she didn't want to go to this thing with me, I wasn't going to back her into a corner. That would just make both of us miserable.

She jerked back at my words, turning her head to look at me, her eyes wide and confused.

"What do you mean? Why would I want to go without you? I didn't think you'd want to go, and I didn't want you to feel like you had to . . ."

She trailed off.

Fucking fuck.

Charlie sounded as messed up about all of this as I was. I liked her family, and dinner was excellent, but at the moment, I wished us back at her house, naked on her futon.

Just like it was before things started to get complicated.

As the word passed through my head, I sighed.

This shit was why I didn't do complicated. Charlie and me naked made sense. Once you threw in the rest of the family, their social status, their past and mine, Charlie and I shot straight past complicated into impossible.

"Is everything set up with Sophie?" Possibly sensing the tension between Charlie and me, Maggie interrupted with a distraction. Charlie let out a breath and leaned forward to meet Maggie's eyes.

"She's moving in the day before Aunt Amelia does. I think she'll work out."

"Have you met her?" Jacob asked Aiden. Aiden nodded.

"She's certainly competent. It remains to be seen if she can keep Amelia under control."

"Isn't your Aunt Amelia in her eighties?" Abigail asked Jacob. He laughed.

"She is. But Amelia's what her generation would have called a pistol. Age may have brought her a few health problems, but she's still trouble."

Vance let out a shout of laughter and leaned forward. "Do you guys remember when she put the rubber snake in Mrs. Williamson's root vegetable basket?"

"Oh my God, I forgot about that," Charlie giggled from beside me. "I can still hear the screams."

Charlie fell into my side, body shaking with laughter. Every other Winters in the room was laughing just as hard.

Jacob, gasping for breath, said, "And then Mom saw it, and she started screaming, too."

"And when Mr. Henried came running and he told them it was a fake . . . I thought they were going to kill Aunt Amelia," Aiden went on.

"But they couldn't do anything because Dad was always her favorite and he never got mad at her. Even the time she ruined the curtains trying to make everyone think the library was haunted," Charlie finished.

"Is Mrs. Williamson going to be okay with her moving in?" Maggie asked after a quick look over her shoulder to make sure the doorway was empty. I shouldn't have been surprised the family would care what their housekeeper thought.

Aiden followed her eyes, still grinning. "I asked her if she wanted extra help, but she said that she was fine, especially with Sophie to take care of Amelia, and that she could certainly handle having more of the family back in Winters House."

"Liar," Charlie said, still giggling. "She'd never admit she doesn't like Aunt Amelia. She's too loyal. I already talked to

Sophie about the pranks and asked her to help watch out for Mrs. Williamson. Sophie knows she'll have her hands full with Amelia."

"I got the impression she was looking forward to it," Maggie said. "Her last job kept her pretty isolated. She said she could do with some excitement."

"I just hope Amelia doesn't scare her off," Vance said.

"Me too." Charlie blotted her eyes with her napkin, still laughing a little.

"Are you ready for the invasion?" Jacob asked Aiden.

I didn't listen to Aiden's answer. I was too lost in Charlie, her smile wide and free, her ocean blue eyes shining with happiness and laughter. Everything about her was luminous. I liked her family, and dinner had been good, but I wanted Charlie to myself.

I checked my watch, ready for the meal to be over, when Aiden cleared his throat.

Conversation stopped.

Clearing his throat again, he lay his palms flat on the table and took a deep breath.

"I called all of you here tonight for a reason. I've already spoken with Holden and Tate before they left for their conference, but I asked them to stay quiet until I could talk to the rest of you together."

"What? What is it?" Jacob demanded.

"Gage is missing."

The silence in the room was deafening. Beside me, Charlie's breath caught in a hitch. Not caring who saw, or what they thought about it, I wrapped my arm around her and pulled her into my side. She pressed her cheek to my chest but kept her eyes on Aiden.

"What happened?" Vance asked in a thick voice.

"As you can guess, they're not sharing a lot of information. All I know is that two months ago, he left on a mission, and a few days later, he stopped reporting in. They won't tell me where it was. They waited almost a month before they let me know he was MIA."

"So they didn't give you anything," Jacob said, his eyes hard and cold.

Aiden shook his head. "Cooper is seeing what he can find out, but he's not optimistic. You know Gage couldn't talk about his work. I wasn't even sure he was still officially with the Army until they called."

"I can make some calls," I offered, surprising myself. "I've been out for a while, but I can guess that Gage and I worked for some of the same people. There's no guarantee they'll talk to me. Better odds that they won't. But I can try."

Aiden gave a grave nod. "We'd appreciate anything you can do."

I had a feeling this explained Aiden's exhaustion, the deep grooves in his face and the circles beneath his eyes. Given the way he watched over his family, Gage going missing must be killing him.

Charlie had said a few things here and there that gave me the impression Aiden and Gage were tight growing up. Until Hugh and Olivia Winters had been murdered, Gage had planned to join the company with Aiden. Before they were cold in the ground, he dropped out of college and joined the Army.

I wished I could do more, but I'd been honest with them. I had connections, and if they were willing to talk, I might be able to get some information, but that was a big *if*.

Gage Winters was most likely already dead, and it was possible his family would never know what had happened to him.

Tears soaked through my shirt as Charlie cried softly

into my chest. I knew she hated the way Aiden tried to coddle her. At that moment, I'd never been more in sympathy with him.

I didn't want her to know about Gage. I never wanted her to hear another piece of bad news for the rest of her life.

How much more was she supposed to take? She'd lost her aunt and uncle, then her parents. She was being stalked. Now, her cousin was missing, probably dead.

Yeah, I got Aiden's urge to wrap her up and keep her safe for the rest of her life.

Her strawberry shortcake abandoned, Charlie looked ready to call it a night. I stood, taking her with me, and said to the room, "We're going to head home. I assume we'll see you all tomorrow?"

"Take care with her," Aiden said. I knew Charlie felt like shit when she didn't respond to the overprotective big brother comment.

I didn't need the warning.

Lately, taking care of Charlie was the only thing that made sense. The only thing I wanted to do.

And that scared the shit out of me.

CHAPTER TWENTY
CHARLIE

I couldn't seem to absorb Aiden's news. Gage was missing. I didn't know a lot about what Gage did, but he'd been a Ranger before he'd drifted into doing things for the Army he couldn't talk about, and I knew there were few people on the planet better trained than he was.

If he was missing, he was probably dead.

My heart and mind refused to accept that.

Not Gage.

Growing up, Vance had teased me, tormented me, and played with me. Jacob had pretended not to have time for me, but secretly, he doted on me, tucking me into bed when my mom was distracted with the other kids and braiding my hair in the mornings before school.

Before our parents died, Aiden had been too busy to bother with me. He'd been an adult to my child, and both he and Gage had treated me with absent affection.

I knew they loved me, they just weren't around much to show it. In my child's mind, they'd both been larger-than-life, tall and strong and smart.

Invincible.

The idea that something could happen to either of them . . . I couldn't force it to make sense.

You'd think after losing so much of my family, I would see death around every corner. I never felt that way, though. What happened to my parents, aunt and uncle had been so shocking, so outside the norm, that it had never felt as if those deaths could bleed into the rest of my life.

Since my mom and dad died, Aiden had stepped up, doing his best to take their place, his natural authority shielding me, buffering me from more loss.

Tonight, when he'd told us about Gage, I'd finally seen him.

Really seen him.

The deep line between his eyebrows. The shadows under his eyes. His cheeks looked gaunt, as if he'd lost weight. I'd never understood the cost of watching over us all, never seen how it weighed on him.

Pulling out my phone as Lucas drove us back to the Highlands, I pulled up Aiden's number in the messaging app and tapped out,

I love you

That was all I had to say.

I loved him and I was sorry he'd had to tell us about Gage. Sorry he had to carry so much on his shoulders.

I let out a sigh. Lucas had been weird when we were at Winters House. Stiff and uncomfortable. For someone who had command of every situation I'd seen him in, seeing Lucas out of step and offbeat unnerved me.

Did he dislike my family?

It's not that I thought we were perfect, but we weren't bad. We complained about each other all the time, but every family did that.

I couldn't remember anyone being rude or saying

anything awkward. Except the whole thing about the benefit. I knew I should've talked to him about it earlier. I just couldn't figure out what to say.

I had no problem stripping naked for Lucas, no issues being vulnerable with him when we were in bed, but when it came to something as basic as asking him to go to a party with me, I completely folded.

Where was my courage? I never had a problem asking for what I wanted. I had issues, but low self-esteem wasn't one of them.

Had I been afraid he'd turn me down?

Stupid question.

Of course I had. We didn't date. We had sex. That was it.

Except it wasn't. It hadn't been *just sex* for a long time. Not since Lucas had spent the night after my stalker jumped me.

We ate together. We were living together. This last month with Lucas had been the best relationship of my life and it wasn't even a relationship.

Now, he was going to the benefit with me, but I wasn't sure if he was going as my date or as my bodyguard. Had he hesitated because he didn't want to go? Because he didn't want to lead me on?

Or was he mad I hadn't asked him myself?

You could talk to him, my good sense suggested.

Or I could avoid the subject and hope it worked itself out.

While I knew option number two was stupid and immature, it was my first choice.

Maybe if I talked to Lucas about all of this, we'd discover that we both really liked being together and were willing to take the risk and turn this into something more.

Or he'd give me a pitying look and explain that he'd been clear with me since the beginning, we were just having fun, and he should've known better than to expect me to handle it like an adult.

I could see that conversation way too clearly, hear it play out in my head.

I wasn't going there.

I wasn't ready yet.

I didn't think I'd ever be ready for Lucas to dump me.

Eventually, we'd catch Hayward in the act, this would all be over, and Lucas would leave.

I wasn't ready now, and I wouldn't be ready then.

We pulled into Lucas's driveway and he parked his truck. I couldn't help a quick glance at the front of my house. The graffiti was gone, hastily covered with a few coats of primer. Lucas or Aiden had taken care of it, and I was grateful.

It wasn't the words spray-painted on the house so much as the aggressive violence of the act itself, the gleeful destruction of something I loved. Now it was erased, the porch light was on, and all was quiet.

After all the time I'd spent wondering why Lucas never asked me to his house, I would've thought I'd be more excited to move in with him.

I wasn't. I wanted everything to go back to the way it was. Staying with Lucas wasn't a progression in our relationship. I wasn't there because he'd decided to let me in.

It was a Band-Aid.

A quick fix.

Just a way to keep me safe.

I didn't intend to speak, but I heard myself say, "If you don't want me to stay in your house, we can always go to a hotel or something."

Lucas went still. His eyes landed on my face, one eyebrow raised. I couldn't decide if he was confused or annoyed.

"What the fuck are you talking about?"

Wishing I'd never said a thing, I shrugged helplessly and said, "Well, I mean, I've never even been inside your house until today. It seemed pretty clear you wanted to keep that distance, and that's okay. I get it. So I'm just saying if you're not good with it, we can go stay somewhere else."

The words spilled out of me, pushing through my defenses, leaving me cold and vulnerable.

Afraid he would see all of the hope I'd been storing in my heart, I refused to meet his eyes.

Finally, he said, "It's fine, don't worry about it. It's not a big deal."

I let out a breath I hadn't realized I was holding. Not exactly the enthusiastic response I was looking for.

This is why we weren't having that conversation about our relationship. Lucas was smart. Lucas was hella smart. He could play at being a dumb guy, but I knew better.

He was well aware he'd never let me across the property line, much less inside his house. We both knew the only reason was because he thought I was in danger.

He didn't really want me there. If I had any pride, I'd go right back to Winters House by myself and let this thing end.

Curiously, I found I had very little pride when it came to Lucas Jackson.

I let Lucas shepherd me into the house, aware he was scanning our surroundings with sharp eyes, his first thought keeping me safe.

I waited for him to shut and lock the door behind us. The second he turned to face me, I jumped him.

I was tired of thinking. After the news about Gage and the weirdness about the benefit and staying in his house, I was done thinking about my feelings, tired of obsessing about my fears and hopes.

I was done thinking at all. I just wanted to feel good.

Lucas had my heart turned inside out, but he was always reliable when it came to my body.

It didn't take much. My hands pulling his face down to mine, my lips against his, his tongue sliding into my mouth.

He caught me as I jumped, closing his hands over my ass, supporting my weight as I wrapped my legs around his waist.

I didn't notice anything about his house as he carried me down the hallway to his bedroom. Everything inside me was focused on Lucas.

I kissed him with frantic desperation, trying to memorize his taste, his smell, the feel of his skin under my fingertips. Ever since we'd argued at the dealership that morning, I'd had the sense things were slipping away, sliding out of my control.

I was losing something I didn't even have. I didn't know how to save it, how to get it back. I only knew that the heart of it was Lucas and I wanted him. I wanted to absorb everything Lucas, to memorize him so I'd have something to remember when he was gone.

He dropped me onto his bed. I tore at his T-shirt. Yanking it over his head, I smoothed my palms down his chest, sinking my nails into his shoulders as I pulled him down on top of me.

I was already working on the button of his pants when he unsnapped mine and shoved them down over my hips.

I wanted us naked.

I wanted nothing between Lucas and me.

I needed him.

All of him.

My knees splayed wide, so wide the stretch of it almost hurt as he settled between them, the head of his cock at the gate of my pussy.

I was ready and wet, my body soft and eager for him. I was always ready for Lucas. I always wanted him. I thought maybe I always would.

Feeling the way he sank inside me, the way he filled me, I couldn't imagine ever wanting to stop.

I clamped my knees to his sides, angling my hips up to take more. Lucas and I had sex almost every way we could— fast and hard, slow and sensual, against a wall, on the floor. I loved it all. Lucas had patience. Even when he was in the mood for fast, he was under control.

Not this time. I had a heartbeat of time to adjust to the sweet stretch of his cock inside me before he thrust his hips hard, filling me, fucking me fast. Just over the edge of rough, he slammed into me over and over, grinding into my clit, driving me higher until I was panting beneath him.

I held onto his shoulders, pleasure blanking out my brain. The first orgasm was a slap, taking me under in a tsunami of bliss that hit out of nowhere. Lucas didn't stop, didn't even slow down.

Blinded by sensation, I reached up to kiss him. At the touch of my lips, he went wild, claiming my mouth in a kiss as rough as his fucking. Low growling sounds rumbled in his chest, the possession of his lips and his loss of control sending me flying over the edge again.

He stiffened in my arms and came with a low shout.

"Charlie. Fuck, Charlie."

I held him against me as he came, the thump of his heart against mine so intimate it brought tears to my eyes. His body relaxed and I became aware of wetness between my thighs.

We hadn't used a condom.

Shit.

Lucas pulled away, realizing our mistake only a second after me.

"It's okay," I said when he turned green eyes filled with guilt in my direction. "As long as you're clean, it's okay. I'm on the pill, and I haven't had sex since I was last tested—except with you."

"I'm clean," he said immediately.

"Okay. Then we're okay."

We'd gone from the most intense sex of my life to chilly and awkward in the space of a minute. I rolled out of bed, suddenly desperate to be alone.

"Bathroom?" I asked. Lucas pointed to a door on the other side of the room. I shut the door behind me, trying to ignore the ache in my heart. This would be so much easier if we'd stuck to having sex.

Lucas's bathroom was masculine and plush, with river rock detailing around his enormous shower and more of those cool poured concrete countertops holding custom sinks of amber glass.

Not eager to face Lucas yet, I stepped into the shower. It took a minute to figure out the dual shower heads, but once I did, I was tempted to stay all night. I didn't. Keeping my hair out of the spray, I washed my body with Lucas's soap, the scent spicy and deep, and braved the bedroom again.

Lucas was tucked into his king size bed, taking the side closest to the door, as he had at my house.

"I put your stuff in the drawers closest to the door," he said.

"Thanks." I got a nightshirt, trying not to enjoy the way my things looked neatly stacked in Lucas's dresser.

It doesn't mean anything, I reminded myself.

Crawling into bed, I rolled to my side and closed my eyes, pretending to sleep. Lucas said nothing, just pulled me across the mattress until he could tuck me into his side.

His body surrounding me with warmth, I fell asleep.

Sometime later, I woke to the discordant tone of two phones sounding the same alarm, but out of sync. My phone and Lucas's phone. The perimeter alarm.

The perimeter alarm at my house.

I shot upright in bed to see Lucas grabbing his phone off the nightstand. He checked the screen, scowled, and dialed.

I couldn't make out everything he was saying as he pulled on his clothes, the phone pinned between his shoulder and his ear. When I started to get up, he spun on his heel to face me. Pointing a finger at me, he wordlessly commanded me to stay put.

I ignored him.

I wasn't going to do anything stupid, but it sounded like people were on their way and I was wearing a nightshirt with a cartoon moose on the front. I needed clothes.

"Yeah, as long as the cameras are recording it, I'll stay put and wait for the black and whites. Yeah. Yeah. You have a clear shot of his face? Yeah. Call me back."

"What's going on?" I asked.

"I told you to stay there," Lucas accused.

"No, you pointed at me. And I'm not going anywhere, I'm just getting dressed. What's going on?"

"Someone is trying to force open your door. They don't know we have them on camera, and he's still there. The police are on their way. Brennan and a black and white. He'll try to keep it quiet."

"Was that Brennan on the phone?"

"No, Cooper. He called Brennan before I called him."

"What are you doing?" I asked, watching him tie the laces of his boots and strap his gun into a side holster.

"Waiting here with you. You're not in danger. We're better off letting the police arrest this guy than for me to go charging over there. The longer he tries to break and enter while he's on film, the better for us."

"Can I look out the window?"

Lucas sighed. "Can I talk you out of it?"

"I don't think so."

"Fine, follow me. Don't turn on any lights."

I followed Lucas through the dark house to the living room. Two floor-to-ceiling windows on either side of the fireplace faced my house. I pressed my face to the glass, but the night was dark and I could barely see anything. A shadowy figure moved on my porch. It looked like they were prying at the door with a crowbar.

What the hell?

That wasn't exactly subtle. It was like he didn't care about being caught. Or he was sure no one was home. But I thought Lucas and Brennan said Hayward knew I had security.

"I can't see anything," I whispered.

"I know. Try this." Lucas pulled me back from the window, leading me back into the hall before passing me his tablet, the view from the security cameras already up.

Evers had installed high-definition night vision cameras. I already knew they looked clear and crisp in daylight. I was shocked how much detail I could see at night.

"I don't think that's Hayward," I said after a minute.

"I'm sure it's not. He wouldn't put himself on the hook for breaking and entering. It's probably someone he hired."

Two cars swung into the driveway out of nowhere. Doors slammed and I heard shouts. A figure vaulted onto the porch and tackled the intruder, startling her into a long, high-pitched scream.

Wait. *Her?* That was a woman's scream.

A woman?

What the *hell* was going on?

Lucas shot for the door, me on his heels.

"Stay here," he ordered.

"No way," I said. The intruder was down, contained by the police. I'd seen it myself. And I wanted to know who she was.

"Goddamnit. Then stay behind me."

It must have been relatively safe. Lucas never would have let me leave the house if it weren't. We raced out the front door and across our driveways to find two uniformed officers standing in my yard and Detective Brennan on my porch putting handcuffs on the intruder.

Once I hit the bottom step and saw her face, I gasped.

"Marissa Archer?" I said in disbelief.

Her head swiveled to face me and her eyes lit with a fervor that had me stepping back.

"Olivia. Olivia. You're dead," she screeched, calling me by my mother's name. "You were murdered. Murdered. No one believes it, no one listens. It wasn't Hugh, it was him. It was him. They knew and he killed them. He killed them all. Olivia."

"What do you mean?" I asked, my head spinning.

Marissa Archer was the last person I would have suspected of stalking me. I barely knew her. We were social acquaintances at best. She'd been friends with my parents when they were younger but they hadn't been especially close. I'd remember that. She was little more than a stranger.

Detective Brennan leaned down to pick something up from the porch while Marissa Archer continued to wail my mother's name. He held up a square envelope.

I'd seen something like that before and I knew what he'd find when it opened it. I was wrong, but not by much.

I'd expected another crime scene photograph of my aunt and uncle's death like those that Jacob and Vance had received.

Almost.

This one was of my parents. I didn't need to see it to know. The way Detective Brennan looked from me to the photo and back told me everything.

"It's my parents, isn't it?" I asked. He nodded.

Marissa was still calling out my mother's name, desperate to make herself understood.

Ignoring everyone else, I stepped closer to Marissa and said, "Who was it, Marissa? Who killed them? Do you know?"

Nodding her head so hard I thought she'd knock herself off-balance, she said, "I know it all. I know all the secrets, I know everything."

"Who was it?" I demanded, my heart surging in my chest. Never in my life had I ever needed to know anything as much as I needed to know this.

Could Marissa Archer really know who killed my parents? It seemed impossible.

Her eyes burning with a desperate fervor, she leaned toward me and whispered, "He knows someone knows, but he doesn't know who. Left me for her. That stupid slut. He killed them. Killed them all. And I'm the only one who knows. The pictures make him crazy. He's scared now."

"Charlie, step back," Lucas said, trying to drag me away from the insane woman on my porch.

I yanked my arm free.

"No, Lucas, I want to know."

He grabbed my arm again and leaned down to whisper in my ear. "Princess, step back. She's nuts. She doesn't have anything to tell you."

"She does, Lucas," I hissed back. "She knows something."

He shook his head. Proving him right, Marissa began to sway back and forth, singing to herself, "All over. All over now. He can't find me, he can't find me."

"Who?" I shouted, trying to break through her descent into madness. "Who killed them? Who can't find you?"

Her head shot up and her bright eyes met mine. The singing stopped. In a clear, level, almost sane voice, she said, "Tell them. Tell them he's still out there. And he's not done. Not yet."

Her head dropped, her eyes closed, and she fell silent.

What the fuck? What did that mean? Okay, it was obvious what that meant. It was either a warning or a threat.

He's still out there. And he's not done.

CHAPTER TWENTY-ONE
CHARLIE

Marissa Archer was brought into police custody and charged with attempted breaking and entering. Attempted because she never managed to use the crowbar to get my door open.

After reviewing the cameras at Jacob's penthouse, the police and the Sinclair team were all confident that she was responsible for leaving the photographs there, as well as at Magnolia's house.

Her son quickly and quietly had her put in permanent psychiatric care. She wouldn't be leaving any more creepy pictures. She wouldn't be doing much of anything. Since she'd told me the killer was still out there, she hadn't spoken a word.

To anyone.

Not the police, not her son, not her lawyer.

No one.

Problem solved. Everyone seemed satisfied that Marissa was my stalker. It made sense. She could have hired someone to leave the note and spray paint my house. She could even have been the one who jumped me, though she could have hired that out as well.

She wasn't young, but she was tall and wiry. Apparently, she played a lot of tennis at the club when she wasn't terrorizing my family.

Lucas had been gone almost all day, leaving me alone at my house. He warned me to keep the alarm on while I was inside, but with Marissa in custody, everyone was less worried about my safety.

I'd told him he didn't have to come to the benefit with me. I still didn't know if he was coming as my bodyguard or my date. I was leaning toward date since he didn't seem to think I needed a bodyguard and had insisted he was coming.

Maggie brought my dress from Winters House and stayed long enough to help me do my hair and grill me about Lucas.

Despite the upheaval of Aiden's announcement that Gage was missing, Maggie hadn't missed the tension between Lucas and me at dinner.

In between twisting and pinning my chin-length curls into a simulation of an updo, she peppered me with questions.

"So, he's still going to the benefit with you?" she asked, too casually.

"He says he is," I said.

"What's the deal? He was all growly and protective last night, and everyone seems to like him. Are you still just friends with benefits?"

"Do I have to talk about this?" I asked. Magnolia Henry was my best friend. If I was going to talk about this with anyone, it would be her. But I didn't want to talk about Lucas. Not even with Maggie.

Proving yet again why she was my best friend, she gave my shoulder a squeeze and said, "No, Charlie, you don't have to talk about anything you don't want to. Did I tell you about my dress for tonight?"

Grateful for her change of subject, I said, "No. Why? What are you wearing?"

"I was going to wear something I already had," she said. "But Vance surprised me and took me shopping, and then he talked me into buying this dress . . . I'm going to be blushing all night, I swear."

"Why? Is it really short?" Maggie had a bombshell figure, all curves. She rarely dressed to show them off.

"No, it's actually pretty long, but it's got a slit up one leg, and a deep V neckline . . ." She trailed off.

"Cleavage?" I asked. Maggie had a lot to offer in the cleavage department, even if she usually kept it covered up.

"Yes. A lot of cleavage. Not tacky cleavage, but still. A lot. And he bought me these crazy shoes. I don't know what he was thinking. On top of that, he made me promise to wear my hair down."

"Like the night you got engaged?" I asked.

"Exactly," she confirmed.

"I bet he drags you out of there before it's halfway over." I didn't have to look at Maggie's face to know she was blushing.

"I'm not gonna take that bet."

"Do you need me to help?" I asked.

I'd done her hair for her the night she'd gotten engaged to Vance. She'd looked like a siren in a black wrap dress and all that red hair in wild curls. I wasn't surprised Vance had begged her to marry him. He was too smart to let go of a woman like Maggie.

261

"Not this time, but thanks. I got a new curling iron and Vance is watching Rosie while I get dressed."

Maggie finished with my hair, gave me a hug, and rushed off to get ready. I didn't spend too long on my makeup. I could do business appropriate makeup in ten minutes and black tie makeup in twenty.

I'd probably look better if I learned to contour and shade and do all those other things to ramp up the glamor, but I'd never learned and tonight wasn't the time to start.

Just before Lucas was due to show up, I finished my face and put on my dress. I'd bought it months before, planning to wear it to a different event, one I hadn't ended up attending. It was formal, definitely black tie formal.

Unlike Maggie's dress, which I suspected was on the slinky side, my dress was a fairytale. Yards of creamy satin in a silver so pale it was almost white, overlaid with a fine netting sprinkled with tiny crystals.

The bodice was strapless and embellished with more crystals and finely stitched embroidery in the palest pink, the back held together with lacing, like a corset.

The dress was more fanciful than those I usually wore, but I'd fallen in love with the sheen of the satin and the sparkle of the crystals the moment I'd seen it.

It had been more expensive than what I'd planned to spend, but I'd talked myself into it when I'd remembered that I had the perfect shoes to match waiting in my closet.

I was halfway dressed when Lucas walked in, already in his tux. Heat flushed my skin and my nipples peaked.

Lucas looked good in anything, but in a tux, he made me crazy. All that black-and-white elegance wrapped around his raw strength. I wouldn't be able to keep my hands off him all night.

When he saw me, his eyes went wide and he froze.

"What? Is the dress no good?" It was a little over the top between the sparkles and the full skirts. Maybe it was too much.

He shook his head.

"Can you help me with the back?" I asked.

There was a zipper hidden in the side seam, but I still needed the wide satin laces tightened so they didn't droop. Lucas moved behind me and went to work, pulling on the laces here and there until he had them in place.

He gave a last tug at the bottom, pulling me backward so I bumped into him. Slowly, he tied the lacing in a bow and secured it, then leaned down to press a kiss to my shoulder.

"You're the most beautiful woman I've ever seen," he said quietly.

I flushed with pleasure.

He straightened and stepped back. "We'd better get going," he said. "If we stay in here much longer, I'll undo that bow, strip off that dress, and we'll never leave."

I took a long look at him in that tux and agreed. If I hadn't promised my family that I'd be there, I'd forget the benefit and jump Lucas. But I had promised, and he was right. If we didn't get a move on, we'd never make it.

Lucas was quiet in the truck on the way to the benefit. He'd been out all day, I thought with Detective Brennan or Cooper, but he hadn't said.

"Did you find out anything else about Marissa Archer?" I asked.

"She's not talking," Lucas said. "She hasn't said a word since last night. But it's looking like she's responsible for everything. The police are ready to pin it on her."

"What about you?"

"I'm not completely sold. She fits, and she had opportunity. She's also bat-shit crazy."

"Does that make her more or less likely to be guilty?" I asked.

I was still thrown that Marissa Archer was involved at all. I knew she'd been friends with my parents back in the day, but to stalk us? Send us pictures of their bodies?

She seemed so certain she knew the story behind their deaths, had taunted me with it, and now she wasn't talking. None of it made any sense.

"Neither," Lucas said in answer to my question. "It just makes it harder to pin down her motive. If she's completely cracked, it could be impossible to determine why she fixated on your family."

"And if she's not completely cracked? If she really does know something?"

"Princess," Lucas said, reaching out to take my hand in his, "I don't want you to get your hopes up. It's possible she does know something. But we can't make her talk, and even if we could, her accusations won't hold any weight. Not with her locked up under psychiatric care."

"I know it wouldn't bring them back," I said in a low voice. "But I still want to know what happened. Someone took them from us—"

I stopped talking. I wasn't going to cry and ruin my makeup. I took a quick breath in through my nose and let it out.

I was fine. Everything was fine. Once I had my roiling emotions under control, I said, "So you guys think she was the stalker the whole time, right? I'm in the clear?"

"That's the working theory," Lucas admitted. "Hayward has had eyes on him nonstop since before you left Winters Inc. If he were pulling the strings here, he did a better job of hiding it than he did hiding all the shit he was up to with his company. Which would be out of character. Still, you should be careful for now. Keep the alarm on when you're home. Carry your panic button. Just in case."

"I can do that," I said. "But you think I'm probably safe now?"

"We'll see," he said, shooting me a sidelong glance.

We pulled up to the valet parking line outside the hotel where the benefit was being held. A few minutes later, Lucas led me inside.

Vance and Maggie were in the lobby, and my jaw dropped when I caught sight of Maggie's dress. Lucas let out a low wolf-whistle. I elbowed him in the side, grinning.

Maggie had been right. She never would've picked a dress like that for herself, but I could absolutely see Vance choosing it.

The navy silk clung to her curves, outlining the hourglass of her figure, a high slit on one side revealing most of her leg, covered in sheer creamy stockings. The deep V of the neckline revealed the inner curves of her breasts. I hoped the fabric was taped in place, otherwise she risked a wardrobe malfunction.

The dress was elegant, classy, yet unabashedly sexy. Around her neck, she wore a choker of diamonds and sapphires, with matching jewels at her ears and on her wrist. Her red hair was a mass of fiery curls, spilling down her back.

Lucas and I joined them and I said, "I like the dress."

Maggie's cheeks went pink.

Vance said, "Told you."

Maggie sent him a mini-glare.

"You look beautiful," Lucas said, and the pink in Maggie's cheeks turned red.

"You really do, Maggie," I said. "You should hire Vance as your personal shopper."

"That's what I keep telling her," Vance said.

Maggie's mini-glare went full-throttle.

"If I let you pick all of my clothes, my breasts would be in danger of falling out every time I lean over," she complained.

"And that's a problem?" Vance asked, laughing.

Vance asked Lucas about Marissa, and we changed the subject. Aiden arrived with a date, some woman I vaguely knew by sight but whose name I couldn't recall.

We said hello, then wandered off to find a drink. There was dancing, and hors d'oeuvres carried around by waiters in white tuxedos, but no sit-down dinner. Along one side of the ballroom, long tables were set up displaying items for silent auction.

Arm in arm, Lucas and I strolled down the line, me sipping champagne and him a beer. Neither of us bid. Aiden had already made a donation on behalf of the family, and I didn't have the extra cash for luxuries I didn't need.

There was a house on the market three streets away from mine that needed a lot of work, but it had potential. I wasn't sure if I could swing it, but if I did, I'd need every spare bit of cash I could get my hands on.

I was just starting to wonder how long we had to stay when a hand closed around my elbow. Beside me, Lucas went stiff. I turned and met a pair of familiar hazel eyes.

Harrison. The first of my ill-fated fiancés.

"Charlie, dance with me," he said. Gently, I extracted my elbow from his grip.

Lucas angled his body in front of mine and eyed Harrison with an unfriendly glare.

"Who are you?" Lucas challenged.

"A very old friend of Charlie's," Harrison said in the cool, superior tone I'd always hated. "And who are you? I don't remember seeing you around."

Lucas declined to answer. Probably for the best, since I didn't know what he would say. To me, he said, "Do you want to dance with this guy?"

I didn't. But I knew Harrison. If I turned him down, he'd be an ass about it. With a tiny shrug, I handed Lucas my champagne and said, "Not really, but I probably should. I'll be right back."

I let Harrison lead me onto the dance floor. He pulled me into his arms and swirled me around the floor, glancing once or twice back in Lucas's direction. I didn't have any desire to spend time with Harrison, but he'd always been a good dancer.

"Who is that guy? Are you two together?"

"That's not any of your business, Harrison. What do you want?"

I was being abrupt, but I knew Harrison. He wasn't being polite. He wanted something.

"I heard Aiden fired you. Are you okay?"

"I'm fine," I said. "It was a shock, but I'm moving on."

"You know, that company was the reason we broke up."

For a second, I lost the power of speech. "No, your repeatedly cheating on me is the reason we broke up. The company had nothing to do with it."

"I never would have slept with anyone else if you'd been around," he said.

I'd heard this before. It wasn't his fault he'd been fucking other women. It had been mine for not taking good care of him, for always working and not being around.

Maybe I had worked too much, but that didn't excuse his cheating on me again and again.

"Harrison, I'm not having this conversation. You need to grow up and take responsibility for your own decisions. *You* are the reason I ended our engagement. If you didn't like me working so much, you should've left me, not slept around."

"You're right. I know you're right. It was immature. We were too young and I was jealous. I should've been honest with you and I'm sorry."

We whirled around the dance floor for another minute in silence.

An apology from Harrison?

In a million years, I never would have expected him to admit he was wrong, much less say he was sorry. He'd broken my heart. Shattered it completely. I'll never forget the stabbing pain when I discovered that lipstick stain on his collar.

Finally, I said, "Thank you. I appreciate your apology."

"But you don't accept it?"

"Why not?" I said, tired of this conversation. "It's been a long time and I don't care anymore. Yes, I accept your apology, Harrison."

Shocking the hell out of me, he said, "I want to try again. Now that you're not with the company, you'll have more time. We can be together. I still love you, Charlie."

I had no words. None.

Whatever love I'd had for Harrison Kenmore was long dead, extinguished in the pain of his cheating and betrayal. There was no way I'd ever trust him again. Even if Lucas hadn't been in the picture, Harrison had no shot with me.

I was trying to figure out the best way to make it clear that we were never getting back together when the song ended. He delivered me to Lucas's side, saying only, "Just think about it, Charlie. Please. Give me a chance."

"What did he mean, give him a chance?" a strident voice

interrupted. I looked up to see Elizabeth, Aiden's ex-wife, standing next to Lucas, her gray eyes cool and her pale blonde hair in a severe twist. She was a stone cold bitch, but she was a beautiful one.

Belatedly, I noticed that Lucas's jaw was set, his clear green eyes hard.

That was Elizabeth for you. She had the unique talent of irritating anyone she spent more than ten seconds with. I hated her. I'd hated her since I was fifteen and she'd never given me a good reason to change my mind.

To Lucas, I said, "How long has she been standing here?"

"She showed up halfway through your dance," he said through gritted teeth. "She's been filling me in on Harrison Kenmore and your broken engagement."

"I'm sure," I said, taking my champagne from him and looping my hand through his arm.

I knew exactly what Elizabeth had been telling Lucas. That it was my fault Harrison and I had broken up, that I'd let my best opportunity for a decent marriage slip through my fingers, blah, blah, blah.

I'd heard it all before. I didn't need a repeat.

"Well?" Elizabeth said impatiently. "Why did Harrison ask you to dance?"

"None of your business," I said. "Why don't you go pester someone else before I throw this champagne on you and you melt?" I said in the sweetest voice I could muster.

Elizabeth sent me an icy look. In one of my fits of teenage rebellion, I'd dumped a bucket of water over the balustrade at Winters House onto Elizabeth when she and Aiden were on their way to a benefit just like this one.

Her filmy chiffon dress had not stood up well to the dunking. Neither had her makeup or her hair. In one glorious rush of cold water, she'd transformed from a movie star to a drowned rat. Aiden had grounded me for a month, but it had been worth it.

"I've been getting to know your new boyfriend," she said, inclining her head toward Lucas.

I tightened my arm around his, tucking myself into his side. The evening had started off promising, but in the past few minutes, the company left much to be desired.

I scanned the crowd for rescue. None was forthcoming.

Damn.

Looking up at Lucas, I said, "I'm sorry I danced with Harrison. He's an ass if he doesn't get his way. It was easier to dance with him than argue about it."

"What did he want?" Lucas asked in a quiet voice. We were both aware of Elizabeth listening avidly.

"Nothing. Just a dance."

Lucas narrowed his eyes at me. He knew I was lying. So did Elizabeth.

"No," she said in that sharp, snotty voice she used when she was about to start telling me what to do. "He wants to get back together with you. Angela said she overheard him telling Brad that he wanted another shot now that you weren't distracted by that company."

Lucas made a sound in the back of his throat I couldn't interpret. Whatever he was thinking, they weren't happy thoughts.

I wished I were still fifteen and reckless enough to shove Elizabeth off her high horse, literally, and storm away. Sadly, my manners had improved in the last nine years.

"I'm not interested," I said, not sure if I was talking to her or to Lucas. "I'd rather die alone than get back together with Harrison. He slept with half the country club when we were together, or don't you remember that?"

The last part was directed at Elizabeth. She sniffed and raised her chin, looking down at me with the haughty know-it-all expression I'd despised through my teens.

"If you'd been home taking care of him instead of wasting your time at the office, maybe you'd be married now instead of single, unemployed, and living in a dump."

"Shut up," I hissed through my teeth. "You have no idea what you're talking about."

"I don't? I know Aiden tossed you out of the company. All those years of sacrifice for nothing. Now look at you." She eyed Lucas with a sneer. "He's certainly nice to look at, but you can't dress up a thug and parade him around like he's *our* kind of people."

I dropped Lucas's arm and raised my hand, so ready to slap her my palm itched for the sting of impact. Lucas grabbed my wrist, forcing my arm back to my side.

"Not worth it, Princess," he said under his breath.

"Are you sure? I think it would be very worth it." Looking Elizabeth in the eye, I said, "Divorcing you is the smartest thing Aiden ever did. You were never good enough for him. You're a cold, manipulative bitch."

Elizabeth's eyes brightened and she leaned in. "That's right, Charlotte, I am. You'd do well not to forget it. I know who your little boy toy is and I'll make you a deal. Stay away from me and Aiden, and I'll keep it to myself."

I tried to step forward, but Lucas wound his arm around me, pasting me to his side. Stymied, I said, "I know who he is too, and you're welcome to tell anyone. I'm proud to be standing next to Lucas Jackson."

The rest of her words filtered through my brain. "What the hell do you mean 'stay away from you and Aiden'? There *is* no you and Aiden."

"Not right now," she agreed in a saccharine voice. "But

now that you're out of the house, I think I can convince him to give me a second chance. Harrison isn't the only one who can beg for redemption. Your brother always liked it when I begged." She slid me a knowing smile.

"You're disgusting," I spat out. I would have said more, but Lucas tightened his grip around my waist and half led, half dragged me away from Elizabeth.

"What are you doing?" I asked as I struggled to keep up.

"Leaving. We're done with this."

"Now?"

"Now."

CHAPTER
TWENTY-TWO
CHARLIE

We didn't run into anyone on our way out. Lucas was silent while we waited for the valet to return with his truck, not speaking even when he helped me into the passenger seat, carefully arranging my full skirts so the door wouldn't damage them.

Finally, when we were halfway home, he said, "Nice den of vipers you call friends, Princess."

"Neither of them are my friends," I said. "Harrison is a tool, and calling Elizabeth a viper is an insult to snakes."

Lucas's only response was a gruff sound in the back of his throat. In fact, he didn't say another word until we were almost home. He'd been so quiet that when he spoke, the sound of his voice startled me.

"Is it usually like that?"

"Like what?"

I wasn't sure what he meant. Was he talking about Elizabeth and Harrison? Or the party itself?

The benefit had been pretty standard as those things went, but Harrison's play for my attention and the scene with Elizabeth were definitely unusual.

"That's what I thought," Lucas said obliquely.

I didn't get it. "What do you mean?" I asked. He just shook his head and fell silent again.

He parked his truck in his driveway. I'd spent the day at my place, but other than my makeup, I hadn't moved my things back to my own house.

Was I still staying with Lucas? We hadn't talked about it. We hadn't talked about anything.

I let him lead me into his house, into his bedroom, and let him strip me of my ball gown in complete silence. Standing before him wearing only a white lace thong and matching thigh-high stockings, I shivered.

His green eyes burned, tracking me from head to toe with a hot, possessive gaze.

I expected him to be rough. Impatient. But Lucas Jackson always seemed to surprise me. He stepped closer, reaching out a hand to trace one finger across my collarbone, leaving a trail of heat in the wake of his touch.

"You're so beautiful," he said in a husky whisper. "So fucking beautiful."

I didn't speak. I couldn't. My heart was in my throat, blocking my words. "Lucas, please."

That was all I could get out. *Please.* I didn't even know what I wanted to say. I knew what I felt. Love and lust. Affection and need. I felt everything for Lucas, and I couldn't tell him any of it.

He was already slipping away. If I laid my heart out for him, he'd disappear.

All I could do was show him. Reaching up, I placed a palm on either side of his face, pulling his mouth to mine. I kissed him with everything I had, gently at first, brushing my lips over his, back and forth, tasting his breath, his heat.

Lucas stepped into me, his big hands coming down on my hips, yanking me into him. He was still fully clothed while I was almost naked. The tips of my breasts rubbed his tuxedo jacket and I leaned into him. He was so tall that at times like this, his size overwhelmed me.

I gave the kiss everything I had, opening my mouth to his, asking him to take what he wanted. Lucas didn't disappoint me. Sex was never our problem.

His fingers grasped my hips, the jut of his hard cock digging into my stomach. His mouth took mine, claiming control of our kiss, of me.

Dropping my hands, I went to work on his clothes, pushing the jacket off his shoulders, tearing at the studs on his tux, suddenly desperate to have him as naked as I was.

I got stuck on his cufflinks, my fingers fumbling with the small metal contraptions, distracted by our kiss and the rasp of his chest hair against my nipples. Abruptly, Lucas stepped back, tearing his mouth from mine.

Eyes hot, hands trembling, he yanked at his shirt, the cufflinks popping free, pinging to the floor. He shoved his underwear down along with his pants. I watched avidly, shedding my thong but leaving the stockings.

"On the bed," he said, the words thick with need. Drawing out the moment, I reached for my hair, pulling out pin after pin, releasing my curls from the elaborate style Maggie had fashioned from my short hair.

Lucas's eyes tracked my every move, his chest rising and falling in deep, harsh breaths. It was costing him to wait, to let me tease him.

It cost me too. Every nerve in my body burned, my breasts swollen and tight, the heat between my legs slick.

Dropping the pins to the floor, I shook my hair back

from my face and stepped to Lucas. He stayed where he was, a fine tremble in his hands where they hung at his sides, his cock so hard it pressed to his abdomen, the tip leaking a bead of pre-come.

Reaching out, I ran a finger along a curving line of ink on his shoulder, following it down his arm to his hand. His skin beneath my fingertip was warm silk covering hard muscle. He was the most beautiful man I'd ever seen.

Aggressive and raw, sculpted from sheer power, yet gentle when he wanted to be.

My fingers interlaced with his and I tugged him to the bed, falling back onto the mattress, taking Lucas with me. I touched him everywhere I could reach, sliding my hands over his body, kissing his jaw, the side of his neck, his shoulder.

Rising over me, he pressed our joined hands to the mattress above my head. Arching my back, I spread my legs, inviting him into me. His cock was so hard, drawn so tight to his body, he had to release my hand to guide himself in.

I'll never forget how perfectly he filled me, the way his cock was made for me, how complete I was when Lucas Jackson was inside me. He took me slowly, gliding in deep and holding still for a heartbeat before he withdrew and rocked in again.

He was killing me, building pleasure in my core with every thrust, driving me closer and closer to my orgasm even as love and pain gathered in a tight ball in my chest, too much for me to contain.

A single tear escaped the corner of my eye.

Lucas dropped his head to mine, kissing away the salty drop. "Charlie," he murmured in my ear.

He didn't tell me not to cry.

He knew.

I couldn't hold him.

I didn't know how.

I had nothing to offer him but what he'd already taken.

My body and my heart.

He'd had all he wanted of the first and he had no interest in the second.

I fought my tears as hard as I fought my orgasm. I didn't want to come. I didn't want it to be over. I wanted to stay like this forever, joined to Lucas, everything I was belonging to him.

All too soon, Lucas reached his limit. With a groan, he moved faster, pounding into me, pushing me over the edge into an orgasm so hard it was a bright flash behind my eyes.

I cried out his name as I came, freeing my hands to hold on to him, my face buried in his neck, my tears streaking his skin.

We fell asleep there, me half on my side, Lucas draped over me, our legs entwined, his arm firmly around me, my back against his chest, my head tucked beneath his chin.

I'd never felt so connected. So safe.

Seven hours later, I woke to see Lucas at his dresser, stuffing clothing in a bag. I blinked, washing the sleep from my eyes as my brain tried to process what he was doing.

He was dressed in cargo pants and a black t-shirt, his gun in a shoulder holster, boots already laced on his feet.

Lucas had been up for a while. My duffel bag sat beside his bedroom door, a plastic bag stuffed with toiletries sitting on top.

This was it. It was over. I closed my eyes, feigning sleep. I'd known something was off the night before. He'd been a little distant all day, but after he'd dragged me from the benefit he'd gone cold and silent.

He'd made love to me—and it had been making love, not

fucking. Not that last time. He'd been drawing it out, trying to make it last.

Okay. Fine. If he wanted this to be over, I couldn't stop him. I couldn't hold him if he didn't want me. At the thought, my chest clenched in pain.

Later. I'd think about it later.

I was not going to cry in front of Lucas Jackson. Not again. Not when it was over.

If I thought I could change his mind, could bare my heart and convince him to stay, I'd do it in a second.

I suspected Lucas already knew how I felt. And he was leaving me anyway.

Lucas wasn't afraid of my love. He just didn't want it.

I dug my fingers into my palms and bit my lip, using my two best tricks to fight back tears. When I was sure I could hold it together. I opened my eyes and sat up.

Lucas turned to face me, his eyes on the wall behind my head.

"You're awake."

"Are you leaving?" I asked, pulling the sheet up to cover my nudity.

"Uh, yeah. I got a call for a job early this morning. Since your situation is under control, I need to get back to work."

"Okay."

Was I wrong? Was he just going out of town for a while? I got out of bed, taking the sheet with me. My ball gown was carefully folded beside my duffel, the sparkle of the crystals flickering like tiny flames against the creamy satin and filmy tulle.

I'd never be able to wear it again without thinking of Lucas.

"I have to head out, but you can take your time. I can lock the place remotely." His eyes skimmed across my body, coming nowhere near my face. Tilting his head toward my duffel, he said, "I got your stuff together."

"Okay." I didn't know what else to say. Lucas wouldn't look at me.

Keeping his eyes on the bag he was zipping shut, he said, "I'll see you when I get back."

"How long will you be gone?" I asked, watching him for some kind of sign. He gave me nothing. When he finally met my eyes, his were flat and blank.

"Don't know. But I'll see you around."

"You'll see me when you get back, or you'll see me around?"

Breaking eye contact, Lucas slung his bag over his shoulder and turned for the door.

"I'll see you around."

"Okay," I whispered, mostly to myself. His feet echoed across the hardwood floor. The front door opened and closed. The engine of his truck rumbled.

He was gone.

Moving stiffly, every step careful and controlled, I dropped the sheet, peeled off the stockings I was still wearing, and got in the shower. Numb, I barely registered the hot water. I ignored the shampoo and bottle of body wash. The last thing I needed was to smell like Lucas all day. Instead, I scrubbed at my skin with my hands, then at my scalp with my fingertips, rubbing so hard it hurt.

When I felt clean, I turned off the water, roughly dried off, and found clothes in my duffel. Lucas had packed everything in neat piles, careful and precise. My eyes prickled. I blinked hard.

No, not yet.

Hefting the bag on one arm, I picked up my ballgown and the bag of toiletries. I could have used the contents in the shower or to brush my teeth. I didn't care. My brain felt wrapped in a blanket, my thoughts sluggish. I just wanted to go home.

Not the house next door. Home. Picking up my tiny purse from the night before, I left, shutting the door behind me. I tossed my stuff in the passenger seat of my truck and got in. Before I left, I texted Lucas.

I'm out.

He wouldn't text back. I knew he wouldn't. Still, I kept looking at my phone in my lap as I drove, the dark screen a reminder that Lucas wasn't coming back. Not really. Not for me.

Aiden opened the door while I was still on the front steps. He took one look at my face and said, "I have something for you."

I followed him to his office.

"Sit." He pointed to the long leather couch beneath the window. I sat.

Aiden poured a healthy slosh of whiskey into the remaining glass from his Macallan set and carried it to me.

"Are you planning to return the decanter and the other glass?" he asked. I took the whiskey and gave him a blank look. The decanter? "Please tell me you didn't smash it in a fit of rage. It cost as much as the whiskey."

"I didn't smash it," I said in a thick, low voice. "I'll give it back."

"Sweetheart," Aiden said in a whisper, sitting down beside me. He took the glass from my hand, helped himself, and handed it back. "Drink."

I took a single sip.

"Drink it all."

I did, my throat burning, the smoky taste tickling my

nose and bringing tears to my eyes. When the glass was empty, Aiden took it and set it on the side table.

"Tell me," he ordered.

I shook my head.

I couldn't. I couldn't tell him. If I opened my mouth and admitted what had happened, it would be real. I wasn't ready for it to be real.

Aiden's arm came around me and he tugged me into his side. My head hit his chest. I tried to breathe, but my lungs were too tight. I heard a low wail and realized it was coming from me.

"Oh, Charlie. My sweet girl." Aiden rested his cheek on the top of my head. "Is this about Jackson?"

I nodded into his shirt.

"Did you break up?" Aiden asked in a gentle voice.

I nodded again. My cheeks were wet. I realized I was crying. I'd cried more in the last month than I had in the last decade.

I wanted everything to go back to how it was before. My body shook in Aiden's arms as great, wracking sobs took me.

I wanted my job back, wanted to work until I was exhausted and forget about dating, about sex. About Lucas. I wanted my boring, stress-filled life to go back to what it was before.

Before I'd bought that house.

Before I'd ever seen Lucas Jackson mowing the lawn with his shirt off.

Before I'd fallen hopelessly in love with him.

Before he'd broken my heart.

Aiden let me cry all over him, his strong arms holding me safe. I'd felt safe with Lucas, but that safety had been a lie. Lucas had torn it away when he was done with me.

"I was so stupid," I stuttered out, rubbing my eyes with

the back of my hand. "We said it was just for fun. I wasn't going to get attached."

"You can't choose who you love," Aiden said. "Sometimes it happens when you don't see it coming."

"I didn't think . . . I just . . . he was hot. And—"

"I don't need any details," Aiden cut in, smothering a laugh. My chest hitched somewhere between a giggle and a sob.

"I wasn't going to give you any," I said. "I was just going to say that it started like that, but then it changed. I liked being with him." I let out a gusty sigh, wiping at my cheeks again. "I just liked being with him. He's a good man. Smart. Gentle. He made me feel safe. And happy. I was happy with him."

"What happened?" Aiden asked in a soft voice.

"I don't know," I wailed into Aiden's shirt. "I think it was that stupid benefit. I didn't ask him, and then he said he'd go but I don't think he wanted to. And then he was weird when we were there. Quiet. Harrison asked me to dance, and while I was gone—"

"What the fuck did Harrison want?" Aiden growled.

"He wants to get back together."

"I'll fucking kill him."

I couldn't help a little giggle. "You'd better watch your own back, big brother. Elizabeth was with Lucas while I danced with Harrison. She said she'd keep quiet about who Lucas was if I didn't get in the way of you two being together."

"She said *what*?"

This time I didn't giggle. I laughed full out. If I'd had a tiny, secret worry that Aiden would fall for Elizabeth's tricks, it was extinguished. His irritated outrage was genuine.

"She thinks that you're vulnerable now that I've moved out."

"Right. Like your living here was the big obstacle keeping us from getting back together."

"You mean instead of her being evil?"

"Yeah. God, she's a bitch." Aiden's arm tightened, and he laid a kiss on the top of my head. "I'm sorry about Elizabeth. I never should have married her. I thought you needed a mom, and it was time for me to find a wife. I fucked up."

"Aiden," I said. He brushed my hair back off my face.

"No, don't. Don't make excuses for me. I fucked up. She made us both miserable and I'm sorry."

"I forgive you," I said immediately. As far as I was concerned, Aiden didn't need my forgiveness, but I'd give it in a heartbeat if it would make him feel better.

"Did Jackson say anything to her?" Aiden asked.

"No. He dragged me out right when I was about to punch her. Then he said my friends were a pit of vipers. We got home and he, um, we went to sleep. When I woke up, he was packing to leave. He already had my stuff by the door. He said he'd see me around."

My breath caught and I started crying again, burrowing into my big brother, borrowing his strength. Mine had carried me home, deserting me now that Aiden was here to hold me together.

My voice a raw whisper, I said, "Why am I so bad at this, Aid? Why can't I find someone? I thought . . . I thought he felt it too."

My breath flooded out in a long, defeated sigh, leaving me feeling empty, compressed, my heart flat and dark.

"It's not you, sweetheart. I promise, it's not you. And if he doesn't feel it, it's him missing out. He's missing out on the best woman I know. And he's not nearly as smart as I thought he was."

"Do you think if Mom was still alive it would be better? I wonder sometimes . . ." I trailed off. Aiden let out a sigh of his own.

"I don't know, Charlie. I wonder that about Dad all the time. Would I have made the same mistakes? Or different ones? Would he be proud of me?"

"You know he would, Aiden. How could he not?"

"I haven't done the best job holding us together," Aiden said. "Annalise is gone, roaming the world, too scared to come home. We almost lost Vance. Gage is missing—"

Aiden's voice choked in his throat and he stopped talking. I wrapped my arm around his broad chest and squeezed. He and Gage had been two peas in a pod growing up, inseparable, their dark heads always together, plotting and planning.

Aiden missed him, and now he felt guilty that Gage might never come home. I got up and grabbed the empty whiskey glass from the side table, filling it from the bottle on Aiden's small wet bar.

"Drink," I said, handing him the glass.

"It's a little early for that," he said, taking it.

"Just drink it." I sat back down beside him, leaning into his side, my head on his shoulder. "You know you're not responsible for all of us, right?"

He finished the drink and set the empty glass down. Shaking his head at me, he said, "Of course I am."

"But this stuff isn't your fault. None of it. You did your best after everything. You made us all go to counseling. You were only twenty, Aiden. What else were you supposed to do? And Gage left you. He should have stayed. I've been so angry with him for leaving us. And now he might not come home."

Tears welled again and I swiped them away. Aiden exhaled in a gust.

"Me too, Charlie. And now I feel like shit about it. I got it. Got why he left. But it still hurt. I have to believe he's coming home."

"He will," I said, but it felt like a lie. Aiden was silent for a long moment, staring at nothing across the room.

"Did I tell you I like your hair?" he asked, reaching over to tuck a strand behind my ear.

"No. Do you really?"

"I do. You look beautiful. Younger. And I love your new house. Even if it means you're not living here where I can keep an eye on you."

"Hmph." I made a frustrated sound in the back of my throat. "I might not go back."

"Sure you will. But stay here for a day or two. Aunt Amelia and the new nurse are moving in next week. Mrs. Williamson could use your help getting them settled."

"I'll stay for a day or two," I agreed. "If it'll help."

"It would. I'll ask Mrs. Williamson to order us a big breakfast to soak up the whiskey and we can go over the logistics, figure out where we should put them and what we need. I could use a hand."

Aiden pulled out his phone and sent a quick message to Mrs. Williamson about breakfast. Back in the day, the house had a complex system of internal phones and bells.

Now we just texted Mrs. W.

So much easier.

Sliding his phone back into his pocket, he started thinking out loud, running through bedroom options for Aunt Amelia and Sophie.

He was distracting me. Aiden and Mrs. W could have handled an invading army without help. They didn't need me for this.

I was grateful for the excuse to avoid my place for a few days. With Lucas out of my life, I didn't think I could face my empty house, knowing that while he'd be back in Atlanta eventually, he was never coming back to me.

CHAPTER TWENTY-THREE

LUCAS

I lay on my hotel bed staring at the ceiling. It was the middle of the night and I needed to sleep. I was ready to wrap this job up sooner than I'd expected. Especially considering that I was a fucking mess.

I hadn't slept more than a few hours at a time since I'd left Atlanta.

Since I'd left Charlie.

Every time I closed my eyes, I saw that fucking look on her face when I told her I'd see her around.

At the time, I thought I was doing the right thing.

I did.

It was harsh, yeah. Breakups were best done fast, like ripping off a bandage. Dragging it out never made it any better. I'd learned that from experience.

What I'd never done was break up with a woman and regret it later.

And I regretted leaving Charlie. It was a fucking ache in my chest, like a rotten tooth, the agony of it blooming with every heartbeat.

I couldn't escape it, even in sleep. I closed my eyes and I saw Charlie, the shocked pain in her blue eyes when I left.

In the brief snatches of sleep I managed, I dreamed of her. Her laugh and the way her skin felt against mine. The silk of her hair.

We weren't supposed to get attached. But we did. I knew goddamn well she had feelings for me. I thought she might even be in love with me, or think she was.

I knew I was in love with her.

It was a fucking disaster. The first time in my life I fall in love, and it's with Charlotte fucking Winters. There was no place for me in her world. That benefit was the nail in the coffin, but I already knew.

I was a rough guy who grew up in a rusted-out trailer. Yeah, I was smart and I could fake it with the best of them. That was part of my job. But the things I'd done . . . where I came from. I'd never fit in.

I didn't give a shit what those people thought of me. I don't need the approval of a bunch of rich people to be happy. But I knew what would happen if Charlie and I hooked up for real.

She'd spend the rest of her life defending me to snobs like Elizabeth, to people who would try to use me to drag her down. And eventually, one day, she'd look at me and all she'd see was a liability.

I couldn't do that to her. I wouldn't. I kept telling myself I wasn't the only guy out there who could make her happy.

Charlie, my Charlie, was perfect. Smart, and feisty, and fucking gorgeous. There were a ton of men, good men, who would kill for a woman like her. Men who would slide into the fabric of her life seamlessly.

That should've been the end of it. I'd walked away, as

good as told her it was finished. She'd move on. I'd move on. Done.

Except that I couldn't sleep, and deep inside, I knew that none of those good men could ever love Charlie like I did.

They'd never be able to protect her like I could, to let her fly but always give her somewhere to land safely. She needed the freedom to be herself. To follow her dreams.

What if the next guy was like Harrison, who cheated on her and wanted her to change for him?

I needed to let her go, but every day we were apart, I missed her more.

Her security system was still connected to the app on my phone. I didn't spy on her. I'm not a creeper. I did get proximity alerts, and I knew when the system was activated and deactivated.

I also had access to the GPS on her panic button, so I knew she'd spent most of the last week at Winters House. The day before, she'd gone home.

I wished she'd stayed with her brother. I didn't like her being on her own, even with the security system and the panic button. Marissa Archer was safely locked away, but something about her didn't ring true for the stalker.

I had no doubt she was the one who'd been delivering the pictures. That part fit perfectly. And she could've been the stalker. There were some interesting transfers going out of her account.

She could easily have paid off the kid who left the note and the one who'd vandalized Charlie's house. She could've paid whoever attacked her, could even have been the attacker herself. She was older, but she was wiry and she had the right build.

The whole thing should've been neatly wrapped up.

When I'd left, I'd been ninety-five percent sure Charlie was in the clear. I wouldn't have gone otherwise.

After too many nights of lying in bed, searching for sleep, the whole sequence of events rolled over and over in my mind and with every day that passed, I felt less certain that Charlie was safe.

Maybe I was making excuses.

It would be so easy to go back, convince her she needed me to watch over her, and get one more taste of Charlie. Just a little more time when I could pretend that she was mine.

I rolled over, punching the flat hotel pillow until it was thick enough to support my neck comfortably. I needed to get a good night's sleep. I needed my brain sharp to finish up this job.

It wasn't dangerous. I was working undercover as a suit in a cubicle, gathering evidence to trap a clever embezzler two cubicles over. I had almost everything I needed for the client to press charges. In another day or two, I could go home.

Home was the last place I wanted to be. I'd kept Charlie out of my house for a reason. Now that I'd let her in, I'd see her everywhere. I'd never be able to look at my bed again without remembering Charlie there, the sheet wrapped around her long limbs, her dark hair spilling across the pillow.

I should've taken her up on the suggestion of a hotel.

I had to do something. I couldn't go on like this, obsessed with a woman I couldn't have. A woman who probably hated me after the callous way I'd walked out on her.

I couldn't get her back, but I could make sure she was safe. Before I went in to my last day on the job, I'd call

Evers. There was no question the Sinclairs had their eyes on her. I could check in and make sure she was all right.

At exactly 8:30 the next morning, I dialed Evers's number. I'd managed to catch a few hours of sleep after I decided to call him.

I was braced for attitude. Charlie was like a little sister to all the Sinclairs and I'd hurt her. She told me the way those guys talked. Given that she'd run straight to her brother, I imagined the assembled Winters and Sinclair crew were out for my blood. It was no less than I deserved.

Evers picked up on the second ring.

"Jackson, I was going to call you today," he said, no hint of anger in his voice. He sounded friendlier than I'd ever heard him.

My guard went up.

"Were you?" I asked evenly. "What about?"

"We'll get to that later. Why did you call me? Something on your mind?" He almost sounded as if he were teasing me. I wasn't going to bite.

"Everything quiet there?" I asked.

"So far. What's bothering you?" Evers's voice sharpened on the question.

"Nothing specific," I admitted. "I just . . . I'm not solid on Marissa Archer for Charlie's stalker. The evidence lines up, but—"

A short gust of air sounded through the phone, as if Evers let out a held breath.

"I'm with you," he said. "We've got eyes on Charlie. Not all the time, but here and there. She still carrying her panic button and being smart about using the system at her house. I want to think all of it was Marissa. Makes it easy."

"But you're not convinced either," I said.

"No. And she's not talking. She hasn't said a fucking

word. The last thing she said was to Charlie. 'He's still out there. And he's not done.' She knows what happened. I believe she delivered those pictures, though I have no fucking clue why. But I just don't see her going after Charlie. The vandalism, that note—those things were personal to Charlie. They had nothing to do with her family."

"It doesn't make sense," I finished for him.

"No, it doesn't."

"Does she know?"

"Charlie? Does she know we're not solid on Marissa Archer? No. Aiden knows. So does Jacob."

"The rest of them?" I asked. If her family hovered, it would drive Charlie nuts, but she was safer if they all knew she might be in danger.

"We're trying to keep it low-key. We don't have any proof that she's still in danger. Nothing's happened since you've been gone. But if you're convinced her stalker is still out there, then why the hell did you leave?" Evers's voice went hard. "Everyone said you two were good together, then you just walked out on her."

"Is this really your business?" I asked. I'd known this was coming, but I wasn't going to talk about Charlie with Evers. Looked like he wasn't going to give me another option.

"Are you fucking kidding me? If you think Charlie isn't my business, you haven't been paying attention. Or you're not as smart as I think you are. Did you get bored? She wasn't enough for you? Or was she too much trouble?"

"You don't know what the hell you're talking about," I said. "It wasn't about Charlie. Charlie is fucking perfect. Anyone who can't see that is an idiot."

"Then what? Seriously, I don't want to do a play-by-play of your whole relationship, but just tell me why you'd walk away from Charlie if you think she's so fucking perfect."

"Because she deserves better, okay? I know you guys checked me out. You know who I am."

"We do," Evers agreed. "Not everything, but we have good access. Birth through your first two years in the Army were easy. After that, the data gets a little sketchy, but we could put together a fairly accurate picture."

"So you know. You know where I come from, you know the things I've seen. The shit I've done. Charlie deserves someone like her. Someone she can be proud of. Someone whose hands are clean. How can you not get that? You should want better for her if you care so much."

"I do. I want the best for her. But what you're describing isn't the best. You think she should be with one of those country club boys? Like the one who cheated on her or tried to drain her savings account? Or the one who tried to use her to get a job? That's what you think she deserves? Because that's what you're leaving her to."

"You don't understand," I said. I didn't know how to explain it to him. How could he not see?

"No, I understand. I do. You've got to figure this shit out for yourself. I don't have any words of wisdom. Except to say—you need to get your fucking head on straight. Do you know why she was so pissed at Aiden when he fired her? If you do, then you know you did the same goddamned thing."

"I'm done talking about this with you," I said, ready to hang up.

"Fine with me. I'm not a relationship counselor. But if you make her cry again, I'll beat the shit out of you."

"I'm scared," I said flatly. I'm sure Evers was trained and a good fighter, but I outweighed him by at least 50 pounds and had a few inches on him. Plus, whoever had trained Evers, I doubted he knew how to fight dirty. Not the way I did.

Evers laughed.

"You should be scared. I'm not stupid enough to take you on by myself. But I have brothers, and so does Charlie. Trust me, you don't want us coming after you."

"Fine. That it?"

"No. I was going to call you later today, but now that I've got you on the phone, we can just talk now," he said, all business.

"What's up?"

"I know you've been freelance since your thing with the Raptors ended. But we're looking to expand in your area. We don't have anyone with your kind of experience. We've got some hackers on the team, and we've got people who can go out in the field. We need someone to lead the new division who can do both. We want you."

That was the last thing I expected Evers Sinclair to say. Did he just offer me a job? And not just a job, but the chance to lead a whole department?

He stayed silent on the other end while I ran through the implications. I wouldn't have the same flexibility I did now if I worked for Sinclair. And they'd have to fork over a hefty salary to match what I could make on my own. But the challenge was intriguing.

I could already see the possibilities in my head, the way I could meld the two sides of my talents into a team. Sinclair Security did good work. The best. If I were going to join a company, theirs would be at the top of the list.

When the silence had stretched out for too long, I said, "That's an interesting offer."

"If it's something you'd be willing to consider, I'll email you a formal proposal. We can talk when you're back in Atlanta."

"That sounds good," I said slowly, still trying to catch up.

"I'll text you my email. I should be back the day after tomorrow. This job is about done."

"Works for me."

Evers hung up.

Now I just had to make one more call. This one, I was dreading. I'd almost asked Evers to pass on the news, but I wasn't a coward.

I pulled up Aiden's number and hit *SEND*. He was considerably chillier than Evers when he answered.

"Jackson. Can I help you with something?"

"Yeah. Look, I'm probably the last person you want to hear from right now. This isn't about Charlie."

"Then why are you calling me?"

It was a good thing we had a few hundred miles between us. If the cold rage in his voice was any indication, Aiden's first move if he saw me in person would involve a swinging fist. Or a bullet.

"I told you I'd do some digging. It took a while, but I managed to get in touch with a guy I know. I don't have any proof to show you, but they're ninety percent sure Gage is still out there."

"They think he's alive?" The relief in Aiden's voice was so sharp it hurt to hear. It killed me to pull him back.

"They intercepted some communications that indicated he was being held. That's all they know. But they haven't heard anything that suggests he isn't still alive. That's no guarantee he's coming home. You know that, right?"

"Yeah," Aiden said, his voice husky. "But for now, they're pretty sure he's alive?"

"For now," I agreed. "Based on what I could find out, if anyone can get free and make his way home, it's your brother."

"Yeah. Thanks. I appreciate your looking into this."

I wanted to ask how Charlie was. Why, I don't know. It would be pouring salt in an open wound, and Aiden would cut me to pieces for daring to say her name.

I couldn't help myself.

"Is Charlie—"

Aiden cut me off. "Stay away from Charlie," he said in a hard voice. "I can guess why you walked, Jackson. I'm even a little sympathetic, considering that I was the last man to fuck up her life because I was sure I knew better than she did about what she needed. She deserves more than a guy she can't depend on. She's had enough of those. You can stop worrying about her. Her family will watch her back."

He hung up. I sat on the edge of the hotel bed, staring at the screen of my phone with blind eyes. That's what Evers was getting at. Aiden had fired her because he thought he knew what was best. And in that case, he had. It didn't make his actions right. He'd taken her choice away. He'd treated her like a child.

Then I'd turned around and done the same thing.

I loved her for her intelligence, her strength of spirit. Her courage.

I was the one who was lacking.

She knew who I was, where I came from. I'd told her. When she was challenged at the benefit, she hadn't hesitated for a second. She could've made an excuse or pretended Elizabeth's insults were a joke.

Instead, Charlie had looked Elizabeth right in the eye and said she was proud to be by my side.

Who was I to tell a woman like her that she couldn't choose who she wanted? If I loved her, really loved her, I'd trust her to make her own decisions.

I fell back on the bed, my head bouncing on the firm mattress, and let out a groan.

I was a fucking idiot.

A stupid fucking idiot. I'd walked away from the only woman I'd ever loved. I'd treated her like a fool.

I'd hurt her. Hurt Charlie. A memory of her shattered eyes when I left flashed through my mind.

Fuck. Of all the challenges I'd overcome in my life, all the battles I'd fought, none had ever been as important as the one that was coming.

I had to get Charlie back. No matter what, I had to convince her to give me another chance.

Chapter Twenty-Four

Charlie

I stayed with Aiden for almost a week. Winters House was familiar. Comforting. And once Aunt Amelia and Sophie moved in, crowded.

It was nearly impossible to be crowded in a house that size, but I felt like crap and I didn't want company.

I adored my Aunt Amelia. She was hysterical and a troublemaker. As Maggie and I had hoped when we hired her, Sophie was the perfect counterpoint. Her quiet, shy nature hid a strong will. She had a dry sense of humor that let her appreciate Aunt Amelia, but her backbone meant she wouldn't get steamrolled. Much.

Aunt Amelia could steamroll anyone, even Aiden sometimes. I was glad my brother had company in the house again. It made it easier to pack my duffel bag back up and come home.

Home. My decrepit house in the Highlands wasn't so decrepit anymore. The floors still needed to be refinished, and I hadn't stripped all of the paint from the trim on the first floor, but I was getting there.

My kitchen was in, and it was spectacular. The bright

white cabinets and marble countertops were perfect. The appliances had been hooked up while I was at Winters House and I stopped at the grocery store on my drive home to buy actual groceries for my real-life, full-size refrigerator.

It took a few trips back and forth to the car to unload everything. I had a bad moment after I unpacked my duffel and put the groceries away when I realized that was it. I was moved in, I was alone, and that wasn't going to change.

Lucas wasn't coming back.

I saw him everywhere I looked. Just the thought of getting back to work on stripping paint made me sick to my stomach. Everything about it, the smell, the feel of the heater in my hands, the sound of scraping the wood—all of it reminded me of Lucas.

I had to get over it.

I was the one who'd messed up. I'd told him, promised him, that our hookup was casual. No big deal. Friends with benefits, except without the friends part. He'd stepped in when I was in trouble, done me a favor. I was the one who crossed the line.

It didn't matter that I was head over heels in love with him. It didn't matter that every part of me yearned for him, missed him with an ache that went down to my bones.

He wasn't coming back, not to me, and I had to get used to it. I wasn't going to spend the rest of my life pining over a guy who didn't love me.

I'd had my heart broken before. I could handle this.

I could talk a good game in my head, but in my heart, I knew this was nothing like breaking up with Harrison.

Then, I'd felt betrayed, angry, and yes, hurt. But not like this. Not like something had been torn away from me, like some essential part of myself was missing, a part I'd never get back. A part that now belonged to Lucas, whether he wanted it or not.

Standing in the middle of my gorgeous new kitchen, I took a deep breath, held it as long as I could, then slowly let it out. I'd cried all over Aiden when I'd shown up at Winters House the day Lucas dumped me.

Not since. I was done with crying.

I was Charlotte fucking Winters, and I'd been through worse than some guy fucking me and leaving me. My heart was broken, sure. I'd lived through that before too. I wasn't going to dissolve into some weeping mess of a woman.

Every time my emotions began to get the best of me, I forced myself to stop and take a deep breath. I was moving forward. I had to.

I had no job, and now I had no heart.

All I had was this house. And maybe, possibly, if everything worked out right, another one. I'd intended to keep this house. I loved it, loved every inch of it.

Now that Lucas was everywhere, had seeped into the grain of the wood, maybe I'd just sell it when it was done and move into the next one. I knew people who did that, moved from house to house, rehabbing and flipping as they went.

It was risky. You never knew when you'd run into serious problems the inspection didn't uncover. I'd been incredibly lucky on this job that everything had gone to schedule. Most of the time, between getting subcontractors and delays on materials, that wouldn't be the case.

Time was money on a flip.

The longer you held onto the house, the narrower the profit margin could get. Definitely a risky line of work.

I wanted it anyway. I loved it. Nothing was like the rush

of satisfaction at taking something neglected and making it new again.

I made myself a quick turkey sandwich and ate it standing at the island in the kitchen. It was time to get back to work. My stomach full, I grabbed my headphones and shoved them in my ears.

The paint was stripped off the trim in the living room, the front hall, and most of the dining room. I could finish the dining room, but I didn't feel like stripping paint. Not yet.

Fortunately for me, all of that cleaned trim needed to be sanded. It was another repetitive, endless job that would be well worth the effort when I was done.

A half an hour later, I was reminding myself how good it would look as my arms ached. I'd only made it up three steps of the staircase.

The detailed carvings on the banister and the spindles were beautiful, but they'd been a pain in the ass to strip and they were just as irritating to sand.

Music pounded in my ears, a hard rock rhythm that suited my mood. No weepy love songs for me. Not for a while. Maybe not ever again the way I felt. Loud, angry rock? I could so work with that.

It was turned up too loud. If I'd had it lower, even just a little, I would've heard something.

I would've been ready.

My only warning was a shadow crossing the side of my vision. Then he was there, sinking his hand into my hair and yanking me back.

I fell on my ass at his feet and looked up to see Bruce Hayward standing above me, a gun in his hand, the barrel pointed at my chest.

"You fucking bitch," he spat out, his eyes wide and wild, the hand holding the gun shaking.

Not good.

I assumed he was here to shoot me, but if he wasn't, I didn't want to be hit accidentally because he couldn't keep his hand steady.

My first instinct was to argue with him, but that would be stupid. As unhinged as he was, I didn't need to push him any further.

I needed to calm him down if I wanted a chance to get away. The panic button was in my purse. Which was in the kitchen.

Stupid, stupid Charlie.

Marissa was in jail and everything had been quiet. I'd thought I was safe.

Suddenly, it occurred to me—my alarm was on and the doors were locked.

"How did you get in?" I asked, trying to keep my voice level and non-confrontational.

Hayward sneered down at me. "You left the door unlocked while you were getting your groceries. I snuck in and hid in your laundry room. Now, we're locked in together. Just you and me."

"What are you going to do?"

I didn't really want to know what Bruce Hayward had planned for me. Still, keeping him talking was a better option than whatever was going to happen when he was done.

"I haven't decided," he said. "I was thinking about killing you."

"Any chance I can talk you out of that?" I said.

Hayward laughed, high-pitched and grating, the gun in

his hand wobbling back and forth as his body shook with amusement.

"My wife left me today, had me served with divorce papers. My kids won't speak to me. My lawyer says I'm going to jail for a long time. What does it matter if I kill you? You think a few more years is anything on top of what I'm looking at?"

"I think murder one is an entirely different thing than a few counts of white-collar crime."

Another unhinged fit of laughter. "It's not a few counts of white-collar crime. That's what *you* uncovered. Once the FBI started digging—"

"Look, I'm sorry," I lied. "I didn't realize it would be this bad. If there's anything I can do—"

"Shut the fuck up, you stupid little bitch. You and your family, you think you run the goddamned world. Think you're better than everyone else. So I was bending the law here and there—everyone does it. Everyone except you and your perfect fucking brother.

"But you had to turn me in, do the right thing, and ruin my fucking life. And now you think I'm gonna buy your fake offer to help me out? Fuck that. When I'm done with you, you and your brother will never forget what you did to me."

That gun swinging back and forth was not good. Hayward was going to shoot me. Either on purpose, or because he lost his temper, or maybe his finger would slip.

It didn't matter.

The shot was coming unless I could figure out a way to escape him. Or call for help. My headphones had been yanked out of my ears when he grabbed my hair, but my phone was still in my back pocket, pinned beneath me. And on my phone was the security app Evers had installed.

There was no way I could pull the phone out and call for help, but if I could turn it on, I might be able to press the app and hit the built-in panic button.

It was a long shot, but it was all I had.

Carefully, I slid one hand beneath me and tugged out the phone, leaving it hidden behind my back.

Hayward started ranting about his son taking over his company, calling him an ungrateful bastard.

Good. The longer he raved about his problems, the more time I had to get myself out of this.

My eyes flicking between Hayward's rage-filled face and his gun, I pressed the *Home* button on my phone, leaving my thumb in place so that my fingerprint could unlock the screen.

It was impossible to tell if it worked without looking. Hoping with everything I had that the phone was unlocked, I pictured the screen in my mind. Evers had put the security app in the center of the bottom row, just to the right.

Feeling my way, I tapped where I thought the app would be. If it had opened, the panic button would be dead center.

The trick was, the panic button in the app needed my fingerprint to activate, a safeguard against calling for help when I just wanted to set the alarm. I tapped the button in the middle of the screen, then pressed my thumb to the *Home* button again.

If it worked, the phone would vibrate twice.

Nothing.

Either I'd never turned the phone on, or I'd hit the wrong app, or it hadn't read my thumbprint.

There was no way to tell.

Hayward was starting to run out of steam, now bitching

about his lying, cheating wife and the lawyer who was sucking them dry.

Any minute, he'd be done with talking. He'd be ready to act.

I clicked the button on the side of the phone to put it to sleep and started the process again.

A click to the home button.

My thumb pressed again for the fingerprint scan.

My heart raced in my chest. Sweat pooled in my armpits and ran down my spine.

I was running out of time.

Again, I pictured the home screen in my mind and tapped where I knew the security app had to be.

One more tap for that red circle that was the panic button and one more press of my thumb.

Nothing.

I squeezed my eyes shut to fight back the rising panic and tried again.

CHAPTER
TWENTY-FIVE
LUCAS

The lights were on at Charlie's house when I pulled in my driveway, home a day later than I'd expected. I'd been driving for hours and I smelled like stale coffee and fast food.

I hadn't figured out what I was going to say to her.

Like the coward I was, I jumped in the shower to delay just a little bit longer. I needed to see her, but I was terrified I'd end up making everything worse.

The shower didn't buy me much time. I changed, rubbed my hair with a towel, and I was ready to go, still with no idea what to say.

I'd have to figure it out when I got there. Maybe I was going to fuck it up again. I didn't have pretty words or a decent explanation for why I'd been such an asshole.

All I knew was that I couldn't wait any longer to see her. If she felt half as miserable as I did, I might have a chance.

I thought about calling first, but she probably wouldn't answer. I wouldn't if I were her.

Groveling was best done in person, anyway. Fully

prepared for her to slam the door in my face, I jogged up her front steps and raised my hand to knock.

From the inside, I heard a voice, a man, yelling. And the beep from Charlie's phone. The proximity alarm. If I could hear her phone through the door, she had to be close.

What the fuck was going on?

I could make out the voice from the other side of the door, but if that was just one of her brothers and they were in the middle of an argument, she would've checked the proximity alert.

Through the door, I heard, "What the fuck is that?"

"It's nothing," Charlie said, her voice thin and strained.

Fuck. I stepped back far enough to clear the sensors, then forward again, triggering them. Another beep from inside the house. I wanted them both distracted while I figured out what was going on.

Pulling out my own phone, I pulled up the cameras at Charlie's house. What I saw sent a bolt of pure terror down my spine.

Bruce Hayward loomed over Charlie, who lay prone on the floor as if he'd thrown her there, a gun in his hand. He was reaching for her. It looked like he was demanding she hand over her phone.

Charlie fumbled with it, and a second later, my own phone lit up. She'd managed to hit the panic button in the alarm system app.

Smart girl.

Now I just had to get in there and save her ass before that fucking maniac shot her.

There was no time for subtlety. I could tell by the way he was waving that gun around that Hayward was not in control of the situation.

I didn't need to give him time to do something crazy.

From the look in his eyes, he was already overflowing with crazy.

I still had the key to Charlie's locks. As quietly as I could, I turned the deadbolt on the front door and swung it open.

Charlie's eyes went wide when she saw me. Hayward swung around, bringing his gun up to my head.

"Move," I shouted at Charlie.

After a second's hesitation, she rolled to the side and didn't stop until she was clear of the front hall. It would've been better if she'd taken off for the kitchen and the back door, but for a civilian, she'd done her best.

I dove low as Hayward swung the gun around, going for his knees. He fired just as I hit him. The bullet buried itself in the plaster above my head, showering specs of white over the hardwood floor.

He fired again when he landed on his back, burying another bullet in the ceiling.

Charlie was going to be pissed.

Hayward was not a fighter. Once I had him down, he went limp and started whining about assault and his lawyer.

I grabbed his gun and pulled it from his hand, flicking the safety on. I slid it across the floor into the empty dining room, well out of reach.

"You okay, Charlie?" I called out. "Did he hurt you?"

"I'm all right," she said, her voice shaky. I looked up to see her getting to her feet. "I tried to hit the panic button, but I couldn't get it—"

The adrenaline was starting to get to her. With Hayward unsecured, I needed her focused. I could hold him down all day, but I couldn't help Charlie if I had my attention on Hayward.

"Can you do me a favor, Princess?"

In a cautious tone, she asked, "What is it?"

I slid my key ring across the floor in her direction. "Go next door to my place. The alarm is off. In the top drawer of my dresser, you'll find zip tie restraints. Bring me back three sets so we can get this asshole locked down."

"Be right back."

I may have fucked everything up, but I knew my girl. All she needed was something to focus her energy on and she was ready to go. She still had a crash coming, but she'd push it off long enough to do what needed to be done.

Straddling Hayward's back, his hands held by one of mine, I had him under control. With Charlie occupied, I pulled out my phone and dialed Brennan.

He answered with, "Got the alert, on my way."

I didn't bother to call Sinclair security. I already knew they'd be racing for Charlie.

She was back a few minutes later, four sets of zip ties draped over one hand.

"I brought extra, just in case." She handed them to me, watching as I secured his hands, then his feet. I dragged Hayward back to the base of the stairs and used the extra zip ties to secure his hands to the thick banister behind him. He wasn't going anywhere.

I wished I'd had a gag in that drawer. He was still mumbling and whining under his breath. Charlie stood in front of him, looking down, her hands on her hips, and opened her mouth to speak.

He glared at her. She shook her head.

"You're not worth it."

She was right. He wasn't. He'd been in deep shit, and with what he'd just pulled, it had gotten immeasurably worse. Every inch of Charlie's house was under surveillance.

No one was watching the cameras live, but they were recording around-the-clock and every second of his attack on Charlie was now on the record in high-definition.

We only had a few minutes before the Sinclair team and Brennan showed up. Closing my hand around Charlie's upper arm, I tugged her gently down the hall.

"He's not going anywhere," I said. She let me lead her to the kitchen, squinting a little when I flicked on the overhead lights. "It looks good in here."

It did, but that's not what I needed to say.

Facing down a guy with a gun—not remotely scary.

Coming clean with Charlie—fucking terrifying.

Time to stop stalling and lay it out.

"I fucked up," I said, meeting her blue eyes directly. I wasn't surprised to see suspicion there. I deserved it. "I broke things off because I'm in love with you."

"What?" She took a step back and threw her arms out to the sides. "What?" She said again, her voice rising, bordering on hysterical.

I sucked in a fortifying breath and said again, "I'm in love with you. And I decided I would rather give you up than run the risk of having you regret being with me."

Charlie crossed her arms over her chest and stared at me, her eyes narrowed on mine. She said nothing for an endless minute.

I had to force myself to breathe.

Finally, she tilted her head to the side and said, "That's the stupidest thing I've ever heard. You're not in love with me. If you were in love with me, you'd trust me to know my own mind. Why would I ever regret being with you?"

Fucking Aiden and Evers were right.

"I do trust you. I fucked up. It doesn't mean I don't love you. It just means I was an idiot."

"So?"

She wasn't going to make this easy on me.

Not that I deserved it.

"I'm sorry. We both know if we try to make something out of this, people are going to talk. I was trying to spare you from that—"

She opened her mouth to speak and I put my hand up to stop her. Surprised, her mouth snapped shut and she glared at me.

"I was wrong. You know what we'd be getting into, and you know what you'll have to deal with. If you're willing to put up with it, that's your choice. I shouldn't have taken it away from you, and I'm sorry."

"I can't stop people from talking, Lucas. If you're worried about what people are going to say, there's nothing I can do about that," she said, sounding so tired I wanted to ditch this whole fucked up apology and pull her into my arms.

That wasn't what she needed. She needed to understand where I stood.

"I don't give a shit what those people say about me, Charlie. I wasn't trying to protect myself. I was trying to protect you."

"You can't," she said quietly. "People will gossip, Lucas. It's human nature. They gossip about us most of all because there's scandal and money and people love that. I've spent my entire life surrounded by it—people who pretend to be my best friend and tear me down the second my back is turned. I don't care about them either. I'm not afraid of gossip. I'm afraid of giving my heart to a man who doesn't believe in me, who doesn't think I'm strong enough to love him the way he deserves."

"Charlie," I said, searching for the right words, the words

that would convince her that I knew I'd been wrong and I wanted to start again. "That's what made me realize I'd fucked everything up. I love you because you're strong and smart. And then I didn't treat you like you were strong and smart. I get that now."

I shoved my hands in my pockets and studied her, searching for some sign she was softening. "If you give me another chance, I promise you, I won't ever underestimate you again, and I'll never let you down."

The front door slammed open and Evers stepped through, followed by Cooper. Brennan was right behind them. Goddammit.

They had the worst fucking timing.

Charlie stepped back and turned to face them. She was going to leave me hanging.

Pretending that the rest of my life didn't depend on her answer, I tried to focus on the problem at hand. Taking out my phone, I pulled up the video feed from the front hall of Charlie's house, selected the section that started when Hayward stepped into view, and emailed it to Brennan, saying,

"If you take a quick look at what I just sent you, I think you'll see enough to bring him in. Breaking and entering, assault and battery. It's a long list."

"Did he hurt you?" Brennan asked Charlie, examining her with his sharp gaze. She shook her head.

"Not really. I tried to hit the panic button but—"

The door swung open again and Aiden stepped into the room, his face pale and his jaw set. When his eyes landed on Charlie, they softened in relief.

He was at her side a second later, wrapping his arms around her and squeezing tight. To Brennan, he said, "I'm taking her home. If you need anything from her, you can get it tomorrow."

"Aiden, I'm okay," she said. Aiden was having none of it.

Brennan said, "I've got plenty to keep me busy until Charlie wants to give me her statement. Bring her by tomorrow."

The last part he directed at me. I nodded. Charlie didn't object, which I took as a good sign, though Aiden, Cooper, and Evers all narrowed their eyes at me.

I ignored them.

Aiden whisked Charlie out of the house and to his car. I could hear her saying that she had to at least get her things, but he must have bullied her into going with him, because the next thing I knew, the engine rumbled to life and his car pulled out of the driveway.

Evers gave me a long look and said, "You fixing that?" I knew he meant Charlie.

"Working on it. I was making progress before you three interrupted."

Evers shrugged, unrepentant. Cooper said, "You take a look at the job proposal?"

I had. The salary was competitive, and the position they outlined would be an intriguing challenge. I missed working on a team, and Sinclair was the best.

"I'll call you tomorrow to set up a time to come in and go over the details, but it looks good."

Cooper grinned and slapped me on the back twice before passing me on his way to the door. "Lock up on your way out."

"Got it," I said, resigned.

Charlie was out of reach for the moment, but this wasn't done. I'd let her brother fuss over her for a night, but I'd be at Winters House first thing in the morning.

We had a future to settle and I wasn't giving up until Charlie agreed to be mine.

For the first time in over a week, I slept well. Charlie hadn't forgiven me, but she would.

I loved her. And she loved me.

I just had to get her to admit it.

I woke up early, as usual, and went for a run to kill some time before hitting Charlie's house next door to pick up the essentials she'd need.

The first hurdle was the imposing outer gate at the Winters House property. The other times I'd visited, the first gate had already been open in expectation of our arrival.

This time, I had to press the button on the intercom to call the house. I wasn't expecting Aiden to answer.

"Jackson. What are you doing here? Charlie's been through enough."

"I have her things," I said. "You rushed her out of her house so fast last night, you didn't give her a chance to get what she needed."

"You going to drop it off? Or do you want to talk to her?"

"I want to talk to her, Aiden. If it helps, I already apologized for fucking things up. I'm in love with her, and I should've trusted her to make her own decisions."

"You told her that?" Aiden sounded like he might be softening. I pressed my advantage.

"I did."

"And what did she say? How do I know she wants to see you?"

"I don't know if she wants to see me. You guys showed up in the middle of the conversation. Look, if she wants to tell me to fuck off, fine. But I want to hear it from her. If she wants more time to think, that's fine too."

Aiden didn't say anything, but the heavy metal gate swung open, admitting me to the Winters estate.

Aiden met me at the door, his chilly expression belied by a speculative look in his eyes.

He took the backpack I held in my hands and said, "I'll give this to Charlie. You can wait in there."

He lifted his chin in the direction of the formal living room.

Sitting and waiting for Charlie wasn't what I was going for, but at least I was in the house. I took a seat on the couch and stretched my legs out in front of me, prepared to wait.

A few minutes later, the housekeeper brought me a tray with steaming biscuits, a pot of jam, and a small silver carafe of coffee. She delivered the food and left without speaking. I wondered if I should worry about poison.

I figured if Charlie wanted revenge, she'd probably poison me herself. The coffee smelled too good to ignore. I'd finished half the pot and polished off the biscuits before the door swung open again.

Charlie stepped through, her hair pinned back from her face, wearing the clothes I'd brought for her, a scoop-neck fitted T-shirt the same blue as her eyes and her favorite pair of jeans.

She closed the door behind her and stuffed her hands into her back pockets, her eyes uncertain.

"Hey," she said.

"We didn't get to finish talking last night."

"I know. I'm sorry. Aiden was freaked and—"

I shook my head. "No, it's better this way. Too much happened last night between Hayward and everything I had to say. It's better to talk about this stuff with a clear head."

"I don't think I've ever had a clear head when it comes to

you," she said. "I had a thing for you before we even met. I used to stand in my window and watch you mow the lawn."

I grinned. "I know."

I'd teased her about watching me mow the lawn before, but Charlie's cheeks still turned red and she dropped her eyes to her feet.

"I used to watch you too," I admitted. "I used to wonder what a woman like you was doing messing around with that disaster of a house. Then I got to know you and I realized that woman, with her pearls and her suits—she's not you, Charlie. Not all of you. There's so much more to who you are. You have courage, and imagination, and strength. I saw that, but you scared the hell out of me so I made excuses and ran away."

"You're not the only one who's scared, Lucas," she said softly. "Sometimes, I think I'm scared all the time. But I've learned that life is too short to be afraid. I've spent too many years doing what I thought I should to make other people happy. None of that worked. I tried to be perfect and I ended up making myself miserable. Now I just want to be Charlie."

"I love Charlie," I said, coming to my feet and crossing the room to her. "I love you. Whoever you want to be, I love you."

She took a step forward and threw herself into my arms. "I love you too, Lucas."

I dipped her back and kissed her, unable to wait a second longer to taste her again. It had been a week and it felt like a lifetime. Her arms wrapped around me, and I lifted her, carrying her back to the couch and sitting, pulling her into my lap.

Opposite me, the door cracked open and an unfamiliar face popped in. A set of sharp, ice blue eyes identical to

Jacob's peered at us, capped by a head of white hair. As abruptly as she'd interrupted, the stranger withdrew, but not before a grin spread across her wrinkled face.

The door shut with a click.

Through the thick wood, I heard her shout, "Charlie's good, but I don't think she's coming to breakfast."

Charlie leaned into me and erupted with giggles.

"Aunt Amelia?" I asked.

She nodded. I cupped her face in my hands and kissed one cheek, then the other.

"We have time for this later," I said. "But I want to show you something now. Will you come with me?"

"Let me just tell Aiden I'm leaving."

I followed her out to the hallway and snagged her back-pack from where she'd left it at the base of the stairs. Good to know she hadn't planned on staying.

She darted into the dining room ahead of me, told Aiden she was okay and she was leaving, then met me in the hall before I could go in. Slapping her palms on my chest, she pushed, backing me up.

"Don't go in there, trust me. If you go in there, Aunt Amelia will invite you to breakfast, Aiden will insist you stay, and we'll be here for another hour."

Seeing the wisdom in Charlie's words, I took her hand and led her out of the house.

We were back in the Highlands twenty minutes later. When I drove past our street, Charlie looked at me, her eyebrows raised. I turned half a mile down from where I usually did and wound through the back of the neighborhood, coming to a stop in front of a mid-century modern house that had seen better days.

That style of architecture wasn't unknown in the neighborhood, and some of them had been rehabbed into works of art, but they required a careful hand or no amount of time and money could keep them from looking outdated.

This was the house Charlie had been stalking on her tablet. I'd looked into it and it had potential. It was a foreclosure, which meant a slow buying process but potentially a great purchase price.

The bank had already done an inspection. It had major issues, one of which was the foundation, but at the right price, we could turn a tidy profit.

I got out of the car and rounded the front to open her door. She stepped out, looking from the house to me and back again.

"What do you think?" I asked.

"What do you mean? I've had my eye on this one, but it's a little out of my price range right now."

"What if we went in on it together?" I asked. "Fifty-fifty. I'm taking a job with Sinclair Security, so my schedule won't be as flexible as it is right now, but I can still do my half."

"You want to buy a house with me?" Charlie asked.

She usually wasn't so slow on the uptake. I pulled her close, tilting her face up to mine. Nothing in my life had ever felt as right as Charlie Winters in my arms. Her gorgeous pink mouth beckoned and I kissed her, at home for the first time since I'd walked out a week before.

Hoping she'd understand, I said, "I want to do everything with you, but we can start with this house."

EPILOGUE
CHARLIE

I couldn't believe our first flip house was finally done. It took five months and more money than we'd planned to spend, but it was a masterpiece. I almost didn't want to sell it.

Lucas and I had fallen in love in this house.

I'd thought we'd fallen in love at my house, while we were pretending we were fuck buddies and he'd helped me strip paint. And we had.

That was where we took those first, hesitant steps toward each other, where we'd realized what we had was so much more than just sex.

But here, in this mess of a rehab we'd bought together, this was where we really fell in love. Not that first flush of fire and heart.

The day to day kind of love.

The kind that lasts.

This house was where I discovered that we were both demons for a schedule, were obsessed with spreadsheets, and went a little crazy when materials were delayed. Where

I'd learned that he could function on almost no sleep, but he discovered the same turned me into a cranky monster.

We'd figured out so many things in the past five months. Lucas was neat. Me, not so much. He didn't mind my being messy, as long as I put away our tools and didn't leave food sitting in the sink. I could handle that. My mess was mostly of the clothes on the floor variety.

I found out that he hated doing laundry and had about eight thousand pairs of cargo pants and an equal number of black t-shirts so he could avoid running out and didn't have to go shopping. Needless to say, I took over washing our clothes.

Lucas still had his place next door, but he'd pretty much moved in with me over the past few months. At first, he'd moved me in with him while my contractors finished the upstairs and the floors at my place. The work was scheduled to take two months but ended up taking three.

That was the only delay we didn't mind. By the time the schedule got pushed back, we'd closed on the mid-century modern and had our hands full.

Lucas was working at Sinclair Security, leading a team of IT specialists who also handled field work. I wasn't exactly sure what that meant. Lucas said I didn't need to know the details, but that it was mostly not-dangerous. I was focused on 'not-dangerous' and ignoring 'mostly'. He loved it, and that was all I cared about.

He worked on the flip house with me after hours, leading to a lot of late nights, picnic dinners on a tarp, and sometimes, spontaneous nakedness. I was taking real estate classes during the day along with managing the renovation, and I was thinking about studying for my contractor's license, though I'd heard the test was a bitch. Maybe not this year, but it was on my list.

Everything had come together so easily. Even moving into my house. Once the upstairs was finished and the floors were done, there wasn't much left other than some details on the outside.

I loved Lucas's place. It was gorgeous and comfortable and it reminded me of him. But my house had been my dream since the first moment I'd seen it. I wanted to live there and nowhere else. But only if Lucas was with me.

As with everything, once we'd finally untangled our fears from our hearts, Lucas made it easy for me. We'd been examining the final touches in the master suite, the blue-grey walls and crisp white trim, when he said, "Do you want new furniture? Or should we just move my stuff in?"

I thought about it, stunned by his offer. He'd renovated his own home from the studs out and I knew he was attached to it. We hadn't talked about what we'd do when mine was finished.

Life had been so good, I hadn't wanted to bring up anything that might cause tension. I should have known Lucas wouldn't let that happen.

"Are you sure?" I asked. He'd pulled me into his arms and kissed me.

When he was done and my knees were weak, he'd said, "I'm sure. You just have to decide about the furniture."

That part was easy. I loved his bed. The dark walnut would look gorgeous against the cool tones of the paint and the white trim.

"Let's move your stuff over," I said. "Your bedroom set will fit in here and we can put the TV and couches in the living room for now."

So we had. Lucas must have wanted to be in my house as much as I did because he had movers scheduled for the next day. Before I knew it, we were really and truly living together.

Quietly, without making a big deal about it, he suggested he put his house on the market. I'd agreed. It sold within a month, and a month after that, we had a sweet family living next door.

Life was just about perfect.

I had Lucas. I was putting together a career I loved. The only cloud in the sky was Gage. He was still MIA, and Lucas's guy hadn't had any good news since he'd first confirmed Gage was alive.

A truck pulled into the driveway beside mine. Lucas, off work early, here to go over the final details on the house before it hit the market. I didn't try to stop the giddy grin that spread across my face at the sight of him.

He unfolded his tall frame from his truck and headed up the driveway, stopping for only a second to send my truck a smug, appraising look as he walked past it.

Did I mention that he bought me a new truck?

I argued for about a minute when he brought it home. It was smaller than his but nicer, with leather, navigation, an upgraded sound system—all the good stuff. He'd driven it home one day and handed me the keys with a long look that ordered me not to say a word.

I tried to tell him to take it back. Lucas was having none of it. He interrupted me with a kiss—Lucas's preferred method of getting me to shut up—and when I was dizzy from his mouth on mine, he said, "Princess, just take the keys and let it go. I hate that thing you're driving. I know you think it's good enough for you. But I don't. Every time I look at it, I want to push it over a cliff."

I'd sighed and taken the keys. I might have argued—I really didn't mind the old truck—but I knew it reminded

Lucas of that miserable week we'd been broken up. Every time he saw it, he turned away.

I'd shoved the keys to my new truck in my pocket and said teasingly, "Okay, but if you think you can solve all of your problems by throwing money at them . . ."

Lucas had growled, "Brat," and dragged me to my new truck, where he proceeded to show me how comfortable the rear bench seat was. Needless to say, we both had very good memories of the day Lucas gave me that truck.

Sophie's car had broken down a few weeks before, and I'd very happily lent her my old truck, glad to have an excuse to get it away from Lucas and help Sophie out at the same time.

I watched him as he made his way up the steep driveway, my eyes eating up his long stride. I never got tired of looking at Lucas Jackson. He hadn't changed in the slightest since going to work for Sinclair Security.

He still dressed like a commando, in his worn cargoes and tight black t-shirts, unless he had work in the field that required a suit, or my secret favorite, a tux. There was still nothing in the universe as hot as Lucas in a tuxedo.

My eyes fixed on the flex of his thighs as he walked. I almost missed the box he held in his arms. He climbed the steps to the front door and set the box on the stoop beside him.

"What's that?" I asked.

Lucas dipped his head for a kiss.

I forgot about the box.

You'd think that with all the sex we had, I'd be bored by now.

Not a chance.

I'd come so close to losing him. That would never happen again, but I knew better than anyone that the good things in life were meant to be savored. And Lucas's kisses were the best.

I fell into him, sliding my arms around his back and tugging up his shirt to press my palms to the warm, silky skin beneath. Lucas shuffled me backward, turning me until my back hit the side of the house.

Against my neck, he said, "I've been in fucking meetings all day, and all I could think about was this."

He tugged at the neck of my blouse, revealing the navy lace bra I'd put on that morning. I'd gone straight from real estate class to meeting the broker who would list the house, so for once, I was dressed up as opposed to wearing the beat-up jeans and shirts I sacrificed to renovation work.

Though the matching lace bra and thong under my suit weren't for business. They were for Lucas.

Deftly, he unfastened the first two buttons and slipped his hand inside my shirt to cup my breast. I vaguely recalled that we were on the front stoop of the house. With Lucas's height and broad frame, he could easily shield me from prying eyes, but not if he stripped me naked.

With obvious reluctance, he withdrew his hand and said, "Let's go inside. I want another walkthrough. What did the broker say?"

I followed him down the hall, into the open space that held the kitchen, great room, and dining room. We'd done an amazing job with the place, in my not-so-humble opinion. Once the foundation had been repaired, almost all of the interior detailing had to go. It had been a lot of work. A ton.

Now, it was a jewel, the ideal example of mid-century modern design, with floor-to-ceiling plate glass windows, bamboo floors, soaring ceilings, and a modern aesthetic. Buyers were going to love it and we'd make a killing.

"She was in line with our estimates on price. We should have the first open house next weekend," I said, watching as he set the mysterious box on the sleek stainless steel of the kitchen island.

"Sounds good. Any news on the offer?"

We'd put in an offer the week before on an arts and crafts bungalow that was part of an estate. I thought we'd end up getting it, but the broker had to talk to all of the heirs to the property, which was taking longer than we'd expected.

"Not yet." My curiosity getting the best of me, I pulled the box toward me and opened it. Looking inside, I asked, "Is this what I think it is?"

A bottle of Macallan scotch sat in the box, nestled in a pile of work rags. Pulling it out, I studied the label. I knew this bottle.

Macallan 25 Year Sar Obair.

Only one hundred and sixty-eight bottles had been produced. Aiden had been crowing about snagging the bottle at auction for a thousand dollars. He'd refused to let any of us taste a single drop. And now Lucas had it.

"How?" I asked.

"We're celebrating," he said.

"With Aiden's whiskey?"

"Forget the whiskey for a second." Lucas lifted me to sit on the island, sliding my skirt up my thighs so he could stand between my legs, bringing us almost eye to eye. His green eyes roamed over my face, resting on my lips, my hair, my chin, before finally meeting my own.

"What's up?" I whispered. He was being weird. Almost like he was nervous, but Lucas didn't get nervous. He was the most confident man I knew. Nothing scared him.

In answer, he kissed me, pressing his lips to mine and

leaving them there, our breath mingling for a long moment before he nipped my lower lip and broke the kiss.

"Before we open the whiskey, I wanted to give you this," he said, pulling a blue velvet box out of his pocket.

My heart stuttered in my chest. My breath froze.

Was that what I thought it was?

Speechless, I looked into Lucas's eyes and saw his heart exposed, overflowing with love, tinged with nerves.

"Lucas?" I managed to ask, afraid to hope too much.

He flipped open the box to reveal a ring.

The ring.

The most gorgeous ring I'd ever seen.

A classic emerald-cut diamond with a halo of pavé diamonds and matching pavé diamonds on the band. Vibrant blue sapphires ran around the sides of the raised mount. From the top, the sapphires gave just a hint of blue, bringing life to the ice of all of those diamonds.

It was gorgeous and sparkly and just on the elegant side of too much. Exactly the ring I would have chosen for myself.

In explanation, Lucas said, "There isn't a gemstone the color of your eyes, so I had to settle for sapphires. Maggie said you liked sapphires."

He'd taken Maggie with him to buy me a ring? I opened my mouth to tell him it was the most beautiful thing I'd ever seen, but no sound came out.

I looked from the ring to Lucas, unable to speak.

"You changed my life, Charlie Winters," he said. "I never thought I could love anyone the way I love you. Every morning, I wake up next to you and think I must be dreaming. There will never be another woman for me. There's only you. For the rest of my life, there's only you. Will you marry me?"

Tears spilled over my cheeks as I nodded, my throat too tight for words. Lucas let out a breath and pulled the ring from the box. He rested his forehead against mine as he slid the ring on my finger. It was a perfect fit. More tears slid down my cheeks.

I'd been wondering, hoping, secretly imagining our future. I'd had no idea Lucas had been doing the same thing.

"I love you, Lucas."

His forehead still against mine, we both looked at the ring on my finger.

"What do you think about a Christmas wedding?" he asked. I gave a watery laugh.

"That's only six weeks away," I said.

"Do you want something big?"

I knew if I said I did, Lucas would agree, though he'd hate the circus of a big wedding. I shook my head, rubbing my forehead against his.

"I really don't," I whispered. "I just want to be married to you."

Jacob and Abigail were planning the wedding to end all weddings, and just the thought of all that work gave me hives. Vance and Maggie's wedding hadn't been huge, and it was beautiful, but it was still more than I wanted. Lucas interrupted my thoughts.

"I want to get married at Winters House," he said. "At Christmas. After Gage is home."

My heart lurched in my chest and I sat back to study his face. "What?"

"I got a call this morning. Aiden will get official word eventually, but my contact told me Gage is in a military hospital. He's injured and not in great shape, but he's going to be okay. And he's coming home. Soon."

I started crying again and launched myself into Lucas's arms, sobbing in relief. I hadn't thought anything could make this moment any better, but Lucas had done it.

Gage was coming home.

Alive.

And in time to watch me marry Lucas Jackson in a Christmas wedding at Winters House.

"I don't think I could be any happier than I am right now," I said into Lucas's neck.

He squeezed me tight before leaning back to wipe my tears with one of the work rags in the box beside me. I took over, trying to keep from smearing mascara all over my cheeks.

I'd never been a crier before I met Lucas. Not since my parents died.

I'd locked my heart away where no one could ever hurt it again. It had taken Lucas to break through. To make me feel again.

Lucas was worth the risk of love.

Lucas was worth everything.

He picked up the crystal decanter of whiskey and twisted off the top. From somewhere in the box, he pulled out a glass from the set I'd stolen the day Aiden had fired me. Cracking the seal on the bottle, he poured a healthy slug in the glass.

"Does Aiden know you have this?" I asked, taking a sip. Amazing. Not as good as the bottle I'd stolen, but nothing was. Lucas shrugged and took the glass, tasting the whiskey.

"Damn, that's good."

"How did you get it?" I asked.

"I went over this afternoon to tell him about Gage and ask for his blessing."

My heart melted. Aiden and Lucas got along better

than I'd expected, but I wouldn't have guessed Lucas would talk to Aiden about marrying me.

"You asked Aiden for his blessing and then stole his best bottle of whiskey?" I asked, torn between a laugh and more tears.

"Of course I talked to your brother, Princess. I wanted to do this right."

I looked from the ring on my finger to the bottle of Macallan.

Nothing could be more us, more right, than Lucas proposing over a bottle of stolen whiskey.

Somehow, I thought Aiden would understand.

I took the crystal glass from Lucas and set it on the counter, sliding it and the bottle a few feet away. Then I pulled his mouth down to mine.

The day we met, we'd stopped with a kiss. One kiss, but it had changed my life. Since the moment Lucas's lips met mine, nothing had been the same.

Here we were, six months later, with another bottle of stolen whiskey.

This time, I wasn't drunk.

This time, we were so much more than two lost strangers.

And this time, we weren't stopping with a kiss.

Turn the page to read a Sneak Peek of Gage's story
The Billionaire's Angel

SNEAK PEEK
THE BILLIONAIRE'S ANGEL

CHAPTER ONE
Sophie

My hands shook as I measured a short length of tape. Staring down at the black cockroach in my hand, I wondered again how I'd gotten myself into this mess.

It's not what you're thinking. The cockroach wasn't real. I've learned how to be brave in the past few years, but not brave enough to carry around live bugs. Yuck. No, this cockroach had been carefully cut out of black construction paper, along with the selection of spiders and crickets spread across the seat of the leather couch.

It was after two in the morning, and I was in my employer's library, fumbling in the dark to tape the fake bugs to the inside of the white silk lampshades. The next person to flip on the lights would be treated to the illusion that huge bugs lurked inside the lamps. I could already imagine the screams that would echo through the house.

It wouldn't be the first time.

I really had to find a way to keep my charge off the

internet. Boredom plus an active mind equals trouble. At least it does when your name is Amelia Winters.

Since Amelia was seventy-eight and her hands weren't as nimble as mine, I got roped into carrying out the pranks she dreamed up. I was supposed to be her nurse, and I was when she needed one.

High blood pressure and type two diabetes meant she needed some supervision, but not enough to require live-in care. Since most of the family had moved out of the enormous house, and Amelia's great nephew Aiden traveled often for work, I was there to keep her both healthy and entertained.

It could have been a lonely job, if not for Amelia. Her pranks aside, she was a blast to work for - funny and loyal and sweet. Her body was slowing down, but her mind was sharp, and she had a wicked sense of humor. Sometimes too wicked.

The pranks, case in point. At least once a week she came up with a new one, sending me out for materials and instructing me on the details of her plans.

At first, I'd worried she was going to get me fired. Since my husband had died, I'd been bouncing from job to job. I'd been more than ready to settle down when I'd been hired here, and I hadn't wanted to be kicked out for lining the hallway with tiny cups filled with water.

Amelia might be almost eighty, but her sense of humor was a lot more frat-boy than elderly matron.

Fortunately for me, the family was well versed in Amelia's ways. Aiden, who'd scared the heck out of me when he'd hired me, adored his great-aunt. She could probably set the house on fire, and he'd laugh and kiss her on the cheek. The rest of them were the same—affectionate and amused by Amelia's antics. The only two exceptions were the housekeeper, Mrs. Williamson, and Aiden's cousin, Gage.

Mrs. Williamson and Amelia were chalk and cheese. Mrs. W was far too proper to admit she didn't love *every* member of the Winters family, but we all knew Amelia drove her nuts. Amelia, for her part, delighted in pestering Mrs. W. More than once I'd heard her mutter under her breath that Mrs. W had a stick up her you-know-where.

She'd never say it, but I'm pretty sure Mrs. W thought Amelia should give in and act her age. I'd only been with the family for six months, but I could have told her that was a lost cause. By all accounts, Amelia Winters had never acted her age, and at seventy-eight, she wasn't about to start.

I adored Amelia, and I had to admit, some of her pranks were funny, but I liked Mrs. W too much to let her think her beloved Winters House was infested with six-inch cockroaches. As soon as I'd taped the last fake insect in place, I pulled out my phone to shoot Mrs. W a warning text.

Sometime tomorrow she'd come into the library on a made-up pretext and let out a very convincing scream. Amelia would get her laugh, and Mrs. W wouldn't have to kill her. Everyone would be happy.

I tapped SEND on my text and went to shove the phone in the pocket of my robe when two arms closed around my chest like steel bars, pinning my hands to my sides.

My phone tumbled from nerveless fingers, bouncing off my bare toes and skidding across the carpet. I froze where I was, my heart thumping in my chest so hard I heard the whoosh of blood in my ears.

Panic shot ice down my spine.

My nerves screamed: DANGER! DANGER!

Head spinning with fear, I tried to think. The long, hard

body pressed to my back made that impossible. Eyes squeezed shut, memories flashed against my closed lids, a newsreel of everything I wanted to forget.

Hard hands grabbing me in the dark, dragging me from my bed. Pain.

It isn't Anthony, I told myself. *Anthony is dead.*

Summoning every ounce of courage I had, I said, "Let me go."

A low, husky voice rumbled in my ear. "Not until you tell me what the hell you're doing in here in the middle of the night."

A hitch in my voice, I said, "Amelia. Amelia sent me."

The words tangled in my throat. I couldn't say more. The heat of a male body so close to mine, the strength of his arms trapping me, his warm breath against my cheek - it was too much.

I hadn't been this close to a man—any man–since my husband had died.

After Anthony, I'd never wanted to be this close to a man again.

In a rush of awareness, I knew this wasn't Aiden. Aiden had always been careful to preserve a polite, formal distance between us. If he caught me skulking around the house in the middle of the night, he'd never grab me from behind. Heck, with the way Aiden adored Amelia he'd probably volunteer to finish the prank himself.

If it wasn't Aiden. It had to be Gage. Aiden's cousin had arrived two days before, when Amelia and I had been out on a shopping trip, picking up construction paper and tape. I met him briefly at the family dinner to celebrate his home-coming, but I hadn't seen him since. Hoping my guess was right, I said, "I'm Sophie. Amelia's nurse."

A grunt in my ear, but the arms around me didn't

loosen. Shoot. I knew better than to struggle. Fighting back only made them hurt you more. My breath shallow, body still, I tried again.

"I'm allowed to be here. I'm not doing anything wrong. Please let me go."

I felt his head drop to my shoulder, the heat of his forehead pressing into my bare neck. He drew in a deep breath.

Was he *smelling* me?

Panic sliced through me again.

No. Please, no. Please don't make me have to leave this place.

I'd thought I was safe here. For the first time in years, I was safe. I didn't want to have to leave.

His heart jackhammered, the echo of its frantic beats fluttering against my back where his chest pressed tightly to me.

"Please," I whispered. The arms around me loosened. I stayed frozen. I was too cautious to move until I'd truly been set free. This could be a trap, and I was too smart to fall for it. Anthony had trained me well.

Warm lips brushed the side of my neck. Another deep inhale. He *was* smelling me. The urge to flee was almost impossible to resist, but I knew in my gut running was the worst mistake I could make.

I wracked my brain for everything I knew of Gage. He was the oldest son of James and Anna Winters, Aiden's aunt and uncle. James and Anna had been brutally murdered when Gage was a child. When Aiden's parents had been killed in an identical crime eight years later, Gage had been eighteen. The day after their funeral he'd joined the army. Until today, he'd never really come home.

Details of his military service were scarce, but Amelia had told me everything she knew. He'd enlisted, gone to

college, then through officer training school, before he'd
joined the Rangers. After that he'd moved into special
forces, his missions and teams so top secret his family hadn't
been sure he was still with the army until they'd called to
tell Aiden that Gage was missing.

For months the family had been stuck in limbo,
swinging between grief and hope, right up until a second
call had informed Aiden that Gage had escaped captivity.
He was coming home as soon as the military hospital
released him, but they'd warned Aiden that the months of
imprisonment had taken a toll.

Gage was no longer the man his family remembered.

Aiden had commented dryly that Gage had been gone
so long, they barely knew him at all. No matter what the
circumstances of his homecoming, to his family, Gage was a
stranger. As my panic ebbed, I realized the man holding me
captive might possibly be more freaked out than I was.

He probably had some form of post-traumatic stress if
he'd been held captive for months. Finding an intruder in
his home was just the kind of thing that would set him off,
especially when his home must seem like a foreign place
after so many years away.

Logic told me that a former special forces soldier
suffering from PTSD was *more* dangerous, not less, but my
guess at what might be going through his head put me back
in control. As a woman alone in the dark, I was terrified. As
a nurse, and a woman used to dealing with volatile men, I
knew what I needed to do.

"Gage?" I asked, careful to keep my voice low and
soothing. "Gage, it's okay. You can let go. I'm Amelia's
nurse. I'm allowed to be here. It's okay."

I kept talking in the same soothing voice, feeling the
tension slip from his body. Eventually, he lifted his head

and stepped back, setting me free. With an odd sense of triumph, I crossed the room before I turned around. I thought he was steady, but I wanted some space between us, just in case.

"I'm going to turn on the lamp," I warned just before I reached beneath the shade and turned the knob. Light flared, blinding me for a moment. A deep chuckle rumbled from across the room.

"Whose idea was it?" he asked.

His voice distracted me for a second, so deep and calm, at odds with the tension that had seized his muscles only a few minutes before. I glanced at the light and saw the shadow of an enormous spider lurking on the inside of the shade.

I stepped away with a shiver before I realized what I was doing. Silly, since I was the one who had taped the bugs in place, but I hadn't expected them to look so real. Amelia was good.

Clearing my throat, I said, "Amelia's. It's always Amelia's idea." I wanted to ask if he was okay, but I held my tongue.

"Clever," he said.

"That's Amelia," I agreed.

"Is this the only room you did?"

"It is." Judging it safe to move, I began to gather up my materials, tucking my phone back in the pocket of my robe and making sure I had all the extra bugs and the tape. A prank was no good if I left the evidence sitting around.

"Mrs. W won't be happy."

I smiled. It was sweet the way the family doted on Mrs. W. I'd always imagined a family as wealthy and powerful as the Winterses would be stuffy, far above those they'd consider the help. Instead, they treated Mrs. W like family and had welcomed me as an equal, insisting I join them for meals and giving me a room in the main house that was bigger than my apartment when I'd been in nursing school.

"I already texted her," I reassured Gage. "She'll make a big fuss tomorrow when she turns on the lights. Unless Aiden does it first."

"Aiden doesn't know?"

I shook my head, picking up the last scrap of construction paper. Suddenly without anything to do, I crossed my arms over my chest. Gage stood in shadow, his features hard to make out, but I was uncomfortably aware I was in my robe, my hair down, looking like an unprofessional mess.

In the six months I'd been living in Winters House, I'd never encountered another soul awake in the middle of the night.

Clearing my throat, I said, "No, Aiden likes to be surprised."

Gage let out a grunt I couldn't decipher. He took a step forward, leaving the shadows of the corner. Light bathed his features, and my breath caught. I'd heard Gage and Aiden were like twins. Everyone else must be blind. To my eyes, they looked nothing alike.

Sure, they both had the same build - tall, broad shoulders, lean hips. The same dark hair. Even their features were superficially similar, with sharp cheekbones, aristocratic noses and full lower lips. Where Aiden's hair had the same auburn tones as his little sister, Charlie, Gage's was a true brown, not a hint of red to be seen.

I'd always thought soldiers wore their hair short, but Gage's was a little long. Shaggy. As if he hadn't had it cut in months. Which of course, he hadn't. I imagined his hairstyle hadn't been a priority when he'd been trying to escape his captors.

He'd probably cut it now that he was home. Maybe with shorter hair, he'd look more like Aiden. I took in the tension in his shoulders, his hands curled into fists.

No. The obvious aside, Aiden looked nothing like Gage.

Aiden was cool. Refined. Controlled.

Standing in the pool of light, his faded grey t-shirt stretched around his biceps, hugging his well-defined chest, Gage was raw, his power barely leashed. Despite his stillness, he vibrated with energy.

I sensed it was taking everything he had to remain where he was. His vivid blue eyes were the least of the differences between Gage and his cousin.

Those eyes were leveled on me, pinning me in place as effectively as his arms had a few minutes before.

Clearing my throat, I said, "Are you going to spoil it for her?"

"The prank?" Gage asked. At my nod, he said, "No."

"Thank you." I started for the door to the library, careful to give Gage a wide berth. I didn't think he was going to grab me again, but it seemed smarter to stay out of arm's reach.

"Tell me next time," he said.

"What?" I stopped at the door, confused.

He was silent for a long moment before answering in a halting voice. "I don't do well with surprises these days. The next time Amelia decides to mess with us, fill me in."

Instantly, I understood. Amelia's plan to duct tape an airhorn to Aiden's desk chair would be a nightmare to a man newly home from a combat zone, even if he *didn't* have post-traumatic stress, and I was betting Gage did.

"Do you have a cell?" I asked.

Gage raised his eyebrows in question. I explained, "I text Mrs. W to warn her. I'll try to talk Amelia out of a few

341

of her plans that might be a problem, but I can text you, too. That way you know what's coming."

"So, Amelia hasn't slowed down. Good to know some things don't change," he said, his voice heavy with something I couldn't quite identify. Regret? Whatever it was, Gage Winters sounded sad.

I had the absurd urge to comfort him.

Absurd because not only did I not know what was wrong, he was a Winters. Yes, he'd been through a terrible experience. But he was alive. He was home with his family, living in this enormous mansion, with a job waiting for him at Winters Incorporated, and more money than he could count stashed away in the bank.

Gage Winters didn't need my comfort. He didn't need anything from me.

He might remind me of a wounded animal, but wounded animals were dangerous. And I'd been bitten enough.

The only person in this house who needs you is Amelia, I reminded myself. *Stay away from Gage Winters.*

"Are you in Vance's old room?" Gage asked.

"I am. Across from Amelia. I guess her room used to be Holden and Tate's?"

Gage nodded. "If you're done with your bugs, I'll walk you back."

"It's just down the hall," I protested.

"All the same. I'll walk you back."

I didn't bother to argue. Gage followed me out the door, turning off the lamp before we left the room. The short stretch of hall outside the library was dark, the doors to the wine room and Aiden's office lost in the shadows.

We turned the corner to the main hall where silvery moonlight streamed through the tall, arched windows, casting the walls in dreamlike shades. Outside, in the center courtyard of Winters House, a fountain burbled, the water flashing black and silver.

I loved this fairy tale of a house. I completely understood why Mrs. W was so devoted to it. How could Gage have left this place and not come back for so many years? In the six months I'd been with Amelia, Winters House had become a haven.

Why had Gage left it just when he'd needed it most?

I couldn't imagine the losses this family had suffered. Not really. I'd lost my mother to cancer when I was a teenager, but Gage had not only lost both his parents as a child, he'd lost the aunt and uncle who'd raised him when he'd barely been a man.

More than once since he'd gone missing I'd wondered what had happened to make the eighteen-year-old Gage flee his family home.

Now that he was back, was he going to stay? None of it was my business, but I couldn't help my curiosity.

Gage kept his distance as we walked down the hall, following just slightly behind me. Our feet shuffled along the polished hardwood floors, almost silent in the sleeping house. This wasn't the first time I'd wandered Winters House in the middle of the night, but it was the first time I'd done so with company.

We reached the door to my bedroom, across the hall from Amelia's. I reached for the handle, and Gage's fingers closed over mine. I started in surprise, letting out a little squeak. I was grateful for the dark as I felt my cheeks turn red.

"I'm sorry about earlier," Gage said in his low rumble. "I wasn't expecting to see anyone in the library and I reacted on instinct. I didn't mean to scare you."

"You didn't," I lied. "It's okay."

Gage dropped his hand and stared at me, his blue eyes gleaming in the moonlight, seeing everything. He knew I was lying, knew I'd been scared. Lips pressed together and eyes wide, I silently begged him to let it go.

Gage took a step back and dropped his hand.

"Sleep well, Sophie," he said, his low voice sending shivers down my spine.

"You, too," I whispered, and escaped into my room.

ALSO BY IVY LAYNE

**Don't Miss Out on New Releases, Exclusive
Giveaways, and More!!**

Join Ivy's Readers Group @ ivylayne.com/readers

THE HEARTS OF SAWYERS BEND

Stolen Heart

Sweet Heart

Scheming Heart

Rebel Heart

Wicked Heart

THE UNTANGLED SERIES

Unraveled

Undone

Uncovered

THE WINTERS SAGA

The Billionaire's Secret Heart (Novella)

The Billionaire's Secret Love (Novella)

The Billionaire's Pet

The Billionaire's Promise

THE BILLIONAIRE CLUB

ABOUT IVY LAYNE

Ivy Layne has had her nose stuck in a book since she first learned to decipher the English language. Sometime in her early teens, she stumbled across her first Romance, and the die was cast. Though she pretended to pay attention to her creative writing professors, she dreamed of writing steamy romance instead of literary fiction. These days, she's neck deep in alpha heroes and the smart, sexy women who love them.

Married to her very own alpha hero (who rubs her back after a long day of typing, but also leaves his socks on the floor). Ivy lives in the mountains of North Carolina where she and her other half are having a blast raising two energetic little boys. Aside from her family, Ivy's greatest loves are coffee and chocolate, preferably together.

VISIT IVY
Facebook.com/AuthorIvyLayne
Instagram.com/authorivylayne/
www.ivylayne.com
books@ivylayne.com

Made in the USA
Middletown, DE
26 August 2024

59712009R00199